W9-AGB-190

Dear Readers:

Charles Dickens had no idea what he was starting.

When Dickens sat down to write *A Christmas Carol* in 1843, he did so because he thought a Christmas story would ease his financial woes. His last book had not done well and his wife was expecting their fifth child.

Dickens worked with an unrelenting passion, and he completed the story in six weeks, but not without a certain amount of revision. For example, Tiny Tim was originally named Tiny Fred.

A Christmas Carol was released a few days before Christmas and was an instant success. And why not?

This is a tale of the true spirit of Christmas. *A Christmas Carol* has inspired readers for more than a century and a half and was my inspiration for this book.

Charles Dickens and *A Christmas Carol* are credited with reviving interest in nearly-forgotten traditions and the celebration of Christmas.

It is a grand legacy for a writer. And a great gift for the rest of us.

Merry Christmas.

Victoria Alexander

Praise for the books of Victoria Alexander

"Warm, witty and wise!"
Julia Quinn

"Victoria Alexander delivers on all counts . . . Inventive, imaginative and intriguing."
Stephanie Laurens

"For love and laughter it doesn't get any better than Victoria Alexander."
Christina Dodd

"A rising star."
Publishers Weekly

By Victoria Alexander

A Visit From Sir Nicholas
The Pursuit of Marriage
The Lady in Question
Love With the Proper Husband
Her Highness, My Wife
The Prince's Bride
The Marriage Lesson
The Husband List
The Wedding Bargain

VICTORIA ALEXANDER

A VISIT FROM SIR NICHOLAS

AVON BOOKS
An Imprint of HarperCollins*Publishers*

This is a work of fiction. Names, characters, places, and incidents are products of the author's imagination or are used fictitiously and are not to be construed as real. Any resemblance to actual events, locales, organizations, or persons, living or dead, is entirely coincidental.

AVON BOOKS
An Imprint of HarperCollins*Publishers*
10 East 53rd Street
New York, New York 10022-5299

ISBN: 0-7394-4721-1

Printed in the U.S.A.

This story is dedicated to the memory of
Rosemarie and Robert Griffin,
who are always in my heart
and taught me everything I know about
the spirit, the hope and the love
that is Christmas.

A Visit from Sir Nicholas

It was a strange figure—like a child: yet not so like a child as like an old man, viewed through some supernatural medium, which gave him the appearance of having receded from the view, and being diminished to a child's proportions. Its hair, which hung about its neck and down its back, was white as if with age; and yet the face had not a wrinkle in it, and the tenderest bloom was on the skin. The arms were very long and muscular; the hands the same, as if its hold were of uncommon strength. Its legs and feet, most delicately formed, were, like those upper members, bare. It wore a tunic of the purest white and round its waist was bound a lustrous belt, the sheen of which was beautiful. It held a branch of fresh green holly in its hand; and, in singular contradiction of that wintry emblem, had its dress trimmed with summer flowers. But the strangest thing about it was, that from the crown of its head there sprung a bright clear jet of light, by which all this was visible; and which was doubtless the occasion of its using, in its duller moments, a great extinguisher for a cap, which it now held under its arm.

Even this, though, when Scrooge looked at it with increasing steadiness, was not its strangest quality. For as its belt sparkled and glittered now in one part and now in another, and what was light one instant, at another time was dark, so the figure itself fluctuated in its distinctness: being now a thing with one arm, now with one leg, now with twenty legs, now a pair of legs without a head, now a head without a body: of which dissolving parts, no outline would be visible in the dense gloom wherein they melted away. And in the very wonder of this, it would be itself again; distinct and clear as ever.

"Are you the Spirit, sir, whose coming was foretold to me?" asked Scrooge.

"I am!" The voice was soft and gentle. Singularly low, as if instead of being so close beside him, it were at a distance.

"Who, and what are you?" Scrooge demanded.

"I am the Ghost of Christmas Past."

"Long past?" inquired Scrooge: observant of its dwarfish stature.

"No. Your past."

—*A Christmas Carol,* Charles Dickens, 1843

Chapter 1

Christmas Past
December 1843

Affectionately Yours, Lizzie.

Lady Elizabeth Effington stared at the words she'd just written and grimaced. No. *Affectionately* was entirely too personal, and *Lizzie* too informal. He'd never called her Lizzie and she doubted he'd start now. Indeed, with one significant exception, he'd never been anything other than completely proper with her. It was most annoying. She crossed out the line just as she had the previous three attempts.

"That was truly wonderful." Behind her, her younger sister, Juliana, sighed with heartfelt satisfaction.

"I knew you would like it," Lizzie said absently and stared at the sheet of white velum lying on the desk in front of her in the sitting room she shared with Jules.

"It was so . . . so . . ." Jules thought for a moment. "Wonderful."

"Quite," Lizzie murmured and wrote *With Sincere Best Wishes, Lady Elizabeth Effington.*

"No, more than wonderful. I daresay it's the best story about Christmas—no—the best story about anything I have ever read."

That wasn't right either. *With Sincere Best Wishes* had an obligatory ring, as if one were writing to an elderly relative one didn't particularly like but was required to be pleasant to nonetheless. Besides, while *Lizzie* might be too personal, *Lady Elizabeth Effington* was far and away too formal for her purposes. She slashed a pen stroke through the bothersome phrase.

"In point of fact," Jules continued in a tone that sounded far more like a literary critic than a mere girl of sixteen years, "I think it's quite the best story Mr. Dickens has written. Of those I've read, of course, but I do think I've read most of his stories as he is possibly my favorite author. It's not as amusing as *Nicholas Nickleby* but a far better ending to my mind than *The Old Curiosity Shop,* although I do so love stories about girls having adventures." Jules paused. "Even if Little Nell's were rather dreadful."

"Yes, well, dying at the end of one's story does tend to make one's adventures a bit less than cheery," Lizzie said under her breath.

With eternal friendship, Elizabeth.

"I dislike books that don't end well. Mother's books always end well. This one does too, in a fashion, although it is something of a pity Scrooge did not discover the error of his ways until he was old. He would have had a rather wonderful life if he had married Belle. Don't you think so?"

"Um hmm."

Friendship was good. Not the least bit improper. And Elizabeth had the right tone. Perhaps . . . Lizzie sighed and crossed out her latest effort. Why on earth was this so blasted difficult? All she was trying to do was come up with an appropriate inscription for a book to give as a gift. Still, her words were as important as the book itself. Even more so.

"I think my very favorite part though," Jules said slowly, "was at the end when Tiny Tim sprouted wings and flew off with Fezziwig and the Ghost of Christmas Past. Don't you agree?"

"Yes. Of course. I . . ." Lizzie jerked her head up, swiveled in her chair, and stared at her sister. "What did you say?"

"I suspected as much." Jules narrowed her eyes suspiciously. "You weren't listening to a word I said, were you?"

"I most certainly was. You said . . ." Lizzie searched her mind. She did so hate to admit that her sister was right, at least in part. "You said you liked *A Christmas Carol* better than any of Mr. Dickens's other works."

Jules snorted in a most unladylike manner. "That was the very least of what I said." She sat upright on the chaise and craned her neck to see around her sister. "Whatever are you doing, anyway?"

Lizzie shifted to shield the paper on the desk and adopted a casual tone. "Nothing of importance really. Just trying to find the right words."

Jules raised a brow. "For what?"

"For none of your concern, that's what," Lizzie said firmly.

"Is it something for Charles?" Jules fluttered her lashes in an exaggerated manner.

Lizzie laughed. "No, it's not. And even if it was, I wouldn't tell you."

"Why not?" Indignation sounded in the younger girl's voice. "I'd tell you what I was giving the gentleman who was about to ask for my hand in marriage."

"Nonsense," Lizzie said quickly. "Charles is not about to ask for my hand."

Jules smirked. "Would you care to wager on that?"

Lizzie stared at her sister, unease settling in the pit of her stomach. "Do you know something I should know?"

"Perhaps." Jules settled back on the chaise and smiled at her sister in that irritating way younger girls refine for the express purpose of torturing their older sisters. "I might know that Charles spoke to Father privately this morning. And I might further know, when Charles came out of Father's library, he had a look of relief and excitement on his face."

Lizzie waved off her sister's comments. "That could mean anything."

"Oh, come now, Lizzie. You can't be the least bit surprised by this." Jules studied her sister curiously. "For as long as I can remember, everyone in both our families has expected a match between you. I rather thought you expected to marry him as well."

"Charles is a good man and an excellent match, and any woman would be honored to be his wife. Indeed, it seems to me there are any number of young women wishing to do just that." Lizzie smiled in a noncommittal manner and hoped her comments would satisfy her sister.

"I know I would. Charles is wonderful." Jules heaved a heartfelt sigh. "He's so handsome, with the brightest blue eyes and the merriest smile and the most charming manner. Indeed, I fear I have a penchant for men with blond, wavy hair. One is hard-pressed to keep from running one's fingers through it."

Lizzie bit back a grin. "You shall have to resist that in the future."

"In the future I shall have a merry, blond-haired, blue-eyed man of my own to wed." Jules cast her sister a wicked grin. "Then I should be able to run my fingers through his hair all I wish."

"I daresay one shouldn't choose a husband on the basis of his hair," Lizzie said wryly.

"I don't see why a man's appearance shouldn't be considered as well as the rest of his attributes. I should much rather marry a handsome man than a homely one." Jules drew her brows together. "Doesn't Charles remind you of Fred?"

Lizzie shook her head. "Fred?"

"Fred. Scrooge's nephew. He was terribly happy and jolly and handsome as well, although he hadn't much money."

"Charles has a great deal of money."

"So much the better. I think it's far easier to be happy and merry if one has money than if one doesn't." Jules thought for a moment. "Although the Cratchits had no money and they seemed happy enough. Except for Tiny Tim, of course. But then he didn't die after all, thanks to Scrooge. Or at least that's what Mr. Dickens implies." Her brow furrowed. "Do you think Mr. Dickens was trying to tell us that if you have enough money you can change your fate so that you won't die young and horribly?"

"Don't be absurd. He didn't mean anything of the sort." Lizzie scoffed. "He was obviously saying that charity and generosity of spirit can make a huge difference in the lives of those who have little. Indeed, I think the moral to the story is that we should all do what we can to help the less fortunate and not just at Christmastime but the whole year through."

"Probably, although I do wish you hadn't said that." The younger girl wrinkled her nose. "I quite liked the story just as it was without concern as to morals or lessons."

"Morals and lessons are good for your character."

"My character has had quite enough, thank you. Between Mother and Grandmother and all the aunts, someone is always trying to tell me something that is good for my character. Or my mind, for that matter."

"Perhaps that's an indication that your character and your mind need improvement," Lizzie said primly.

"I would scarcely comment about the need to improve one's character or one's mind if I were you."

"Juliana Effington, how can you say such a thing?" Lizzie gasped in mock dismay and clasped her hand to her throat. "There is absolutely nothing wrong with my character or my mind. I am intelligent and well-read, honest and forthright, and my moral standards are beyond reproach."

Jules eyed her sister wryly. "Then it must be exceedingly difficult to fool the entire world, as you, among all the varied and assorted Effington and Shelton cousins, are considered perhaps the merriest and the most frivolous."

"Indeed it is. I work very hard at it." Lizzie nodded solemnly, then met her sister's gaze, and both girls burst into laughter. Lizzie sobered and sighed. "In truth, Jules, I learned long ago that in this world a woman, as opposed to a man, is judged far more on her appearance than her intelligence, and men quite prefer a frivolous nature to a serious one. Someday, when I am old and long married, I fully intend to allow my mind free rein and explore all sorts of fascinating interests."

"I do hope I live long enough to see that." Jules thought for a moment. "Still, I doubt that Charles would object. I daresay you could do almost anything and Charles wouldn't mind in the least."

"He is a wonderful man," Lizzie murmured.

"Indeed he is. Aside from the dozens of blond-haired, blue-eyed children you shall have—"

"Dozens?" Lizzie raised a brow.

"Well, perhaps not dozens, but several." Jules shrugged.

"You and he are well suited. Everyone has always said so. Why, I believe you and Charles are fated to marry."

"Everyone has always said so." Lizzie echoed her sister's words.

She too had always assumed she would marry Charles. Had, in fact, loved him in a fashion since childhood.

Charles Langley was heir to a sizable fortune and respectable title. His family had long been friends with her own. Indeed, Charles was one of her older brother Jonathon's closest friends. He would make an excellent husband and father, and no girl could ask for more. Why, he was quite simply wonderful.

But his eyes weren't dark and smoldering. And his demeanor wasn't overly serious and somber. And when he stole a kiss in the shadows at a party, it was quite nice, but it didn't curl her toes and snatch her breath from her lungs and make something deep inside her melt with a heretofore unknown yearning.

"Do you know who reminds me of Scrooge?" Jules said thoughtfully. "Nicholas Collingsworth."

"Nicholas?" Lizzie drew her brows together in a forbidding manner and ignored the way her heart skipped a beat at the mere mention of his name. "What a terrible thing to say! He's not the least bit like Scrooge. He's kind and generous and—"

"He's stiff and proper and far too serious and somber and not at all fun," Jules said firmly. "Why, his only redeeming quality is that he is so devilishly handsome."

"Jules!"

Jules continued without pause. "And I don't care what you think, he reminds me very much of Scrooge in his younger days. I don't know why Jonathon and Charles consider him such a good friend. They haven't the least bit in common."

"They have been friends for years, and it is lucky for him that he has friends who are not so critical as you," Lizzie snapped. "You must not forget, his life has not been as pleasant as ours."

"Yes, yes, I know, he's an orphan and all that," Jules muttered, sinking deeper into the chaise. "Obviously my character needs more work. Still, if the man would simply smile now and again . . ."

"He does smile now and again," Lizzie said more to herself than to her sister. And it was a smile made all the more wonderful for its rarity.

Nicholas Collingsworth had entered their circle of acquaintances more than a decade or so ago after the death of his parents. The orphaned boy had come to live with his bachelor uncle, the Earl of Thornecroft, who, in turn, was a longtime friend of Lizzie's parents, the Duke and Duchess of Roxborough. Jonathon and Charles had immediately accepted the young man as one of their own, and the trio had been inseparable in their youth, attending the same schools and spending holidays variously at one of their respective families' estates or another. Nicholas was somewhat more reserved than the other boys, and Lizzie had paid this friend of her brother's, as she'd paid all her brother's friends, scant attention. He, like Charles, was simply always present and, unlike Charles, of no real significance.

Three years ago, Nicholas and his uncle had gone off on a Grand Tour, not simply of Europe but of the entire world. They'd returned four months ago. The earl was unchanged by their travels, as friendly and jolly as ever, if a shade older in appearance, but Nicholas was not at all as she'd remembered.

The boy she'd paid no heed to had become a man she could not put out of her thoughts.

He was strong and handsome and even mysterious, with a jaw chiseled by determination and a look in his dark eyes of purpose and resolve. He seemed to stand apart from the rest of them, in truth from the rest of life really, as if he were an observer rather than a participant and was indeed as somber and serious as Jules had claimed. But it was a sobriety born of desire and ambition. She had never known anyone with the ambition of Nicholas Collingsworth.

He was the only heir to his uncle's wealth and title and had no need for more, yet he was set on making his own fortune. Jonathon had told her it was a point of honor and pride.

Nicholas wanted to atone for the failures of his father, who had also sought to make his own fortune but had been trusting and naïve and unsuccessful in every venture he'd attempted.

From the very moment Lizzie had laid eyes upon Nicholas again, she'd been intrigued and curious. Soon after his return to London, she had made it a point to come upon him alone on the terrace at some now-forgotten event. For the first time in their years of acquaintanceship they'd spoken of matters not relating to friends or the weather or other polite utterances. Her well-practiced flirtatious banter had faded under the assault of his steady, assessing gaze, and she'd found herself asking about his travels and confessing her envy at what he as a man could do and would do and she could not.

He'd talked of lands as yet unexplored and endless possibilities and his own awe at the carefree nature of her family and their obvious affection for one another. She'd spoken of wishes and desires and the curiosities life might hold. He'd responded in kind with his own hopes and dreams and his determination to make his mark on the world beyond what he would achieve by virtue of who he was rather than what he was.

He'd spoken to her as he might have to her brother or his friends. As if she were not pretty and frivolous and lighthearted but rather intelligent and competent and of an interest beyond her blond hair and green eyes and dowry. No man had ever spoken to her like that before.

But then she had never known a man like Nicholas Collingsworth before.

It had been the beginning of these odd feelings for him that now churned within her and the start of a friendship that was odder yet. More and more she'd found herself seeking him out, and she'd fancied he'd sought her out as well, for a continuation of their private discussions about their lives and their futures, their opinions and reflections. And more, they'd spoken of art and music and even politics and the state of the world. And the wonders it might hold.

Their conversations in the presence of others had remained of little significance. They would dance together, on occasion, no more or less often than she would dance with any other young man. And if he'd held her during a waltz a shade tighter than the others or murmured polite, proper phrases with an underlying meaning only she could understand, no one had known it save Lizzie and Nicholas.

Nothing improper or personal or untoward at all had passed between them in public. Nothing anyone could raise an eyebrow at, nothing even the most ardent gossip could speak about in hushed, smug tones. But her gaze would meet his across a room and her heart would leap in her throat, and she'd known, with a certainty that had come from somewhere deep inside, that what she'd been feeling had been shared.

Until finally, inevitably perhaps, they had met privately at some gathering or another and their voices had faltered. For the first time they'd been awkward and ill at ease, as if what had been silently growing between them had sprung now full blown. There had been a hundred things, a thousand things she'd wanted to say. A thousand things she'd wanted to hear in return, yet the words would not come for her or for him. She'd turned to leave and brushed against him, and his gaze had met and meshed with hers in an endless instant of recognition and desire and even, perhaps, love.

Then she'd been in his arms and his lips had crushed hers in a kiss that had stolen her breath and her heart. A kiss she had never imagined possible save in her dreams. A kiss that lingered in her soul.

It had lasted forever and no time at all. When they'd parted he'd looked as shocked as she and as moved. He'd muttered a polite apology. She'd waved it off with an awkward laugh. And they'd pretended it hadn't happened and had gone on as before save they did not meet privately again. But she could not forget his kiss or the look in his eyes or the tremulous feelings he'd aroused within her.

"He's leaving London, you know," Jules said with a casual shrug, as if Nicholas Collingsworth's leaving was of no importance whatsoever.

"So I have heard." Lizzie's tone was as casual as her sister's, belying the urgency that Nicholas's plans triggered within her. "Jonathon said he's sailing tomorrow. For America, I believe."

"Well, I for one shan't miss him, although I daresay he'll be here tonight. I can't imagine anyone missing the Effington Christmas Ball."

"It would be most impolite of him." And disastrous to Lizzie's plans. She had to know if what she felt about him was real or imagined. Simply a momentary lapse in judgment, and nothing at all serious, or lasting and important. And if her feelings were real, did he feel the same?

"I can't wait for tonight." Excitement sparkled in Jules's eyes. "This will be the very first Effington Christmas Ball that I won't have to watch in secret."

For as long as Lizzie could remember, the younger Effington children and their cousins had watched the Christmas ball festivities from a hiding place in an unused balcony overlooking the ballroom. Although to say they watched in secret was not entirely accurate, since every year, promptly when the clock struck ten, whatever governess was in residence at the time would fetch them and send them off to bed.

"I still can't believe Mother is allowing you to attend. She did not allow me to attend until I had come out in society, and you won't do that until spring."

"But I am nearly seventeen and Mother is not tied down by antiquated conventions. She is a modern woman," Jules said loftily, then grinned. "In truth, though, I think I simply wore her down."

"I know the rest of us have certainly been worn down," Lizzie said wryly.

Jules's campaign to be allowed to attend the grand party had begun in earnest two years earlier, when Lizzie, at age seventeen, had been allowed to attend her first Christmas ball. Jules's unending assault on her mother was a subject of great amusement in the household, if a bit trying.

"Besides, Lizzie"—Jules leapt to her feet and twirled about the room—"it's Christmas and anything is possible at Christmas. Anything at all."

"I do hope so," Lizzie murmured.

Jules stopped abruptly and stared. "Whatever is the matter with you? You've been exceedingly quiet and even thoughtful in recent days. Not at all like your usual self. One would think you had a world of troubles on your mind."

"Not at all," Lizzie said firmly. "Why, what on earth could possibly trouble the frivolous Lizzie Effington?" She forced her brightest smile. "And you're right, it is Christmastime, and anything is indeed possible at Christmas. Now, shouldn't you be getting ready for tonight?"

"I most certainly should." Jules nodded and headed toward the door to her room. "I have a scant six hours, and as this is my first Christmas ball, my first ball ever, I want to look my best. Better than my best. I want to look," she tossed her head and cast her sister a wicked look over her shoulder that was far more adult than was seemly for a girl her age, "better than you."

Lizzie raised a brow and bit back a grin. "Oh?"

"You may well be the Effington everyone considers the most fun, but I fully intend to be the one most sought after." Jules grinned, then sobered. "This will be a night I shall remember always, Lizzie. I'm certain of it." She nodded, turned, and swept from the room.

Lizzie laughed. When Jules set her mind on something, there was no stopping her. If she was indeed determined to become the belle of London, she would succeed. Lizzie had no doubt that Jules would do whatever she wished to do in this life.

As for Lizzie's own life, she had never once doubted where she was headed and what would become of her. She couldn't remember ever being confused or uncertain.

Until Nicholas.

Now, she wasn't certain she knew either her own mind or her heart. She loved Charles. She always had. There wasn't a question at all about that. But did she love Nicholas as well? Was it even possible to love two men at the same time? One who warmed you with the comfort of his presence and the other who made you tremble at the mere sound of his voice?

She had to find out, and tonight would be her only chance. Before Charles asked for her hand. Before Nicholas left London, left her life, possibly forever.

Lizzie turned to the paper on the desk, thought for a moment, then penned a few lines. She sat back and studied them.

Personal, but not too personal. Affectionate, but not overly so. One could read her words in any number of ways depending on the reader's own feelings. Yes, it would do.

She pulled open a drawer and drew out the book she had purchased. She'd been lucky to find one still available. The bookseller had said they could well be sold out entirely before Christmas. She opened the small volume, drew a deep breath, then carefully wrote the decided-upon lines on the flyleaf and waited for the ink to dry.

It was the perfect Christmas gift for a man she might or might not love. A man who might or might not love her. The perfect gift for an old family friend about to embark on endless travels or someone who might well be very much more than a friend.

She closed the book gently and studied the red cloth cover with the words *A Christmas Carol by Charles Dickens* emblazoned in gilt and encircled by a gold wreath.

Jules was right.

One way or another, this would most certainly be a night to remember.

Chapter 2

"There's no reason for you to leave, none at all." Frederick, the Earl of Thornecroft, sat in his favorite chair in his favorite room at Thornecroft House, sipping his favorite brandy with his favorite and ever-present cigar in his hand, and glared at his favorite, indeed his only, nephew. "You'll have my money and my title as well when I'm gone."

"Ah, but the key there, Uncle, is that you should have to die first," Nicholas Collingsworth said mildly, prowling the perimeter of the Thornecroft library in a manner even more restless than usual. "And I am far and away too fond of you to wish that."

"That's something, at any rate," Frederick muttered. "Still, I can well provide you with whatever you desire in life, and glad to do it."

"You have provided for me since the day my parents died. It's past time I provided for myself."

"You're just like your father, you know."

"Thank you." Nick flashed the older man a grin. For a moment, uncle and nephew fell silent, each with his own memories: one of a cherished younger brother, the other of a beloved father taken far too soon. "Still, I hope we are not too much alike."

His uncle considered him thoughtfully, as if comparing father to son in his own mind. "James was a good man, but he had no head for business."

"He was a dreamer," Nick said absently, stepping around a precarious tower of books stacked unsteadily on the floor. The untidy appearance of the library was a constant source of dismay for Mrs. Smithers, the housekeeper. While the room was officially forbidden territory for Mrs. Smithers and her staff of maids, Frederick and Nick knew full well she managed a bit of clandestine cleaning nonetheless. "He refused to see past the dream of an endeavor to the reality."

"And you are far more practical?" It was as much a statement as a question.

"Indeed I am," Nick said, deftly skirting a pile of correspondence and unread manuscripts. Uncle Frederick had a secret passion for all manner of scientific and scholarly pursuits, especially those of a historic nature. While few of his social acquaintances knew of this more serious aspect of his character—indeed, he was better known for his pursuit of women than for anything else—in certain amateur academic circles, he was considered something of an expert on the flora and fauna of ancient Egypt.

"With more desire as well," Frederick said under his breath.

It was not a new thought for the older man, and Nick had accepted the truth of it a long time ago.

As the second son of the Earl of Thornecroft, James Collingsworth, Nick's father, had been heir to nothing beyond the family name and had always seemed to have few aspirations beyond that. No one had been more surprised than his brother to learn of James's determination to make his own fortune independent of his family. His quest had taken him, and his wife, away from England to America. Unfortunately, James's desire had not coincided with either his ability or his nature. His disposition had been more suited, as Nick's mother's had, to a life of frivolity and gaiety. His had not at all been the kind of temperament needed to succeed in anything of a financial nature save the inheritance of great wealth. Even then, Nick had often wondered, after he'd come to live with his uncle, whether the family coffers would have been sorely depleted—indeed, would have survived at all—had his father been the oldest son.

Still, James had been a good man with a kind heart and generous spirit. Nick's memories of his parents were shaded by laughter and love. And if their lives had been built on credit and the financial support of his uncle, as a child Nick had only been vaguely aware of his father's failures. And as none of them had seemed important to his parents, why should they have seemed important to him?

It was only after their deaths in a flu epidemic that Nick had learned of the extent of his father's incompetence. Knowledge gained not from his uncle, who Nick suspected would defend and protect his younger brother to his own dying day, but from James's own words in long saved letters to Frederick and various papers and files and notes of indebtedness.

Nick was determined to succeed where his father had failed and, in doing so, redeem him, even if Nick realized the irony of such a pursuit. No one would have found more amusement in the idea of Nick following his father's path in the pursuit of James's redemption than James himself.

"It's that American influence no doubt." Frederick glared at his nephew. "All that land of opportunity business. The absurd notion that a man can become whatever he wishes if he works hard enough. I thought I'd managed to overcome the ill effects of those years you lived in America, but they've ruined you, my boy. Damn egalitarian nonsense."

Nick laughed and pulled a volume from the shelves, more from a need to do something with his hands than the desire to read anything whatsoever. "You don't believe that. Any of it."

"I bloody well believe some of it," Frederick snapped, then sighed. "I believe you should stay here and learn what you must of necessity learn to be the next Earl of Thornecroft."

"You have already taught me well. Indeed, I am more than prepared to take on the responsibilities of your title and wealth when the time comes." He caught his uncle's gaze. "A time, I might point out, that will be very far from now."

"Yes, yes." Frederick waved off Nick's comment. "You wish me to live forever."

"You've barely passed forty-eight years of age and, I daresay, you have a good many years left in you." Nick flipped open the book, glanced at the title page: *The British Flora; or, Genera and Species of British Plants: Arranged after the Reformed Sexual System; and Illustrated by Numerous Tables, and Dissections by Robert John Thorton, M.D.* and grimaced. "Of course, stuff like this may damn well kill you from sheer boredom alone."

Frederick ignored him. "You're not behaving at all as a proper Englishman and heir to a long- established and respectable title should behave."

"And a proper Englishman heir to a long-established and respectable title would stay here?" Nick paged through the book idly. "Squandering your wealth while waiting for your demise?"

"It's not uncommon," Frederick said under his breath.

"Then I fear indeed I am not a proper Englishman. Besides, Uncle, you would hate that." He snapped the book closed, then met his uncle's gaze. "I have heard your comments, rather scathing I might add, about men who do nothing more with their lives than count the days until their father's passing. You have no tolerance or patience for such wastrels." He aimed the book at the older man. "And you would be damnably disappointed in me if I chose that path."

"One of the blackest days in a man's life is when his son, or in your case the child he's always thought of as a son, throws his own words back in his face," Frederick said grimly. "You have principles and honor, my boy. I have obviously done something right in raising you to this point. To my eternal regret."

"I shall miss you too, Uncle." Nick laughed, then sobered. "I do admit it is difficult to leave you here alone."

"Then stay."

"Uncle."

"Very well. Abandon me. Toss me to the wolves of loneliness and despair." Frederick heaved an overly theatrical sigh.

"I daresay you will not be entirely alone." Nick bit back a grin and replaced the volume on the shelf.

"Not entirely." The corners of Frederick's mouth rose in an

altogether wicked manner. "There is an actress at Drury Lane who does not seem especially adverse to men of my years. Or my wealth."

"Take care, Uncle, that you do not fall into bad habits." Nick laughed and continued his aimless circle of the room. He would miss his uncle, and leaving him was far more difficult than Nick had anticipated. But now that he had decided to leave, it seemed pointless to linger any longer than necessary.

"One could say my habits could scarcely be worse than they are now." Frederick puffed at his cigar and blew a perfect ring of blue smoke into the air.

"One could definitely say that if one was of a particularly narrow-minded nature."

Those not bothered with such a nature would note only that Lord Thornecroft was a wealthy, unmarried gentleman with a taste for fine wine and good cigars and lovely ladies.

"Perhaps it's the young lady who should be warned."

"Perhaps." Nick grinned.

They could well joke about Frederick's amusements and how the rest of the world might view them, but he had been as responsible and good a parent as anyone could ever ask. From the day Nick had walked into his life, Frederick had been more father than uncle to the boy.

"I do regret leaving you alone, you know, but it's your own fault. You should have family around you, children of your own, a loving wife."

Frederick chuckled. "I don't think this particular lady is overly interested in marriage and family."

"Probably not." Nick paused to choose his words with care. He was to leave tomorrow, and in spite of the thirteen years spent living with this kind and warm-spirited gentleman, a man who had very much taken the place of his father and done so with grace and affection, there were still things left unsaid between them.

"Why did you never marry?" Nick's tone was casual, as if neither the question nor the answer was of any significance.

Frederick's voice was as unconcerned as the younger man's. "Marriage has never especially appealed to me. Shackling yourself to one woman for life and all that. Never found the right woman worth sacrificing my freedom for, I suppose."

"Except my mother," Nick said quietly.

Frederick's brow rose slightly in surprise. "You know about that, do you?"

Nick nodded. He'd known for years the story of how his mother had been betrothed to his uncle but had instead run off with his uncle's younger brother. Frederick had never said a word, nor had he ever said anything implying that either Nick's father or mother were anything other than honorable. Indeed, given his uncle's obvious affection toward his parents, learning the truth had come as something of a shock for Nick.

"I forgave them, you know. Rather quickly, if I recall. There was no need for them to leave England. Certainly, I was angry at the time. It's bloody hard to be tossed aside for your younger brother. But I cared too much for your mother not to want to see her happy, and I dearly loved your father. I realized they were meant for one another, and she would not have been truly content with me. I wonder, even now, if I would have been happy with her as well. Our marriage might well have been an enormous mistake for all three of us. Regardless . . ."

He heaved a sigh at the memories. "I wrote to him, to them, over and over urging them to return home, but your father had that damnable notion of making his fortune in his head and refused to so much as consider giving it up. He was always certain the next venture, the next speculation, the next investment would be the right one. He and your mother were as stubborn as their son."

"Thank you, Uncle," Nicholas said with a wry smile.

"I had enough then to take care of us all, as I have enough now to take care of you."

"Uncle." A warning sounded in Nicholas's voice.

"Damn it all, boy." A scowl furrowed Frederick's forehead, and he studied his nephew. "I thought traveling the world would settle you down. Make you see that your duty and responsibility lie here in England. Indeed, I thought I had fairly well convinced you somewhere along Calcutta, I think, or perhaps it was in Cairo, to abandon this whole idea."

"It was Casablanca, Uncle," Nick said mildly. "And it was a momentary aberration. I decided upon this course for my life years ago."

"Still, when we returned to London, I was confident you had decided to stay. Yet in the months since our return . . ." Frederick paused and stared for a long moment.

"Yes?" Nick turned toward his uncle. He knew that look and was not particularly fond of it.

Frederick shook his head, his words slow and measured. "I simply find the method in which history chooses to repeat itself exceedingly odd."

Nick raised a brow. "You expect me to fail then? As my father did?"

"On the contrary." Frederick's gaze was steady and level, as if he could see right through his nephew. Knew, in fact, his very thoughts. "I expect you to own the world by the time you return."

"Fine words, Uncle, but I recognize the look in your eye. You have come to some sort of realization."

"Sometimes one fails to see what is right under one's very nose," Frederick murmured.

"Sometimes one's elders are as obtuse as a stone." Nick's tone was sharp, and he adopted a lighter note. "Come now, what are you thinking?"

Frederick flicked an ash at the saucer provided for that purpose, ignoring the fact that he missed it entirely, then narrowed his eyes and gazed at the younger man. "Your father left England to seek his fortune."

Nick crossed his arms over his chest. "As I am doing."

"And failed."

"As I shall not." Nick's voice was as firm as his conviction. "You shall not see a repeat of history in that respect."

"James left as much because of a woman, your mother, as any desire to make his own way in the world."

"There you have it, Uncle." Unease twisted Nick's stomach, belying the cool smile he forced to his face. "I am not repeating my father's history, as I am not running off with my brother's fiancée. Although, I confess, I too have an actress . . ."

Frederick gazed at him silently.

"Very well, then." Nick rolled his gaze toward the ceiling. "It's most distressing to admit, but there is no lady in my life at the moment. None whatsoever."

"I know you better than anyone in this world, and I daresay no one else has noticed, but I have seen the way you look at her," Frederick said quietly.

"I have no idea what you're talking about." Nick met his uncle's gaze directly. "Or whom you're referring to."

"You do not lie well, boy." Frederick chuckled. "You have never been able to lie to me."

Their gazes locked for a long moment. Frederick was right. Even when Nick had been a child, the older man had seen right through whatever tale the boy had concocted. And when his uncle's knowing brown eyes had fastened on Nick then, as they did now, confession had poured from his very soul.

"If you're speaking of Elizabeth Effington, I look at her the way any man looks at a beautiful woman." Nick turned to peruse a shelf of books and clasped his hand behind his back. "It scarcely matters. She is to marry my best friend."

"They are not betrothed."

"Yet." Nick shrugged. "They will be. Before this Christmas has passed, Charles has vowed to ask for her hand."

"I wondered why you were so intent upon leaving before Christmas."

"It seems best." Nick glanced at his uncle over his shoulder. "I will confess, I am intrigued by her, even enchanted. But each minute spent in her presence is a temptation I am hard-pressed to resist. The best way to deal with temptation is to remove it—or, in this instance, remove myself from the temptation."

Frederick considered him in silence.

"You needn't stare at me like that, Uncle. Elizabeth is a charming, lovely creature. You cannot fault me for wanting her. But Charles is my closest friend, and she . . ." Frustration surged through him, and he laughed it away. "This is what was meant to be. For as long as I've known him, Charles has planned to wed Elizabeth. Jonathon expects it, as does everyone in both their families." He shook his head. "Charles is a far better match for her than I in temperament and heritage and all those other things that are taken into account when entering a marriage. Besides, he has loved her always, and I—"

Frederick raised a brow. "Have loved her nearly as long?"

Nearly.

"Love? Don't be absurd." Nick snorted in amused disdain, as if the very concept of his loving Elizabeth Effington at all, let alone for much of his life, were ridiculous.

But he had.

She'd been a child when they'd first met and he barely a few years older. She'd ignored him, of course, and he'd ignored her equally well. Jonathon and Charles had become his friends and constant companions. In spite of that, between the years of school and travel, his path had crossed hers infrequently. And while she'd paid him no particular notice when it had, and he, in the way of his male friends, had not deigned to pay her heed, he had always been all too aware of her presence. Of the spark of gaiety in her lovely blue eyes and the joy that echoed in the ring of her laughter.

Yes, he had loved her nearly always.

"And what of Elizabeth?" Frederick said slowly. "Does she care for you?"

"Of course not. She loves Charles. She always has. She . . ." Nick shook his head. "I can't imagine that she has any affection for me at all."

Nick didn't know of her feelings, not really. Did a scant handful of conversations that had begun innocently enough and ended with his revealing things he had never told a soul, thoughts and dreams he hadn't realized he'd had until he'd gazed into her lovely face and heard her own candid responses indicate affection on her part? Did the fact that inevitably when he glanced at her across a room, her gaze would meet his again and again, as if she were looking for him just as he was looking for her, signify a longing that matched his own? And was the shock in her eyes after he'd dared to kiss her maidenly outrage or a silent admission that she'd been as shaken by the moment as he?

It scarcely mattered.

"I daresay if she has any feeling for me whatsoever, they are perhaps those of confusion." He chose his words carefully. "I have not always been as circumspect with her as I have wished. But she is young, and a bit of confusion regarding her feelings in response to the unwarranted attentions of another man, any man, is to be expected."

Confusion brought by his glance and his kiss and a yearning he knew full well he could keep from his face but feared it did indeed show in his eyes.

Frederick snorted. "You are scarcely much older than she."

"Three years, Uncle." Nick set his jaw firmly. "There is a great deal of difference between a man of two and twenty and a woman who is barely nineteen."

"Ah, yes, what was I thinking?" Frederick puffed his cigar in the methodical manner that signified serious thought on the older man's part. Nick braced himself. This discussion was obviously far from over.

"Then you have not spoken to her of your feelings?"

"I have no feelings for her."

His uncle ignored him. "Don't you think you should? Speak to her, that is."

Nick grit his teeth. "No, as I have said repeatedly, I have no feelings for her."

Frederick pressed on. "But if she feels the same it would be the height of fool—"

"Damn it all, Frederick, I am not my father." Nick glared at his uncle. "I will not fail where he failed, and I will not steal the love of another man's life from him. A man who has been as close to me as any brother."

"You would deny Elizabeth the happiness your mother found with your father?"

"No!" Nick raked his hand through his hair. "I will ensure her happiness. I will guarantee it by leaving her free to be happy with Charles."

"And what of your happiness?"

"Achieving my ambitions will make me happy." Nick turned on his heel and paced across the room, ignoring a question in the back of his mind.

Was he trying to convince his uncle or himself?

"And who knows what may happen in the future. I may find not only my fortune but a wife in America." He pulled up short and cast his uncle a wicked grin. "Or I may live all my days as you have, with an assortment of women to warm my bed."

"Yes, well . . ." Frederick cleared his throat. "That is not precisely . . ." He glared. "I have no particular regrets about how I have lived my life, and that is not the topic at hand. We are not discussing my life but yours."

"Indeed, and you would do well to remember that. I have made my decision, and I believe with all my heart it is best for everyone concerned." Nick lightened his tone. "Come now, Uncle, it's Christmastime. There is singing on every street corner, and goodwill hangs in the air between friends and strangers alike. It's the last such season we shall see in one another's company for Lord knows how long. I should hate to spend our final day in argument."

"It needn't be our final day," Frederick muttered, then rolled his gaze toward the ceiling in surrender. "However, I shall say no more on the subject." He aimed his cigar at his nephew. "But I vow, boy, to include a plea for your return with every letter I write to you."

"I expect no less."

"As you will not be here for Christmas Day, I assume you will at least attend the Effington Christmas Ball tonight."

"I would not miss it, Uncle," Nick said with a smile that belied the churning in his stomach. He would not, could not miss the opportunity to see her one last time.

He didn't know how she felt and probably never would, but he was certain he couldn't bear to hear from her own lips that she cared nothing for him. Nor could he stand to watch her pledge her heart to another. In many ways, he was something of a coward.

And if indeed she did declare some affection for him? It was of no real significance. She had loved Charles all her life, and even if she thought she cared for Nick, it could not possibly be more than a fleeting attraction probably brought on by the enormity of her impending betrothal. There was not the slightest doubt in Nick's mind that she belonged with Charles and with Charles was where her happiness lay.

Besides, he would not break his best friend's heart, and he would not follow his father's path.

"Very well then. I will concede defeat, as I am left no other choice." Frederick heaved a sigh, rose to his feet, and crossed the room to settle behind a rosewood desk carved in the Egyptian revival style popular at the beginning of the century. "However, there are any number of issues we must settle here and now, letters of credit, the transfer of funds—that sort of thing."

Nick braced his hands on the desk and leaned toward his uncle. "I vow I shall pay you back. Every penny."

"It is every bit your money as much as it is mine. Always has been and always will be." Frederick's cool brown eyes gazed up at his nephew. "Be rest assured, Nicholas, I have no doubt of your success."

Something akin to pride flooded Nick, coupled with affection for this man he did indeed love as a son loves a father. "Thank you, Uncle."

"A word of advice, though, before we leave off other subjects altogether and turn our attention to finances. If I may."

Nick shook his head and straightened. "If I said no, would that stop you?"

Frederick grinned. "My boy, it would scarcely slow me down."

"Very well then. What sage words of wisdom born of your vast years of experience have you for me, Uncle?"

"Nothing you don't already know, I suspect. Simply keep in mind that any number of women may warm your bed, but it is the rare woman who can warm your heart."

"Wise words indeed, Uncle, and I shall be wise in turn to remember them." Nick's laughter belied the vague ache in the back of his throat.

There would indeed be women to warm his bed in the future, but his heart? No. He couldn't imagine anyone ever filling this empty void that currently lingered in the vicinity of his heart. And if his heart was empty, his ambition would fill his life.

He had found the love of his life and she could never be his. It was a nasty quirk of fate, but there it was. In many ways, Frederick was right about history repeating itself, but the end result would not be the same.

Nick would make his fortune and add to the wealth and prestige of the Collingsworth name.

He would not break another man's heart for the sake of his own.

And he would not, he would never, be the man his father had been.

Chapter 3

Holly and ivy, evergreens and all manner of fruits and berries, caught with wide silk and satin ribbons in shades of red and gold and silver, hung in great festoons and massive swags along the grand stairway at Effington House. Every doorway and each window was framed with an overabundance of greenery, as if they were portals not to another room or the out-of-doors but entry to a secret world of magic and joy and all that was Christmas.

A huge kissing bough hung beneath the chandelier in the foyer that led to the ballroom. While it was not the most discreet spot to share a kiss, Mother insisted it be placed prominently so that friends and acquaintances could embrace publicly in the spirit of the season. There were, of course, bunches of mistletoe hung here and there throughout the house for more private moments of affection, even if Father heartily disapproved, pointing out that he had two daughters and, worse, a son, and mistletoe was not especially conducive to proper behavior. Mother disagreed, and Mother, being Mother, as well as furthermore voicing complete confidence in the character of her offspring, always had her way in such things. And Father, even after long years of marriage, still being thoroughly besotted with his wife, grudgingly allowed her whatever she wished.

Even the ancient family portraits of long dead and perpetually scowling Effington ancestors lining the walls of the open gallery overlooking the first floor were bedecked with fir branches and ivy and ribbons. If one was particularly fanciful, one might imagine their countenances a bit less forbidding, the suggestion of a smile on their lips, even the hint of a twinkle in their eyes in celebration of the season.

Lizzie smiled at the thought and started down the broad double stairway that swept in a gracious curve to the ground floor. It had always struck her as exceedingly odd that those long-ago Effingtons had chosen to be preserved for eternity in such serious expressions. Not at all accurate, given everything she had heard through her life about those who had preceded her; stories of swashbuckling privateers, proud, stubborn women, spies and patriots, lords and ladies and those substantially less than noble, and all sorts of other fascinating characters.

The great doors to the ballroom were flung open wide, and even the landing at the foot of the stairs was crowded with guests. Laughter and calls of "Merry Christmas" rang out over the sounds of the orchestra from the ballroom. The Effington Christmas Ball was, as always, a huge crush and unqualified success.

Lizzie had slipped away to her room to fetch the book she wished to present to Nicholas, even if doing so had been rather more difficult than she had imagined. Thus far she had danced every dance with one gentleman or another and two with Charles, who was as charming and thoughtful as ever, although he gave the distinct impression of being a bit nervous. In her experience, Charles had never been anything but thoroughly lighthearted and completely confident. She feared that his odd manner tonight was indeed an indication of his intention to ask for her hand, and, at the moment, she had no idea how she would respond.

Lizzie hid the book in the folds of her gown and headed toward the library. She navigated her way through the crowd milling in and out of the ballroom and acknowledged various greetings politely but without overt encouragement. She had no desire to waste time with anything akin to a conversation at the moment. She was altogether too anxious to engage in mindless pleasantries. Still, she could not help but overhear any number of comments in passing, most about the two small fir trees on linen-covered tables that flanked the entry to the ballroom. They were bedecked with sweets and flowers, garlands of ribbons and tiny candles, unlit as a precaution against setting careless guests aflame.

"The Queen has had trees like these in celebration of Christmas since, oh, 1841, I believe," one lady said to her companion. "It's the Prince's German background, no doubt."

"I quite like it," the second lady said firmly. "It's exceedingly festive. I shall have to have a tree in my own home next year."

"As will I." Her friend studied the closest tree. "The duchess says, regardless of what the Queen chooses, she may well have a larger tree with decorations in the future. One that does not sit on a table but rather stands on the floor and reaches toward the ceiling."

"A full-size tree? In the house?" The other woman snorted. "Absurd idea."

Lizzie bit back a grin. If her mother, Marianne, the Duchess of Roxborough, wished to have a full-size tree, or an entire forest, in her house at Christmas or any other time of the year for that matter, she most certainly would do just that, regardless of what anyone else might think.

Lizzie reached the library, and all thoughts of Christmas and fir trees vanished. She drew a deep breath, pushed open the door, and stepped into the room.

The huge library was shadowed, the endless shelves of books little more than a hint of scent in the air, the gas lights dimmed. For a moment she was afraid that he hadn't come. That he wouldn't come. Or perhaps this emotion that pooled in her midsection was relief that she had arrived before him. Or relief that he might not come at all. It would certainly make her life easier. She could push these disquieting feelings she had for him aside, lock them in a place in her mind reserved for other discarded and fanciful notions, and go on with her life exactly as she, and everyone else, had planned. Marry Charles, the man who had always loved her. The man she had always loved. Until Nicholas.

"Good evening, Elizabeth." Nicholas emerged from the shadows on the opposite side of the room near the desk.

She started, as much from her own nerves as his sudden appearance. "Good evening, Nich-olas." She forced a casual note to her voice. "It's a wonderful party, don't you think?"

"It always is. Indeed, I have long thought of your family's ball as the highlight of the holiday season."

"Yet you did not hurry back from your travels last year or the year before or the year before that to attend." She kept her tone light and teasing. "Indeed, by my count, you have missed the last three Effington Christmas Balls."

He raised a brow. "And you were counting?"

"Of course." She smiled. "You and your uncle are as much a part of the family as if you were blood relations. You have both been sorely missed these past years."

He chuckled. "It is always nice to be missed."

"I understand we shall soon be missing you again," she said as if it were of no importance whatsoever. As if it didn't matter. As if she didn't care.

"I leave tomorrow." He studied her for a moment. "I must confess I am rather surprised by your appearance. I am waiting for Jonathon. A servant said he had asked to meet me here to discuss my trip."

"No doubt he will be here any minute." Lizzie shrugged and resisted the impulse to confess that Jonathon had no idea whatsoever about this meeting in the library. "Until then, why don't you tell me of your plans?"

He laughed softly, and the sound echoed through her veins. "There is nothing to tell, really. I propose to seek out those investments of my father's that may still be feasible and see if there is anything of worth to be salvaged. Beyond that, I intend to make my own fortune in shipping or the import of goods or something of that nature."

"Is it that easy then?" She tilted her head and considered him. "Does one simply say, 'I shall make my fortune' and then go out and do just that?"

"Exactly." He nodded somberly, but there was a distinct twinkle in his eye.

"Exceedingly odd then that there are not more fortunes being made, don't you think? I mean to say, if it is indeed that easy, surely there would be no more poor? One and all would be successful and wealthy."

"I am mistaken then, it is obviously not at all easy." He sobered. "In truth, Elizabeth, I do not know if I can succeed. However, as I do not intend to fail, there is no other option." A half smile quirked his lips. "Nor do I intend to return until I have accomplished all I have set out to do."

"Must you really go?" she blurted and stepped toward him. "Couldn't you make this fortune of yours right here in England? Besides, you will be the next Earl of Thornecroft with all the wealth and prestige that accompanies the title. Surely, that is enough for any man?"

"It's not a question of wealth, although it may well seem so. It's more a matter of, I don't know, of . . ." He searched for the right words.

"Honor?" she said, hoping he would deny it. Honor was one thing she knew she could not fight.

"Exactly." He smiled and her heart sank. "Or rather that's part of it. Pride plays a part as well, I suppose." He thought for a moment. "I wish to atone for my father's mistakes, and that is obviously a point of honor for me. I wish to achieve success because of what I am rather than who I am."

"Pride?"

He nodded. "I don't want my life to be simply handed to me through a whim of blood and fate. Through no effort of my own. I know it is the way of the world we live in; still, I find it somewhat distasteful. Odd, I know, but there you have it. Oh, certainly when the time comes I will be happy to accept the title because it is my duty to my family and it is what my uncle wishes and I care for him very much."

"Yet you are willing to leave him and everyone you care about. Everyone who cares for you."

"I admit it's difficult, but this is what I was meant to do. I know it now as I have always known it. I cannot refuse to follow the dictates of my heart. Wherever they may lead." His intense gaze caught hers. "Can you understand that?"

"No," she said quickly, then sighed. "Yes, I suppose I can, although it would make no sense coming from anyone but you."

He laughed. "Is that a compliment?"

"You may take it as such." She forced a lighthearted smile. "However, as you insist on leaving us, I have a small token for you. A farewell gift, as it were." She held out the book. "It's Mr. Dickens's new Christmas story."

He accepted the book and turned it over in his hands, the gilt lettering winking in the dim light. "I have heard talk of it. It's supposed to be quite good."

"Oh, it is indeed wonderful. It may well be the most wonderful story about Christmas that has ever been written. I liked it enormously."

He stared at the volume in his hand. "I shall treasure it always."

"I hope it will be a comfort when you are far away from . . . us." She gazed up at him. "I thought it would serve to remind you of Christmas here in London and your uncle and—"

"And all I hold dear?" His gaze met hers, and her breath caught.

She nodded slowly. "What do you hold dear, Nicholas?"

"I . . ." He drew a deep breath. "Jonathon isn't coming, is he?"

"No," she whispered and stared into his dark eyes. "I didn't think you would meet me if I simply requested it."

"You were right. It's most improper to be here alone with you."

"Nonsense. We have been alone any number of times. Besides, we have known one another since childhood."

"But you are no longer a child." His gaze darkened with what was surely desire or need or longing. *Or love?*

"Neither of us are children." She stared up at him for a long moment. "I could not let you leave without a moment alone. Without the opportunity to convince you to stay or, failing that, to say good-bye."

"Why?" His tone was hard and demanding.

"Because I . . ." She swallowed hard against the ache in the back of her throat. "Must you go? Must you leave?"

He drew a deep, shuddering breath, as if it were as difficult for him to say as it was for her to hear. "Yes."

"Why?"

"I told you. I cannot explain it better than I already have. This is something I must do. My destiny perhaps."

"Then let it be my destiny too. Take me with you," she said without thinking. "There is something between us, Nicholas. Something that has hovered unspoken since the very moment you returned to London. You cannot deny it."

"Perhaps—"

"No!" Her voice was sharp with pent-up longing, and she moved closer. So close she could see the rise and fall of his chest and feel the heat of his body a hair's breadth from her own. Desperation vanquished any modicum of caution.

"Why are you so stubborn? There is no 'perhaps' about it. You kissed me as I have never been kissed before, and that I cannot forget. I do not believe you can forget it either. You have feelings for me, Nicholas, I know you do, and once you leave there will be no opportunity for you, for us, to determine if those feelings are of importance or nothing of significance at all." Her gaze searched his with a yearning born of an awful, aching wonder deep inside her. "I have to know what you think, how you feel, what you want—"

"What I want?" He stared at her in disbelief. "What I want, what I have always wanted," he yanked her into his arms, "is you."

He pulled her hard against him and crushed his lips to hers. He tasted her, devoured her, and she responded in kind. His chest was hard against her breasts, and she could feel his heart beat against her in measure with her own. Passion she had never suspected could exist surged through her, and she clung to him with a need so great that it overwhelmed reason and conquered rational thought and swept away resistance. She thought she would surely die from the sheer intensity of his lips meeting hers, her body molding against his as if they were halves of the same whole. As if this was where she belonged. It lasted a moment or a lifetime or forever, and she vowed never to let him go.

Without warning, she felt his body stiffen. He released her and stepped back.

"Forgive me, Elizabeth." He nodded in a curt and formal manner, as if they were mere acquaintances. As if he had not just claimed her soul. "I should not have taken such liberties. Please accept my apologies."

She struggled to catch her breath. "What?"

"I have no excuse, of course, suffice it to say I was simply carried away by your loveliness and," he waved absently at the room, "the festive nature of the evening."

"You . . . you . . . you're apologizing?" She widened her eyes in shock. "For kissing me?"

"Yes, of course." He shook his head. "It was decidedly improper, especially here, alone, your reputation—"

"You don't have feelings for me?" Disbelief coursed through her. Surely, no man kissed like that without emotion, without *love*, involved. "You don't care for me? You don't want me?"

"I most certainly do. A man would have to be long dead and moldering in his grave not to want you. It is sheer desire that has simmered between the two of us. Only a fool would deny it. And given the way you kiss . . ." He chuckled wickedly. "Good God, Elizabeth, you're lovely and charming and have a passion within you I confess I never so much as suspected. You would be most amusing."

"Amusing?" Her voice rose. "I would be amusing?"

"*Most* amusing." His gaze raked over her, as if thoroughly assessing her charms. "We could have a very good time together, you and I. I learned a great deal on my travels about men and women and the very, very good times they could have together. My uncle is extraordinarily knowledgeable about such things. He has been an excellent guide."

"Has he?" Was that the answer then? Did his kiss curl her toes and sap her will only because he did it so very well? Was it the result of experience and practice rather than any affection on his part? And was her response that of any inexperienced woman to a man of his skills?

"Most certainly. My uncle is a man of the world, and he has introduced me to . . . well, I suppose that's neither here nor there."

"No, it isn't." Her words were stiff, her tone overly proper, and even to her own ear did not sound like her at all.

"However, I must admit," he narrowed his eyes thoughtfully, "your proposal to accompany me is most intriguing."

Fury welled within her, and she raised her chin. "I don't—"

"You're the daughter of a most prestigious and wealthy family. Your dowry and your family's influence, together with my uncle's money, are most appealing." He nodded in a considering manner. "Indeed, I am more than a bit tempted to say honor be damned. To abandon this making my fortune nonsense and stay right here."

"Nicholas!" She stared in horror. As much as she wanted him to do just that, the tone of his words, as well as the calculating look in his eye, were not those of the man she knew. Or thought she knew. Or thought she might love.

"Still," he shrugged. "It would never work. I am committed to this quest of mine, and were I to marry at this point, it would be to a wife who was willing to work by my side to achieve my goals. As charming as you are, I need a wife far more serious and far less frivolous than you."

"Frivolous?" She tried not to choke on the word. She had thought he knew her better than that.

"Come now, Elizabeth, surely that estimation of your character does not surprise you? In point of fact, I suspect you have actively cultivated just such a manner."

She stared at him for a long moment. Regardless of what they'd shared, what she thought she'd felt for him and what she'd been confident he'd felt in return, she obviously didn't know him at all. He was a stranger. And she would not now, not ever, allow him to see how devastating his callous words were.

She cast him a blinding smile that belied a rising tide of anger and an equally powerful sense of hurt and betrayal. "You have found me out, Nicholas. It has long been my experience that men are far more interested in women who have little more on their minds than the latest fashion or the current social season than they are in those who are serious and dreary.

"And dear, dear, Nicholas, I fear you have misunderstood me as well." She lowered her voice in a confidential manner. "I was not actually suggesting marriage."

"Oh? You would be content to come with me without benefit of marriage?"

"Don't be absurd." She forced a lighthearted laugh. "I really wasn't suggesting anything at all beyond the kind of companionship you and I have shared. I was simply carried away by the prospect of your adventures."

"Were you?" He raised a skeptical brow.

"I was indeed. Why, you are off on adventures that I, as a woman, shall never be privy to. For a moment, and no more than a moment, mind you, the idea of leaving behind London and the life I have always known to set off on the unknown challenge of making your fortune was quite irresistible."

She raised a shoulder in a casual shrug. "I am sorry if I misled you. I would have come to my senses in no time at all. Even as"—she braced herself against the irritating word—"*frivolous* as I am, I know accompanying you, regardless if it was only as a mere companion, would be a dreadful mistake. Besides, who would believe there was nothing more between us than mere friendship? My reputation, my very life, would be ruined. As for marriage, why, you and I would never suit."

"No, we wouldn't."

"But I can certainly understand how you would think I was suggesting marriage or something substantially less respectable. Frivolous or not, it's precisely what you would expect from someone of my family and background." She heaved a theatrical sigh. "I must confess, I am really rather embarrassed that I said anything at all, but you know how women of a frivolous nature are. And I, in particular, do tend to speak before I think. It's a dreadful flaw in my character and one I shall have to work on."

"Indeed you shall." His voice was light, but his eyes smoldered. "The next man you offer to accompany on his"—he cleared his throat—"*adventures* may not be as understanding as I. He might well accept your offer."

"Come now, Nicholas, I daresay I have learned my lesson and shall never do anything of the kind again." She met his gaze directly. "If I could take back my words, all of them, I would."

"Of course," he murmured.

She had to escape his presence, now, before her resolve crumbled. Before she turned into a quivering mass of despair. Still, she could not allow this ill-advised meeting to destroy her life and her future. "I do hope you will not tell—"

"It shall be our secret," he said firmly. "You have my promise."

"And you are a man of honor, aren't you?"

He grinned. "Always about my word, if nothing else."

"Thank you." She cast him a relieved smile. "I must return to the ball. I daresay Charles will wonder where I've gone to."

"Yes, of course . . . Charles."

She turned to go, stifling the impulse to run, to flee as fast as she could. Lizzie stepped to the door, then drew a deep breath and turned back to Nicholas. "I suspect we shall not see each other again, at least not for a very long time. I do wish you well, Nicholas. I hope you get everything you've always wanted."

The enigmatic half smile that did delightfully unpleasant things to her insides lifted the corner of his lips, and she steeled herself against it. "Ah, Elizabeth, I cannot possibly get everything I want. Some things were not meant to be."

Her breath caught, but she forced a smile to her face. "And some things were."

She pulled open the door and started out.

"Thank you again. For the book, that is." His voice was soft behind her, and her heart twisted.

"Merry Christmas," she tossed over her shoulder. She couldn't bear to look back at him again. She stepped through the doorway and pulled the door closed, his final words lingering behind her.

"Merry Christmas, Elizabeth."

She leaned back against the closed door and struggled to catch her breath, fought to hold back tears.

How could she have been so wrong? About him, and worse, about herself?

Obviously her feelings for him were no deeper than his were for her. How could they be otherwise, now that he had revealed his questionable character? He was right, of course. What simmered between them was nothing more than desire. Lust. She had never tasted it before and therefore had no defense against it. Nicholas was mysterious and handsome, and only a woman long dead and deeply buried would fail to succumb to his charms. And his kiss. No doubt nothing more than the result of his travels through the world and the guidance of his uncle, a delightful gentleman but one any respectable woman would be wise to stay far away from.

As humiliating as the last few minutes had been, at least she knew now. Nicholas Col-lingsworth might have been the biggest mistake of her life, and she should be—no—she was grateful to him for letting his true nature show. She could go on with her life now without doubt or regrets. She squared her shoulders and headed back to the ballroom.

And if there was a certain amount of pain involved, so be it. It was a small enough price to pay for peace of mind.

She slipped into the ballroom, the festive gathering a balm to her wounded feelings. Her wounded pride more than likely and absolutely nothing more than that. She would not allow it to be more than that from this moment forward.

"Lizzie." Without warning, Charles appeared at her side. "Wherever have you been? I have been looking for you everywhere."

"I was simply . . ." She looked into his clear blue eyes and shook her head. "It was hot, and I—"

"It scarcely matters." He grinned and grabbed her hand. "I must speak with you."

"Charles, I—"

"Privately," he said firmly and started off, pulling her along behind him.

"Where are we going?" She laughed in spite of herself. Of course, Charles could always make her laugh. Her heart lightened.

"Where we shan't be disturbed. And if there is mistletoe," he cast her a wicked smile, "so much the better."

"Charles!" She laughed again and realized that the simple fact that she could laugh at all was obviously an indication of where her true affection lay.

He pulled her into an alcove off the side of the ballroom, a fairly secluded spot for an intimate conversation, and drew her into his arms so quickly that she had no time to protest. His lips met hers in a kiss warm and tender. A kiss that spoke of an ease between them and long acquaintence and . . . love. Not the kind of passion that melted her knees and seared her senses but rather a gentler affection that warmed her heart and comforted her soul and promised to be true forever.

He pulled away, and she stared up at him with mock suspicion. "I see no mistletoe here, Charles. I fear you have taken inappropriate liberties."

"Not at all." He released her, reached into his waistcoat pocket, then drew forth a bedraggled twig of limp leaves and drooping berries, which he presented with a theatrical flourish. "I brought my own."

"I see." She raised a brow. "And do you carry it with you in the event an opportunity to use it presents itself? In which case I fear I shall have to warn every unsuspecting female in the house as to your wicked intentions."

"My intentions are indeed wicked." He laughed and tossed the withered twig onto a nearby bench. "But only in regards to you."

A teasing note sounded in her voice. "I'm not entirely sure if I should be shocked or flattered."

"You should be . . ." He paused, and his expression sobered. "Lizzie, your father wishes to make an announcement, and I . . ."

Her heart stilled. "An announcement?"

"You see, I . . . that is to say . . . I did speak to him but I haven't been able to . . . well the words, you see . . . with you I can't seem . . ." He blew a long breath and took her hands in his. "Dash it all, Lizzie, I love you. I have always loved you and I wish to marry you."

She sucked in a sharp breath. She'd known this was inevitable. Still, she hadn't really thought his proposal would come tonight. Here. Now.

"Surely you know how I feel about you." His worried gaze searched hers. "I know we have never spoken of our feelings, not really, but I always thought you had some affection for me."

"Oh, Charles, I—"

"I shall get down on one knee if you like, or both if you prefer. I'd be happy to grovel at your feet if you wish."

"You needn't—"

"I know this is what everyone has always expected, but I'm not asking out of any sense of obligation or because this will make both our families happy but," his grip on her hands tightened, "I want this, or rather you, more than I have ever wanted anything. I cannot live without you, Lizzie. I vow I shall make you happy from this very day forward and I promise we shall have a wonderful life together. Will you make me the happiest man in the world? Will you agree to be my wife?"

"I . . ." She stared up at him for a long moment, and the oddest sense of pieces of a puzzle clicking smoothly into place filled her.

Some things were not meant to be.

And some things were.

"On one condition," she said slowly.

"Anything."

"Never again carry mistletoe in your pocket." She adopted a stern expression. "One never knows who might try to take advantage of such a thing, and if I am to be your wife, I should hate for other women—"

He laughed and gathered her into his arms. "Mistletoe or not, there shall be no other women. There shall be one woman and one woman only for the rest of my days."

"The rest of our days," she echoed as her lips met his once again and she firmly set aside any lingering thoughts of dark, smoldering eyes and unrelenting longing and a kiss that melted her bones.

Some things were not meant to be.

And some things were.

This, Charles, was meant to be. He was her fate, her future, and for now and forever, he would be her life. And she would indeed make him happy for the rest of their days. He deserved no less. She deserved no less.

She would put all thoughts of Nicholas Collingsworth away with the other remnants of this Christmas and go on with her life. A good, full, happy life.

Exactly as it was meant to be.

Elizabeth was a terrible liar.

Nick stared unseeing at the library door.

Fortunately for them both, he was very good at deception. He had never suspected he had such a skill. No doubt it could come in handy in the future.

He had hurt her, he could see it in her eyes, but he'd had no choice. Any feelings that she thought she'd had for him couldn't possibly be anything of significance. She'd loved Charles and Charles had loved her all of their lives. Nick was nothing more than an intriguing moment of confusion in a young woman's mind, or possibly her heart.

Besides, while he knew in many ways the notion was ridiculous—his uncle was an earl after all—he couldn't escape the nagging suspicion that he was not entirely worthy of her.

She was an Effington, one of England's most powerful families. Her father was the Duke of Roxborough, as had his father been before him, and her brother was a marquess. He was the son of the youngest son of an earl, a man who'd been scarcely better than a wastrel, really. A man who had professed to want to make his own way in the world yet had done little to achieve that goal. Certainly, he had had a fair amount of bad luck, but it had long bothered Nick that his father's failures hadn't seemed to bother his father at all. It was now Nick's duty to atone for his father's sins. And he would do so alone.

But if he was wrong? If she indeed truly loved him?

Nick swept the question aside. Elizabeth's feelings would surely pass once he was gone from her life, and he would not do to her what his father had done to his mother. He would not take her from her home and her family and all she held dear for an insecure future regardless of love. And he would not betray his friend. No, this was the right thing to do. Nick knew it as strongly as he knew his own path in life. Elizabeth would be happy with the life she was always meant to have.

And what of your happiness?

He would be happy with success, he asked no more than that.

It was done then. He had made certain of it. Elizabeth would forget about any ill-advised affection she might have had for him and marry Charles. Her future was assured.

As for his future, Nick shrugged and started toward the door. He had no desire to return to the festivities. No desire to see Elizabeth in Charles's arms. He would return at once to his uncle's house, prepare for his departure, and pen brief notes of farewell to Jonathon and Charles complete with an apology for not bidding them adieu in person. Nick simply didn't know if he could keep up the charade of not caring for Elizabeth if he looked into her green eyes one more time.

Hurting her with his hateful comments had been the most difficult thing he had ever done. He was confident she would never forgive him and confident as well that he would never get over the look in her eyes and the unrelenting pain in his own heart.

Still, it was a small enough price to pay for doing what was right. Indeed, there was no better way to start his journeys than with the sure and certain knowledge that the woman he loved would be safe and happy and loved.

He gripped the book in his hand tighter. He needed no reminder of this night, this Christmas, but he would cherish the gift always as a token of her affection, no matter how misplaced it might have been. He would keep it close to his heart, as he would keep the memory of her laugh and her kindness and her kiss, and it would warm him as he went on with his life. Alone.

And that too was meant to be.

The moment Scrooge's hand was on the lock, a strange voice called him by his name, and bade him enter. He obeyed.

It was his own room. There was no doubt about that. But it had undergone a surprising transformation. The walls and ceiling were so hung with living green, that it looked a perfect grove; from every part of which, bright gleaming berries glistened. The crisp leaves of holly, mistletoe, and ivy reflected back the light, as if so many little mirrors had been scattered there; and such a mighty blaze went roaring up the chimney, as that dull petrification of a hearth had never known in Scrooge's time, or Marley's, or for many and many a winter season gone. Heaped up on the floor, to form a kind of throne, were turkeys, geese, game, poultry, brawn, great joints of meat, sucking-pigs, long wreaths of sausages, mince-pies, plum-puddings, barrels of oysters, red-hot chesnuts, cherry-cheeked apples, juicy oranges, luscious pears, immense twelfth-cakes, and seething bowls of punch, that made the chamber dim with their delicious steam. In easy state upon this couch, there sat a jolly Giant, glorious to see: who bore a glowing torch, in shape not unlike Plenty's horn, and held it up, high up, to shed its light on Scrooge, as he came peeping round the door.

"Come in!" exclaimed the Ghost. "Come in. and know me better, man!"

Scrooge entered timidly, and hung his head before this Spirit. He was not the dogged Scrooge he had been; and though the Spirit's eyes were clear and kind, he did not like to meet them.

"I am the Ghost of Christmas Present," said the Spirit. "Look upon me!"

Scrooge reverently did so. It was clothed in one simple green robe, or mantle, bordered with white fur. This garment hung so loosely on the figure, that its capacious breast was bare, as if disdaining to be warded or concealed by any artifice. Its feet, observable beneath the ample folds of the garment, were also bare; and on its head it wore no other covering than a holly wreath, set here and there with shining icicles. Its dark brown curls were long and free: free as its genial face, its sparkling eye, its open hand, its cheery voice, its unconstrained demeanour, and its joyful air. Girded round its middle was an antique scabbard; but no sword was in it, and the ancient sheath was eaten up with rust.

"You have never seen the like of me before!" exclaimed the Spirit.

"Never," Scrooge made answer to it.

—A Christmas Carol, Charles Dickens, 1843

Chapter 4

Christmas Present
December 1853

"I wondered if you were ever going to return home." Frederick puffed on his cigar and studied his nephew. "It has been a very long time."

"Nonsense." Nick settled deeper into the library chair that matched his uncle's, a glass of excellent brandy in one hand, a fine cigar in the other. "Why I was here a mere four years ago."

Frederick snorted. "Scarcely worth mentioning, I'd say. You were in London for no more than a handful of days. Barely long enough to attend your own investiture."

Sir Nicholas grinned. "Who would have imagined the furtherance of steam transport between England and North America would be considered service to the crown."

"Business is exceedingly important in this day and age, and Her Majesty knows it. While the significance of that visit is not diminished by its brevity, to my mind, it scarcely counts." Frederick aimed his cigar at the younger man. "Ten years is an exceptionally long time to remain away."

"Not at all. At least, not in the way in which the world judges time." Nick shrugged. "It's all relative, Uncle. As history goes, a decade is a mere blink of an eye."

"Well, in my history, it's been a bloody long time." Frederick's voice softened. "I have missed you, my boy. It is good to have you home."

"It is good to be home." Nick's tone matched his uncle's.

He sipped his brandy, the mellow warmth of the liquor matching the equally comfortable warmth of his mood. He would not have believed it when he'd left ten long years ago, but he'd missed London and this house and this man more than he had thought possible. This was the only real home he had ever known, and he'd had no idea it meant so much to him until he was no longer here.

Aside from a bit more gray on his uncle's head, nothing had really changed. The library, indeed all of Thornecroft House, was exactly as he remembered. Even the disarray in this particular room appeared untouched, although Nick suspected that in the last decade, Mrs. Smithers had surely managed regular, if surreptitious, cleanings. Still, the look, even the scents of beeswax and cigars and times long past were exactly as he'd remembered when he'd closed his eyes at the end of a day. This was the very essence of comfort and belonging and home and precisely what he had missed in those endless years alone. It was indeed exceedingly good to be back.

"You have made quite a name for yourself, Nick." The older man's eyes glowed with pride. "Why, I don't know of a single person in all of London who isn't aware of the fortune you've made or the success you've achieved."

Nick laughed. "And no doubt I can credit you for that."

"Perhaps." A gruff note sounded in Frederick's voice, and Nick bit back a smile. It was obvious that his uncle had made it a point of trumpeting Nick's financial triumphs through the years. "I see no reason to keep your success a secret, especially as you have made me a far wealthier man in the process." Frederick grinned. "And I am most appreciative."

"It's the least I could do, Uncle. After all, you gave me the funds to start with."

"Nonetheless, you've worked tirelessly, and you've earned everything you have."

"Even the notoriety?"

"There's nothing particularly distasteful about notoriety of an affirmative nature. You've become extremely successful, and the world, at least the rarefied, refined world of London society, should be aware of it. I don't mind telling you that the notion that the only honorable wealth is that which has been in a family for generations is complete and utter nonsense. We should applaud man's ingenuity rather than his ability to outlive wealthy relations. I'm damnably proud of you, Sir Nicholas, and I don't give a fig who knows it."

"Thank you, Uncle." Nick raised his glass. "I will confess," he flashed a grin, "I'm rather proud of myself."

"As well you should be." Frederick nodded and returned the salute.

Nick had indeed earned his success. What he had been able to locate of his father's investments, given James's random record keeping, had proved worthless. Nick's own ventures into shipping and exporting had produced a steady profit with equally steady, but only moderate, growth. It was when he'd invested and then become a partner in a new steamship line to transport not only goods but also passengers that his fortune had truly been made.

Steam-powered ships crossed the Atlantic from England to America in a mere eleven days rather than the thirty-five or more required for a crossing by sail. The combination of speed and novelty had proved irresistible to a public eager for a faster, more convenient, and, ultimately, economical means of travel and transport from one continent to another.

"I had rather thought you might return for good three years ago," Fredrick said casually. "When Lord Langley died."

Nick raised a brow. "Now, why would I do that, Uncle?"

Frederick shrugged. "As I said, it was just a thought."

Charles's unexpected demise in a carriage accident had been both a shock and a tragedy. He'd left not only a wife but two young sons. Nick had mourned the loss of his old friend and regretted the years apart. In spite of his words to the contrary, he had indeed considered returning to London, but to what end? To console Charles's widow? Charles's friendship alone deserved more than that. Nick's loyalty to his childhood companion did not end with his death. Besides, Elizabeth was surrounded by family and friends, and he would have been nothing more than an unwelcome interloper. Nick had avoided both Charles and Elizabeth on his brief visit home, and given their parting, he could not imagine Elizabeth greeting him upon the death of her beloved husband with anything less than disdain. Indeed, he might not have returned now had it not been for a letter from her brother.

"I wasn't certain you even knew of his death."

"As his solicitor located me in America through your solicitor and as you mentioned Charles's death in your letters, I could hardly avoid knowing," Nick said wryly.

"Still, correspondence goes astray."

"Jonathon wrote me as well when it happened." Nick blew a long breath. "I could scarce believe it then and even now find it difficult to accept. I had not seen Charles in years, yet I do miss him. I had always assumed he, Jonathon, and I would be friends in our dotage just as we had been in our youth. I shall miss that as well." Nick's thoughts drifted back to his younger days and the golden-haired boy with the generous nature who had befriended him. "Friends one can count on are rare in this world.

"However," Nick pulled himself firmly back to the present and fixed Frederick with a steady gaze, "at the moment, Uncle, let us not talk of the past but of the here and now. Since my arrival last night, we have spoken of nothing but me. My life and travels and adventures. Surely, the years have not stood still for you?"

"Would that they would have, but the years march on inexorably, etching themselves in the lines on my face and the gray upon my head." Frederick heaved an overly dramatic sigh. "I am growing old even as we speak. I shall soon be doddering and inept and require a nursemaid simply to feed me."

"Come now, your fate is not that dire." Nick laughed. "Why, you are the very picture of health."

"Only at the moment, my boy." Frederick's voice was grim, but a twinkle shone in his eye. "One should be prepared for the future. I already have my eye on a nursemaid who would prove most . . . efficient."

"Oh?" Nick drew his brows together in concern. "Is there something you haven't told me? Are you ill, Uncle?"

"Not today, but tomorrow . . . It is always wise to be prepared." Frederick leaned back in his chair and blew a smoke ring that hovered in the air for a moment before fading away to oblivion. "For example, this nursemaid I mentioned would need a fair amount of training. Her current position does not demand the skills I should require. Or perhaps," he smiled wickedly, "it does. I daresay, in many ways, she might be well versed in the care of older gentlemen such as myself."

Nick stared for a moment, then grinned. "She is on the stage then?"

Frederick nodded. "The woman has the most magnificent pair of . . ." He cleared his throat. "Legs. For a nursemaid, that is."

"Of course." Nick's grin broadened. "For a nursemaid."

"Or a goddess." Frederick chuckled and flicked the ash of his cigar in the general direction of the ever-present saucer. Inevitably the ashes drifted to the floor.

Nick laughed. "It is good to know some things never change."

"You, however, are not the same man who left here a decade ago."

Nick aimed his cigar at his uncle. "That, Frederick, was the whole purpose of my departure."

"I am not speaking of wealth or success." Frederick studied him for a moment. "I see a marked difference in your manner."

"Older and wiser I should hope."

"As do we all, but that's not what I mean." Frederick considered him thoughtfully. "Ten years ago, even on your last visit, you would not have sat calmly in your seat without fidgeting or leaping up to pace the room. You are far less restless than you once were. There is a distinct air of calm about you."

"I have conquered my doubts, the demons of uncertainty that have long haunted me, if you will." Nick's voice was casual, as if his words were of no consequence—and perhaps, at this point in time, they weren't.

Nick had always known it was important to him to succeed where his father had failed, but he'd never quite understood how deep that desire was until he had achieved success. It was as if with success came peace. "Indeed, one could call me satisfied with my life. Even content."

"As admirable as that is, there is more to life than the accumulation of wealth. Or at least there should be," Frederick said. "A man needs a wife and an heir to make his life truly complete."

"Yet I see you are no closer to marriage now than you were a decade ago."

"And I freely admit there is an element lacking in my life that I regret rather more often than I should like to acknowledge. However, I am not dead yet." Frederick's voice was cool. "I confess I have kept my eye on a lovely young widow of late."

Nick laughed. "Excellent, Uncle. I am glad to hear it. Perhaps this one will finally get you to the altar."

"I wouldn't wager on it," Frederick murmured. "My interest in her is not of that nature."

"Why not?"

"We simply do not suit. I have known her for much of her life, she is the daughter of old friends. I have a difficult time thinking of her as a grown woman even though she most certainly is."

"Who is this widow?" Nick said slowly.

"She has two sons," Frederick continued without pause, "and while I am not opposed to children in a theoretical sense—they are the future of the nation and all that—I am not entirely certain I wish to play the role of father at this stage of my life."

"Uncle." A warning sounded in Nick's voice.

Frederick ignored it. "Regardless, she is still eminently eligible, of good family and an excellent disposition. Beyond that, the years have been most kind to her. The lady is every bit as lovely now as she was, oh, say, ten years ago. Possibly more so."

Nick raised a brow. "Are you quite finished?"

"For the moment." Frederick pointed his cigar at his nephew. "But only for the moment."

"Then am I to understand that this is a beginning of a campaign on your part?" Nick downed the rest of his drink.

"I hadn't thought of it as a campaign, but," Frederick shrugged, "that's not entirely inaccurate, and I rather like the way it sounds."

"Then be prepared to accept defeat." Nick forced a casual note to his voice, placed his cigar in the saucer on the table beside him, and got to his feet. "I have no intention of pursuing Lady Langley."

"Why not?"

Nick crossed the room to the decanter of brandy on the desk. "Charles was one of my closest friends."

"And?"

"And nothing, Uncle." Nick drew his brows together. "I cannot betray his memory by pursuing his wife."

"His *widow.*"

"Semantics." Nick shrugged and refilled his glass. "She was, and always will be, Charles's wife."

"He's dead and gone now."

"From her life, but not from her heart." Absently, Nick moved to the nearest bookshelf and perused the titles.

"Perhaps."

Nick glanced at his uncle. "What do you mean, 'perhaps'?"

"Nothing really. Rumor, gossip, innuendo, nothing of significance, no doubt."

Nick narrowed his gaze. His uncle was not usually this vague. "What are you trying to say?"

Frederick shrugged. "Only that one truly never knows what goes on behind the closed doors of a marriage. What transpires between a man and a woman in the privacy of their own home."

"I had understood they were quite happy together." It was as much a question as a comment. Without thinking, Nick held his breath. Not that his uncle's response mattered, really. Ten years ago, Nick had made certain Elizabeth would put aside all thoughts of him and turn to a life with Charles, where she belonged. He had done what he believed—no—he'd known was right for her future and her happiness, and it was far too late to question that decision now.

And if that decision had been wrong?

"As I said, one never knows the truth of a private relationship." Frederick thoughtfully drew on his cigar. "I can only tell you, to my personal knowledge, they did indeed appear the perfect couple. I never saw anything to indicate otherwise."

There was a tone in Frederick's voice, no more than a hint really, that all might not have been as it had seemed between Lord and Lady Langley. Still, what relationship between a man and a woman, any man and any woman no matter how well suited, was ever without a certain amount of discord? It was only natural and, indeed, to be expected. Nick pushed aside a vague sense of unease. Besides, there was nothing he could do about it now.

He stared unseeing at the row of books in front of him.

Nick had spent the last ten years putting Elizabeth firmly and thoroughly out of his mind and out of his heart. And he had succeeded as admirably in this as he had in everything else. While he had not loved another woman, he had certainly not been celibate, and he'd even toyed with the idea of marriage when the occasion, and the lady in question, had warranted it. The fact that he had never taken that drastic step had had nothing to do with Elizabeth. She was a part of his past and nothing more to him now than the wife—or rather the widow—of a good friend.

He wandered absently around the fringes of the room. Oh, certainly, there had been the odd moment through the years when another lady's smile would remind him of her smile or a laugh heard in a crowded theater would be reminiscent of her laugh or the green of seawater just under the crest of a wave would be the very shade of the color of her eyes. But those moments were as rare as they were unexpected, and Nick was confident his feelings for Elizabeth were as distant as the years and the miles that had separated them.

"What are you going to do about Lady Langley?"

"What?" Nick pulled up short. His startled gaze jumped to his uncle's. "What do you mean, *do* about her? I plan to *do* nothing whatsoever about her. I just told you I have no plans to pursue her. She is not a part of my life, nor do I intend for her to become so."

Frederick raised a brow. "That's not what I meant, but I do

find your overly vehement response rather telling." He waved his cigar at the younger man. "You protest too much, boy."

"Then what did you mean?"

"Charles's will. What will you do about that?"

"Nothing." Nick swirled his brandy and watched the amber liquid coat the inside of the glass. "As I understand it, Jonathon has handled Elizabeth's finances and her sons' inheritance since Charles's death. I see no reason to change that."

"Charles explicitly requested you take over that responsibility whenever you returned to England." Frederick studied him thoughtfully. "He came to talk to me when he decided to include that clause in his will. Charles could think of no one better suited to watch over the financial resources of his wife and children. He, too, was proud of your accomplishments." Frederick paused. "His decision to put his family's financial fate in your hands had to do with your success and abilities and friendship and nothing beyond that."

"I never even considered the possibility that it did." Nick noted the ease with which the lie slid smoothly off his tongue and avoided meeting Frederick's gaze.

The moment Nick had learned of his old friend's wishes he had wondered if Charles had indeed suspected Nick's long-ago feelings for Elizabeth. Still, Charles had given him no indication of that in his infrequent correspondence through the years.

"Regardless of Charles's reasons, Jonathon is her brother and I am little more than a stranger." Nick shrugged. "It's best to leave things as they are."

"Still, you speak of being unwilling to betray his memory, yet you are more than willing to ignore his final wishes on a matter that I know was of the utmost importance to him."

"It's two entirely different things, Uncle." Nick shook his head and without thinking moved to stand before a painting of hounds and horses and red-coated riders. He stared at it as if he had not seen it countless times before. "However, I am not unaware of my responsibilities, especially as Jonathon's last letter to me reiterated them. It was he who suggested I visit London to make certain for myself that all is well." In truth, Nick had jumped at the excuse to return home. He had been away far too long. "I plan to meet with Jonathon tomorrow to ascertain precisely the state of Charles's estate."

"It's the least you can do," Frederick murmured.

"It's the best I can do," Nick said sharply, then sighed and cast his uncle an apologetic smile. "I simply don't think there will be a need for me to do anything beyond confirming that the finances of Charles's wife and sons are in good hands. I could be wrong, of course, but I doubt it. Forgive me for snapping at you, Uncle. I am obviously still fatigued from my long journey home."

"Yes, of course. Precisely my thought." Frederick puffed his cigar. "I didn't for a moment think it was the subject of Lady Langley that caused your irritation because you still harbor a certain amount of affection for her."

Nick scoffed. "As I have never harbored any affection whatsoever for Lady Langley save that of friendship, that would indeed be ridiculous."

Frederick nodded. "Ludicrous."

"Absolutely," Nick said staunchly.

"Preposterous."

"Most certainly."

"Or possibly most perceptive on my part."

Nick glared. "Or possibly simply a case of you seeing only what you wish to see."

"Come now, my boy. In spite of your protests I know you cared for her ten years ago when you left London. I know you avoided her and virtually everyone who knew her—or you, for that matter—on your lone visit home. And I am firmly convinced your feelings have not changed."

"Regardless of whether or not I cared for Elizabeth when I left England, which I will say for the last time I did *not,* that was a lifetime ago. She is most certainly different, as am I."

"You said yourself some things do not change."

"My point exactly." Nick nodded. "There was no future to be had between the two of us then, and that has not changed now."

"Nonsense." Frederick snorted. "Everything has changed regarding the two of you. Life has moved on and pulled you both in its wake. You were barely more than children a decade ago. She is not the same woman who wed Viscount Langley, and you are not the same man who left to make his own way in the world. You have both grown, and while much of the rest of the world hasn't changed, you and she have."

"Indeed, Uncle, I am not a child. I know my own mind and—"

"Do you know your heart as well?"

"Yes," Nick snapped.

"Do you?" Frederick raised a brow. "I doubt it."

Nick heaved a long-suffering sigh. "Why?"

"For one thing, there's a look in your eye whenever Elizabeth's name is mentioned."

Nick snorted. "Don't be absurd."

"For another." Frederick blew a perfect ring of blue smoke, drew on the cigar again, and puffed a second ring that sailed through the first, suspiciously reminiscent of an arrow piercing a heart. "Your restlessness is back. I'd say the demon that has haunted you has returned. Or perhaps," he flashed his nephew a knowing grin, "she never left."

Chapter 5

Elizabeth, Lady Langley, slammed open the door of the Effington house library and noted with satisfaction how it smacked against the wall and the way the sound reverberated through the room and, with luck, the entire house.

"How could you, Jonathon?" She stalked into the library, waving the papers in her hands and resisting the urge to fling them at her brother. Jonathon Effington, the Marquess of Helmsley, sat behind the desk, his eyes wide at her sudden appearance.

"For three years you haven't so much as hinted at this! I'm your sister after all, and I should think that alone would provoke a certain amount of loyalty on your part! How could you not have told me?"

Jonathon laid his pen down on the paper in front of him, no doubt his latest literary effort, cast it a longing look, and rose to his feet in his best someday-I-will-be-the-Duke-of-Roxborough manner. In spite of his demeanor, a mix of inevitability, resignation, and a distinct touch of trepidation showed in his eyes. Good. He should be uneasy. Very uneasy. He'd be wise to be afraid as well.

"I did tell you," he said in an altogether too collected manner for a traitor. "You obviously have the papers I sent you right in your hand. Therefore you cannot complain that I did not tell you."

"Oh, I most certainly can," she snapped. It was just like Jonathon to try to smooth things over by taking her words literally. He knew full well exactly what she was asking. "Then allow me to rephrase my question. Why didn't you tell me before now?"

"Ah yes, well, that is an entirely different question."

"Isn't it, though?" She glared at her brother.

"Indeed . . ." Jonathon studied her cautiously, as if he was concerned she might launch herself over the desk at any minute and fasten her hands around his neck. "I must say you are even angrier than I anticipated."

"Am I?" She flung the papers down on the desk. "Did you imagine for a moment that I wouldn't be livid?"

"I had hoped . . ." He shrugged in the helpless way even the most competent of men adopts when faced with a righteously indignant woman. And Elizabeth was far beyond indignant. "With any luck at all . . . possibly . . ."

"Jonathon! That's quite enough. You have avoided this for years, and I shall not allow you to avoid it one second more." She moved toward him in as menacing a manner as she could muster. Not a difficult task as, at this particular moment, strangling him with her bare hands was indeed tempting. She would, in truth, never do such a thing. Probably. "I deserve an answer, and by all that's holy I bloody well intend to get one."

"Such language, Lizzie." Jonathon shook his head disapprovingly. "What would father think?"

"As father is not here at the moment and as I am a woman of nine-and-twenty, a widow, mother, and Viscountess Langley, father's opinion as to the words I choose to use doesn't matter in the least!"

Elizabeth brushed aside the lie and peeled off her gloves. The opinion of her father, Thomas Effington, the Duke of Roxborough, was always of importance to her regardless of her age or situation in life. She loved her father—and her mother too, of course—but she'd always rather liked them as well. Neither parent had ever believed she was incompetent simply because she was pretty and enjoyed the fun life had to offer, although apparently her late husband had. She dropped the gloves onto a chair and untied the ribbons of her hat.

"I suspect if father knew precisely what prompted my language he would have a few choice words of his own." She pulled off her hat and paused. "Or does he know about this?"

"He hasn't an inkling, as far as I know." Jonathon shook his head firmly. "Charles didn't want to have to argue with anyone about the merits of his actions, although I will tell you I lodged a firm protest."

"Not firm enough obviously." She tossed her hat in the general direction of her gloves. "So who does know?"

"An insignificant number of people, really," Jonathon said brightly, as if the fact that few living souls knew that her deceased husband had not trusted her with her own fate made it more palatable. "I didn't feel it was anyone's business but yours and his."

"Oh, and I do so thank you for that small consideration."

She discarded her cloak, draping it over the back of the chair. She'd been far too angry upon her arrival to concern herself with her outer garments. Indeed, it was only at the insistence of her butler and housekeeper that she'd bothered to don a cloak at all, but the early December morning was gray and cold and bearable only because the brisk air brought the promise of Christmas to come.

Jonathon ignored her. "Charles's solicitor knows—"

"*My* solicitor." Elizabeth's tone was grim. She would sack the man as soon as possible. And do it with a great deal of relish.

"I believe Charles also discussed it with Lord Thornecroft before he put the provision in his will and, upon his death, I felt compelled," Jonathon looked as if he would rather be anywhere but here, "to write to Nicholas and inform him myself."

She gasped and moved toward him. "You did not see your way clear to tell me, your own sister, about actions that would impact my well-being and that of my children, yet you informed Nicholas Collingsworth? A man you have not seen for ten full years?"

"It was only seven at the time."

"Nonetheless—"

Jonathon squared his shoulders. "It was my responsibility to tell Nicholas."

She wanted to smack him or scream or both. "And where was your responsibility to me?"

"I fulfilled my responsibility to you." Jonathon's voice was firm. "I watched over your finances until I was confident you could do so yourself. Frankly, there was a great deal of doubt on that score as to whether you could indeed handle estate business and the boys' inheritance and Charles's investments."

Strangling was too good for him. She leveled him a lethal glare.

"Not on my part, though," he said quickly. "Precisely why I told Charles from the very beginning that it was not necessary. I always knew there was far more to you than the frivolous, flighty creature you presented to the rest of the world."

"And for that you have my undying gratitude." Sarcasm dripped off her words. She would not be mollified by a mere compliment from her brother. He could be as charming as he wished and it would not change the facts of the matter. "However, you—"

"I didn't tell you because, blast it all, Lizzie, I didn't know how." Jonathon ran his hand through his hair. "Charles included this clause in his will a year or so before his death, right around the time Nicholas was knighted. Although I know they didn't meet, I suspect the knighthood is what gave Charles the idea in the first place. I probably didn't argue with him about it as much as I should have because I never expected him to die before you had both reached ripe old ages. It would be moot by then.

"It didn't seem appropriate to tell you right after Charles died, and then, as you took over more and more of the management of your affairs, it simply seemed pointless to bring it up. But I swear to you, it has weighed heavily on my conscience."

She snorted in disbelief.

"It has," he said firmly. "I have managed to live with it, but it's been difficult." He heaved a dramatic sigh. "The guilt, you know."

She raised a brow.

"Perhaps guilt is not entirely accurate." He rolled his gaze toward the ceiling. "Perhaps, as Nicholas did not seem likely to return to England, and you had proven more than competent to handle matters, it seemed little more than an unnecessary detail. Revealing it would do nothing but upset you, so I simply disregarded it. I might have even, well," he grimaced, "forgotten about it entirely."

She stared at him for a long moment. Elizabeth knew full well her anger was directed as much at her late husband as it was at Jonathon—if not more. Pity Jonathon had to take the brunt of it. Still, he wouldn't be in this position now if he hadn't held his tongue for so long.

"I suppose I can accept that." She drew a deep breath and forced a measure of calm. "Now that you have revealed some of the truth," she picked up the papers and waved them at him, "I need, I deserve, a more detailed explanation than I have received thus far. Honestly, Jonathon, do you really think a copy of a portion of my husband's will, a clause I had no idea existed, and a cursory note from you would suffice?"

"I thought I explained it all rather well," Jon-athon murmured.

"Then you were mistaken." She narrowed her gaze. "Somewhat cowardly of you to inform me of my husband's lack of faith in me in a letter rather than in person, don't you think?"

"Good God, yes." Jonathon nodded vehemently. "In fact, calling it cowardly is putting a good face on it. I confess, I have never thought of myself as a coward, yet when it came to telling you of Charles's last wishes, obviously I am. I daresay I'd rather face pistols at dawn than face you. At least about this. You've always had something of a temper, you know, and you are prone to throw things, even if you have been more reasonable and even-tempered in recent years. Besides, I had rather hoped by the time you had made your way here after reading my letter, you would be substantially calmer and rational. Apparently, I was wrong."

"Apparently."

"However, although I did underestimate your ire, I was still fairly confident your initial reaction would not be pleasant, and in that, obviously"—Jonathon cast her the all too engaging and charmingly boyish grin that had been the downfall of any number of unsuspecting women—"I was right."

"Indeed you were." Elizabeth resisted the urge to return his smile.

This wasn't really Jonathon's doing, and it wasn't entirely fair to vent on him alone the fury and unrelenting sense of betrayal that had burned within her since she'd read his note a scant hour or so ago. That he had not seen fit to inform her of Charles's wishes was not nearly as maddening as the discovery of Charles's wishes in the first place. And the fact that Charles had chosen Nicholas Collingsworth of all people to oversee her finances only compounded her anger.

She crossed her arms over her chest. "Well?"

"Well?"

She huffed. "The explanation?"

"Of course. It's really quite simple." He shrugged. "Charles was impressed by Nicholas's financial success and the knighthood of course, and decided he would be the best man to oversee the financial future of his family. However, he was also well aware that Nicholas might not return to England permanently, therefore he requested I manage your affairs until such time as Nicholas did return home, if ever. Or the boys reached their majority and received their inheritance. Or," Jonathon paused, "you remarried. If said marriage was to someone approved of by myself and Father, the management of his fortune, your fortune really, would be turned over to your new husband."

Elizabeth had gathered as much from her brother's note, but not until she heard it from his own lips did the import of Charles's action truly strike her. She sank into the nearest chair.

"So have I ever really been in control of my finances?" she said slowly. "My life?"

"You most certainly have." Jonathon pulled up a chair and sat down beside her. "Essentially, in Nicholas's absence, Charles put everything in my hands. You recall how after the shock of his death had passed, you began taking over more and more?"

She nodded. "But I was under the impression you were simply handling things out of familial concern because I was unable to do so at that particular time, and not because Charles had designated you some sort of legal overseer."

"As much as Charles was my dear friend, he never quite understood that there was far more to you than anyone ever suspected." Jonathon grinned with brotherly affection. "I, however, knew better."

"That's something, at any rate," she muttered. "Why wasn't I told this when Charles died?"

"It didn't seem particularly wise." Jonathon chose his words with care. "Grief is a dreadful thing, Lizzie, particularly as there is little anyone else can do to help. Charles's untimely death was a shock to everyone, but, if you recall, you were not at all your usual self for several months."

"Yes, of course," she murmured.

Elizabeth had not forgotten those dark days after Charles's demise. Days filled with unyielding loss and an odd sense of regret and startling revelations. About the man she had married but more about herself.

She was exceedingly proud of the fact that she had survived at all and prouder yet that she had grown and become strong and confident. Still, she'd only really done what she'd had to do for her sons and herself. It dawned on her now that if Jonathon had revealed how Charles had intended to safeguard his family's fortune after his demise, she might never have become the woman she had, but would have continued to depend on the men in her life to take care of her every need.

"Lord, Jonathon." She shook her head. "I was such a fool. I paid no attention whatsoever to matters of finance when Charles was alive."

"In that, you are not unlike most women."

"I am not most women." She met her brother's gaze directly. "I didn't truly realize that before Charles's death. I have always understood that I am a descendent of generations of independent, headstrong Effington women, but I never realized the legacy of those ladies until I was forced to draw upon the strength inherent in my own nature. I remember when I was young, vowing that someday I would call on the reserves of intelligence and competence I knew lay within me and live life precisely as I saw fit. I never did when Charles was alive because there was no need for me to do so. Even so," she smiled wryly, "it's extremely upsetting to realize my husband did not know me well enough to trust me."

"Charles was a fool," Jonathon said in a voice far harder than necessary.

Her gaze shot to her brother's.

"Not to have recognized your intelligence and competence, I mean," Jonathon said quickly. "I, however, coming from the same Effington stock and therefore sharing those gifts of intelligence and competence, not to mention charm," he flashed a quick grin, "can see what a lesser mortal cannot."

She laughed. "I suppose it scarcely matters now. All is said and done, and now that I know—" A thought struck her, and she drew her brows together. "Jonathon—"

"I'd say a brandy is called for at this point." Jonathon jumped to his feet and fairly sprinted toward the cabinet that held Father's supply of fine brandy, and other spirits.

She raised a brow. "It's rather early in the day for brandy isn't it?"

"It's later than you imagine," he muttered and pulled open the cabinet doors.

"Even so, I don't understand what you think we should be celebrating."

"Sibling affection." His back was to her, and his voice was muffled. "The binding ties of blood. Loyalty."

"All that and it's barely midday." A teasing note sounded in her voice, but she studied him curiously. "Whatever are you up to now, dear brother?"

"Affection. Blood ties. Loyalty." He returned to his chair, two glasses in one hand and a decanter in the other. "The idea that one should never kill the messenger." He poured a glass and thrust it at her. "Forgiveness."

"Very well, you have my forgiveness." She accepted the glass reluctantly. "But I really don't think—"

"Do go on, Lizzie, you like brandy. You always have."

Jonathon poured a glass for himself and tossed back a long swallow.

"As do you, apparently." She took a cautious sip of the liquor. While it was far and away too early in the day for such libations, the brandy warmed her nicely. "This is rather lovely on a dreary day like today."

"Isn't it, though?" Jonathon smiled pleasantly, but there was a distinct glimmer of apprehension in his eyes. "Perhaps you'd like more?"

"This is quite enough, thank you." She laughed. "Honestly, Jonathon, one would think you were trying to get your own sister soused."

He laughed, a sort of odd, squeaking, uncomfortable sound. "What an amusing thought."

"Brandy always produces such a pleasant feeling of warmth and well-being within me. It's really rather difficult to be angry about anything, no matter how distressing, if one has had enough brandy." She took a small sip. "You should have tried this before you sent me your note."

He smiled weakly.

"I should probably apologize to you as well. None of this is really your fault." She settled back in her chair and cupped her hands around her glass. "Oh, certainly you should have told me the truth long before now, but I can see where you have believed everything you've done has been in my best interests."

"Keep that in mind," he said under his breath.

"I shouldn't have been as angry as I was. On reflection, I am most appreciative of your efforts on my behalf."

He downed the rest of his brandy and poured another glass. "More?"

"I've barely touched what I have." She studied him for a long moment. He was most definitely nervous. "What on earth—" The question he had forestalled her asking earlier returned. "There is more, isn't there?"

"Nearly half a decanter."

"Not more brandy." It wasn't like Jonathon to be quite this evasive. It was extremely suspicious. "More that you haven't told me."

Jonathon shrugged. "*More* is such a vague term."

"*More* is quite specific."

"You won't like it." He shook his head in a mournful manner, and she might well have felt sorry for him if it had not been for the weight growing inevitably in the pit of her stomach.

"I don't expect to." At once she realized exactly what he was trying so hard not to say. "Jonathon, why did you decide to tell me about Charles's will today?"

"It was past time?"

"Jonathon?" She held her breath.

"Nicholas is back," he blurted.

Her heart caught. "Back?"

He nodded. "In London. He arrived only yesterday, I believe."

"I see." Her voice was remarkably calm, belying the thudding of her heart and the roar of her blood in her ears. "Well, that does complicate matters somewhat, doesn't it?"

His eyes narrowed thoughtfully. "I don't know. Does it?"

She tossed back the rest of her brandy. "It does if he thinks he can step into my life and take over my affairs."

"Is that all?"

"Of course. What more could there be?" A distinct challenge sounded in her voice.

Jonathon blew a long breath. "I have yet another confession to make."

"So many in one day?" she snapped. "Have you been saving them up as a special treat in preparation for Christmas?"

"I know that you and he once shared some affection for one another," he said quietly.

"Don't be absurd." At once, she got to her feet and stalked across the room. Absolutely no one knew how she had once felt about Nicholas. Or rather how she'd thought she'd felt. Jonathon's comment was little more than speculation on his part based on nothing of substance. "Nicholas and I shared nothing whatsoever but a casual sort of friendship. I have not given him a second thought since the day he left."

It wasn't the truth, of course, yet it wasn't entirely a lie. It had taken far longer than she'd expected, but she had managed to put Nicholas out of her mind for the most part. After all, she'd had Charles, a man who, in spite of his faults, had indeed loved her, and she'd loved him as well. They'd had an excellent life together. Pleasant and comfortable, and if it had not been as perfect as she had once thought it was, it had hardly been dreadful. And Nicholas had had no place in it.

And if, perhaps, on a rare occasion, she had glimpsed a man who resembled Nicholas on a busy street and her heart had twisted slightly, or if she had heard a voice in the crush of guests at a party and her breath had caught for the barest fraction of a second, or if she'd awoken from a dream with a sense of loss so profound there was the briefest ache in her throat, they'd been mere aberrations. Memories of a disloyal heart that had had no more substance than gossamer and had been just as insignificant. He had no place in her heart or in her life. And he never would.

Nicholas Collingsworth had come very close to breaking her heart. Indeed, would have done so without a second thought if her feelings for him had been at all real. Which, of course, they had not been. He had, however, embarrassed and humiliated her. She would not allow him to do so again.

She whirled back toward her brother. "It's ridiculous, of course, but why ever did you think there was something between us?"

Jonathon rose to his feet and drew a deep breath. "Because I heard you. You and Nicholas."

Her eyes widened. "What do you mean, you heard us?"

"In this very room. The night before he left England."

She sucked in a hard breath. "You were eavesdropping? On a private conversation? How could you?"

"I wasn't exactly eavesdropping, I was trapped. It was most inadvertent on my part." Indignation sounded in his voice. "You are not the only one who has arranged assignations in this room on occasion, you know. Indeed," an expression somewhere between sheepish and proud crossed his face, "one way or another I seem to have some sort of tryst in the library during every Christmas ball."

"It was not a tryst!"

"It would have been if you'd had your way," he said with a smirk.

She gasped. "I should have strangled you a few minutes ago when I had the chance!"

"Idle threats did not work when we were children, and they will not work now. Besides, I am out of reach and I intend to remain out of reach."

In spite of his words, he grabbed his chair and whipped it around in front of him in the same manner in which he had done so as a child, when his teasing would drive her to retaliate. She wouldn't be at all surprised if he stuck his tongue out at her at any moment.

"Now then, as I was saying, I had arranged a meeting with a charming young woman. I can't recall her name now, but she was amusing." A smile curved the corner of his mouth. "Most amusing."

"And?"

"And when I heard Nicholas coming, I hid behind the sofa, because I thought it was her, you see. I had hoped to surprise her."

"That sofa?" Elizabeth nodded at the sofa at the far end of the wall.

For as long as she could remember, the sofa in the library had sat in that very spot facing the fireplace, providing a delightful place for intimate conversations between friends or for a young girl to read and consider her future or even for children to hide from unrelentingly vigilant governesses. While her mother had refurbished any number of rooms in Effington House since she'd become the Duchess of Roxborough, the library was sacrosanct to the Effington men, who considered it their personal domain. Elizabeth wouldn't have been at all surprised to learn that the sofa, or its predecessor, had been in precisely the same position since the house was first built.

"That very one. You can certainly imagine how the surprise was on me when I realized that instead of a delectable young lady—"

"Whose name you cannot remember," she said pointedly.

"Perhaps she is more delectable in hindsight." He shook his

head. "At any rate, Nicholas was in the library. I scarce had a moment to consider how to make my presence known when you arrived. As I had no idea how to extricate myself without a great deal of embarrassment on all sides," he shrugged, "I decided silence was the wisest course."

She grit her teeth. "So you were there the entire time?"

He nodded.

"Yet you've never said a word to me about it." She crossed her arms over her chest. "Why?"

"Because, at the time, I thought Nicholas was right." He squared his shoulders slightly, his gaze met hers, and for a moment he was every inch a future duke and not merely an annoying older brother. "I agreed then that whatever had occurred between the two of you was insignificant compared to what you shared with Charles. Looking back on it now, I think, perhaps," he blew a long, resigned breath, "I might have been wrong."

"What?"

"I am confident there was affection between you and your husband, but I am not as sure it was," he paused, "a grand passion."

"A grand passion?" Her voice rose. "Are you mad? *A grand passion?* I cannot believe you are spouting something so ridiculous. Obviously you have read too many of Mother's novels and too much of Father's poetry."

"And you have not read enough."

"Grand passions are the stuff of books and poems and have no place in the reality of life." The words came out of her mouth without thought, and a voice in the back of her mind wondered when she had become so staid and stuffy. "Although I'll have you know the passion between us was exceedingly grand."

"I stand corrected." His tone was cool, but there was a skeptical gleam in his eye. "Still, I'm not sure if you have been as happy, perhaps, as you could have been."

"What utter nonsense." She jerked her chin up. "I loved Charles and he loved me, and it was indeed the grandest of passions. We were quite, quite happy together. Why, *blissful* does not begin to describe our lives. If he hadn't died, I daresay we would have been ecstatic to the very end of our days!"

"Probably why you feel compelled to tell me this at the top of your lungs," he said mildly.

Once again, she wanted to hit him. "You are infuriating, Jonathon, and I have had quite enough."

She grabbed her hat and cloak and started toward the door. If she stayed one moment longer she would no doubt throttle her brother, and she hadn't the time or the patience to waste on him now. No, Elizabeth had spent far too long putting Nicholas out of her life to allow him back in without a fight. If she was going to do battle with a man who had achieved all that Nicholas—*Sir Nicholas*—had, she would have to use every weapon at her disposal, and she hadn't a moment to lose.

Lady Langley, Elizabeth Langley, was a woman of accomplishment and a far cry from the frivolous Lizzie Effington. And more than a fit opponent for Nicholas Collingsworth.

"Where are you going?"

"First, I'm going to inform my solicitor, that traitorous, vile rat of a creature, that his services are no longer required. Then I am going to pay a visit to father's solicitor, who has served my family and my family's interests—not Charles's, not Collingsworth's—well for countless number of years to see if there is anything that can be done about this."

She whirled toward her bother. "Regardless of what Charles and I shared, I shall not allow him to reach out from the grave and put me in the nice, pleasant, mindless niche he thinks I belong in, like I was a porcelain doll. And I will not allow an arrogant, high-handed stranger interested in nothing more than the increase of his own fortune to control my life and the future of my sons."

"Good for you, Lizzie." Admiration sounded in Jonathon's voice. "You may count on my assistance should you require it."

She cast him a scathing glare. "It's the very least you can do."

"And I stand ready to do the least whenever possible." He grinned. "You could always throw yourself on Nicholas's mercy, you know."

"Never!"

"*Mercy* is probably the wrong word. But he's a highly intelligent man and a man of business as well. If you—or rather we—simply show him how well you have done thus far with Charles's—or rather your—finances, perhaps he will agree to leave things as they are. Even better, send over your account books and I shall present them to him myself."

"I shall have them sent over at once." She met her brother's gaze. "Do you really think there is so much as a remote possibility he'll leave things as they are?"

"I have no idea. But, don't forget, he was my friend as well as Charles's. He was a good man and honorable then, and I can't imagine he has changed substantially."

"Do you think anyone who has acquired the kind of fortune he is reputed to have can remain a good and honorable man?"

He paused for a mere fraction of a second, then nodded firmly. "I do."

She snorted in disdain. "Well, I do not. And I do not intend to risk all on the possibility that Nicholas Collingsworth is a good and honorable man. Besides, in my experience, even good and honorable men rarely look beyond a pretty face."

Again she started for the door, then stopped and turned back to her brother. "That is everything, isn't it?"

Jonathon drew his brows together in confusion. "Everything?"

"There is nothing else you have kept from me, is there? Nothing I should know?"

He shook his head firmly. "Absolutely not."

"I'm not entirely sure I believe you."

He gasped in feigned dismay. "You wound me deeply, dear sister."

"I would certainly like to." She huffed with exasperation. "If your ability to keep secrets is any indication as to how well you will perform when you inherit father's title, you will certainly make an excellent duke." She pulled open the door. "If you are permitted to live that long."

His laugh trailed after her. "It should be an interesting Christmas, Lady Langley."

Christmas was the last thing she wanted to think about at the moment. It would be her fourth as a widow, and in the years since Charles's death, in spite of her resolve, each had been more difficult than the last.

In the foyer, Elizabeth called for her maid, requested her carriage to be summoned, and tried to be as pleasant as possible. Given the myriad of thoughts churning in her head, it was not an easy task.

When Charles had been alive, it had been easy to push aside all thoughts of the last time she'd seen Nicholas. Besides, he'd been very far away and therefore easy to ignore. But since Charles's death it had been increasingly difficult to disregard the memories that nagged at the back of her mind at every Effington Christmas Ball or surfaced unbidden whenever *A Christmas Carol* was read aloud.

Increasingly difficult not to wonder what her life might have been like if she had not chosen the comfort and security and unquestioned affection of one man over the adventure and excitement and, yes, uncertainty of another, even if Nicholas had essentially given her no real choice. She'd told herself that night and in the ten years since she hadn't really cared for him at all.

What if she'd been wrong? Then and now?

What if he'd been wrong?

How much more difficult would those memories and those doubts be to ignore with Nicholas back?

Nonsense, she hadn't been wrong. She would not permit herself to consider otherwise. Besides, it scarcely mattered now. She wanted nothing to do with him, and no doubt he wanted nothing to do with her as well. If she could not find a legal means of escape, there was always the possibility Jonathon was right. Nicholas might well jump at the chance to relieve himself of a responsibility he had never asked for.

And if he didn't?

She would be compelled to do whatever possible to make his life a living hell. She had no idea how to make a man's life a living hell, but surely it couldn't be all that difficult. However, the details were of no significance at the moment.

She raised her chin and cast a brilliant smile at the footman holding open the door. She was, after all, the Viscountess Langley, who successfully handled her own finances, and the daughter of the Duke and Duchess of Roxborough, and surely blood would tell. Her father wrote bad poetry and her mother wrote novels of romance and adventure, and no doubt some of that vast reservoir of creativity surged through her veins as well. When the time came she would come up with a plan.

Nicholas Collingsworth hadn't the faintest idea what he was about to face.

Lizzie Effington was now Elizabeth Langley.

And Elizabeth Langley was a force to be reckoned with.

Chapter 6

"Everything appears in order." Nick scanned the final page in the ledger book but, after having assessed the entries leading to this point, was more than confident everything was in perfect order. "Charles's assets have not merely been maintained but his investments have grown substantially."

Nick flipped the book closed and glanced up at Jonathon, who stood before the desk in the Effington House library with a distinct air of good-natured innocence and a brandy in each hand. In their youth, Jonathon had never been as innocent as his appearance, and Nick suspected even the advance of years had not changed that. The fact that his friend adopted just such a manner now did not bode well.

"In addition, I found nothing amiss in the household accounts nor for the estate. Indeed, there have been a number of improvements made that are quite progressive and have proved most beneficial. You've done an excellent job."

"While I do do an excellent job in many things"—Jonathon handed Nick a glass and sat down to face his friend across the desk—"I cannot take the credit for this."

"Don't be modest." Nick leaned back in his chair and sipped the liquor. The duke's fine brandy was as good as always. Yet another thing that had not changed with the passing of years. "I know the increase of one's fortune or, God forbid, the earning of money is frowned upon, but you should be proud. Obviously, you have inherited your father's skills at investment."

While it was certainly not public knowledge, Nick was well aware that the Duke of Roxborough had dabbled in various investments including real estate and publishing for much of his adult years and had, for the most part, been quite successful. In an age in which many of the long-held fortunes of the landed gentry had dwindled, Effington wealth had increased.

"Indeed, I have. I have turned a tidy profit in several successful ventures, and I am most immodestly proud of those. And while I'm also proud of the brilliant handling of Charles's fortune as well—"

Nick laughed. "Brilliant?"

"Brilliant," Jonathon said firmly. "The fact remains that it is not my doing."

"No? Your father's then?"

"Elizabeth has handled everything herself." Jonathon's expression was decidedly smug.

"I see," Nick said slowly, not that he was surprised. The surprising aspect of all this was that Charles had appointed someone to manage his affairs in the first place instead of leaving them in his wife's eminently capable hands.

"And I see no reason why she should not continue to do so."

"Nor do I." Nick studied his friend for a long moment. "Nor do I see any reason why I should have received from you a letter implying all was not well with Lady Langley's finances."

"Lady Langley?" Jonathon raised a questioning brow.

"Lady Langley," Nick said, ignoring Jonathon's unspoken question. He had absolutely no intention of having anything other than a cursory, businesslike relationship with Jonathon's sister. Charles's wife. Lady Langley. Calling her—indeed, thinking of her—by anything other than her title was starting down a path he refused to tread. "And you have not answered my question."

"I know." Jonathon grinned and raised his glass in a salute. "I'm very good at evading questions. Indeed, I consider it a gift I have honed to a fine art."

Nick tried not to smile and failed. Jonathon too had scarcely changed with the passage of years.

"And, as impressive as that skill is, I still want to know why the letter you wrote me carried the vague, but no less unmistakable, message that something was amiss with Lady Langley's finances."

"I thought it was time you came home for something longer than a mere visit," Jonathon said simply.

It was Nick's turn to raise a brow. "And you took it upon yourself to make certain I did so?"

"Someone had to. Why not me?"

"Perhaps I was not ready to return."

"Perhaps you were simply too stubborn to return." Jonathon cast him a pleasant smile.

"Stubborn?" Nick gasped in feigned indignation. "Me?"

"You've always been stubborn and you well know it. Besides, you could have come home and stayed four years ago when you were knighted. By my observations, that's approximately when you had more money than Croesus and your accomplishments publicly acknowledged. That, old friend, is when you had achieved all you had set out to achieve."

"You seem overly aware of my success." Nick wasn't entirely sure if he was annoyed or flattered.

"Your uncle took it upon himself to make certain we were all aware of your accomplishments. Besides, it's difficult to hide a knighthood even if you did not remain in London long enough for your friends to applaud your success. I know I probably mentioned it in a letter, but I should add my congratulations in person."

"Thank you," Nick murmured, pushing aside a touch of guilt at his elusive behavior on his last visit.

"Beyond that, as I had my own investments, I could not fail to note the success of yours. You will find I have followed your lead and hold stock in several of the same areas you have shown an interest in, including," Jonathon grinned, "your steam-ship line."

"Are you serious?" Nick stared in amused disbelief.

"Wickedly clever of you, I thought, to use the new docks at

Southampton rather than London, what with the convenience of the railway lines and all."

"Ships are getting bigger," Nick murmured, then shook his head. "Surely I would have noticed if you were among my investors."

"You have always been far more aware of obstacles in your path than anything or anyone trailing along behind you."

"Even so, I would have noted your name on the lists of stockholders."

"Not if I used another name." Jonathon got to his feet and offered his hand to Nick. "May I introduce Mr. J. E. Shelton."

"You are J. E. Shelton?"

"At your service."

"You are a devil, Jonathon." Nick stood and clasped his friend's hand.

Mr. J. E. Shelton's share of stocks in Nick's company was indeed substantial, and Nick had long wondered about the man. Since the purchases had been made through brokers and solicitors, Nick had been unable to track down the mysterious Mr. Shelton and had finally abandoned the quest, in part because he had had other matters to attend to, but primarily because his investor had shown no interest in the company beyond the income his shares produced.

"Why didn't you tell me? Why keep your identity secret?"

"You might well have refused my investment. All that making your fortune on your own nonsense. You accomplished that, you know, and made me remarkably wealthy in the process." Jonathon chuckled. "And I am most appreciative."

"Glad I could be of assistance. Now." Nick met Jonathon's gaze directly. "Why did you lure me home?"

"I wouldn't say I lured you. Do give me some credit, after all. If I had wished to lure you, I wouldn't have been nearly as subtle as I was. All I did was remind you of the responsibilities placed upon you by Charles's will. I was very careful on that score not to go too far. You read into it exactly what you wished, and what you wished was to come home. I simply provided the impetus." Jonathon shrugged in an all too satisfied manner. "Nothing more than that."

Nick studied the other man for a moment. Jonathon, just like his sister, was far more intelligent and perceptive than anyone gave him credit for. It gave him the upper hand more often than not, as well as the potential to be a powerful enemy. And an invaluable friend.

"I suppose I should thank you."

Jonathon grinned. "It's the least you could do."

"As for the finances of Lady Langley and her children," Nick nodded at the papers on the desk, "I had decided before my arrival here that, barring any unforeseen problem, management should remain in your hands. Even now that I know your sister is handling her affairs herself and, I might add," he shot Jonathon a rueful smile, "brilliantly, I see no need to change that decision."

"Excellent." Jonathon heaved a sigh of relief. "Especially as it was not until this very day that I told her of the clause in Charles's will regarding her finances."

Nick blew a long, low whistle. "I can't imagine she would take that well."

"Not taking it well is an understatement." Jonathon grimaced. "She was furious, and I can't blame her. It would be different if she were indeed a simpering idiot, but anyone with half a brain should be able to see beyond her pretty face. Particularly the man who had married her. Don't you agree?"

"Most certainly," Nick murmured.

Indeed, the Elizabeth Effington Nick had known wouldn't for a moment appreciate the fact that her husband had not left her in charge of her own fate. Of course, the Elizabeth he'd known had been a far cry from the lighthearted, flighty creature she'd appeared to be to the rest of the world. He'd wondered, on those rare occasions when he'd thought about her at all, if it was his own reserved, serious nature that had brought about the more thoughtful side of her character. Still, how was it that her own husband had not seen what Nick had?

"She'll be most relieved to know you do not intend to take over."

Nick grinned. "No doubt the least I can do."

"A joke, Sir Nicholas?" Jonathon raised a brow. "You have changed with the years."

"Come now, Jonathon, I joked." Nick winced with the memory of a far too serious youth. "On occasion."

"You have, I don't know, mellowed, I think. Like a fine wine or a good cheese."

"Or an excellent brandy." Nick raised his glass and laughed.

He had most definitely changed with the passage of time. Life no longer seemed quite as dire, as serious, as urgent as it once had. He was very much a man different from the one who had left here ten years ago. An annoying thought nagged in the back of his mind. Had Elizabeth changed as well?

Jonathon sobered. "There is, however, something you have not yet seen in the records you've perused that I think you should note."

"Oh?"

Jonathon circled to the back of the desk and opened a drawer.

"I did indeed handle Lizzie's finances in the first months after Charles's death. It was not particularly onerous; his record keeping was surprisingly meticulous." He pulled out a stack of what appeared to be paid bills, receipts, and other documents. "Frankly, anyone with half a brain could have picked up where he left off.

"He apparently never considered for a moment that his wife might take over, or surely he would have disposed of, or at least hidden"—Jonathon's voice hardened and he dropped the papers on the desk—"these."

"What are they?" Nick rifled through the receipts. "They appear to be nothing more than ordinary bills."

"Indeed they are. For milliners and dressmakers and butchers and greengrocers."

"Fairly basic for a household, I should think." Nick shook his head. "I still don't understand."

"They are not for his household. Or rather Lizzie's household."

"Not for . . ." Nick's gaze met Jonathon's, and he blew a long breath. "I see."

"I didn't believe it at first." Jonathon shook his head. "I realize it is not uncommon for a man to support a mistress, and according to these papers, this had gone on for years. But I did expect better of the man who had married my sister. One of my closest friends. A man who had always claimed to have cared for her since we were children."

"Charles always was the most charming among us," Nick murmured.

"The one women always seemed to find irresistible."

"If he had married anyone else, we would not have found this the least bit surprising." Nick shook his head. "I gather you had no knowledge of this?"

"I had heard an occasional rumor, just as I have heard rumors about nearly every married man I know, but, as there was never anything of substance, I disregarded them. I realize now I should have confronted Charles, but, blast it all, Nick," Jonathon blew a long breath, "I trusted the man."

"Did Elizabeth know?"

"To be honest, I don't know, but I assume not. I can't imagine her allowing such a thing while he was alive, and I made certain she has not seen any of this since his death. Still, her pride is such that if indeed she does know, she might well never say a word."

"She would prefer the world think she was ignorant as opposed to betrayed," Nick said.

"You know her rather well." Jonathon studied him curiously.

Nick ignored the implication. "Not really. But I am observant enough to know the accuracy of your assessment."

"My initial impulse was to destroy these the moment I found them, but, as Charles named you as overseer of his financial affairs, I did not feel quite right about doing so until you had seen them."

"And, as I have now seen them," Nick held out his hand, "there is no time like the present to destroy the evidence."

"Excellent idea." Jonathon smiled with relief and handed Nick the sheaf of papers.

Nick strode toward the fireplace at the far end of the room, then paused. "What of the woman in question?"

Jonathon shrugged. "All the bills were handled through a

solicitor, and I have made no effort to contact him. Nor, in the three years since Charles's death, has the lady ever made her identity known to me. I have always assumed she learned of Charles's demise and was discreet enough, or intelligent enough, to realize whatever promises he might have made regarding her support were no longer valid."

"That's something, at any rate." Nick nodded and skirted the sofa, bending low to toss the pages on to the banked fire.

While he had no intention of intruding in Elizabeth's life, and, despite his uncle's encouragement and this revelation about Charles's infidelity, no plans to involve himself with the woman in any manner whatsoever, he could spare her this. It was indeed the least he could do. He watched until the receipts caught to make certain not one piece of incriminating evidence remained.

"I cannot believe this, Jonathon, any of it."

It was the last voice in the world Nick expected to hear at the moment. The last voice he wanted to hear. And the last voice he thought could ever make his heart leap. Again.

He straightened slowly.

Lady Langley, Elizabeth, swept into the room, anger apparent in the very line of her body, her gaze pinned firmly on her brother. She was exactly as Nick remembered.

"I have had the most frustrating afternoon, and it was all to no avail." She yanked her hat off impatiently and flung it onto the chair. "My solicitor, or rather Charles's solicitor, that vile, despicable beast of a creature, says I cannot discharge him. Only you or Collingsworth can do so, and he was unforgivably smug about it." She planted her hands on the desk, leaned forward, and glared at her brother. "I wish you to do so at once, unless you'd rather shoot him for me. That would be my preference, but I shall allow you to choose, as there are those pesky legal issues of prison to contend with should you murder him. Although I daresay an argument can be made for the elimination of vermin! However, if you simply wound him, I suspect a respectable amount of money would ease his pain. He would be expensive, of course, but well worth it, I think."

"Thank you for considering all the possibilities." Jonathon grinned.

"I could certainly shoot him myself, I suppose." At the moment she looked more than capable of doing so, and Nick stifled a laugh.

But he was wrong, she wasn't exactly as he remembered. The girl who'd haunted his dreams was a pretty and vivacious creature, charming and amusing with an innate intelligence she did not display to the rest of the world. The woman he saw now carried an air of grace born of maturity and experience and confidence, and had, if possible, grown lovelier with the years. This woman was vivid in character, filling the room with her presence, and exuded life as if her body could not quite contain her spirit. And no one would ever think her frivolous.

Every feeling he'd thought long since dead swept through him with an unexpected ferocity, and he knew, with a clarity he had rarely experienced in his life, that he had made a dreadful mistake.

"Lizzie, you should know—"

"And then there was Father's solicitor, *your solicitor*, a member of the firm that has served the entire Effington family for generations." She straightened and yanked off one glove. "In a nasty twist of fate, he is also the solicitor for Lord Thornecroft and, need I say it aloud? Nicholas Collingsworth!" She smacked the glove against the palm of her hand for emphasis.

Not that her words needed emphasis. Elizabeth was nothing short of magnificent in her fury. And best of all, she had no idea Nick was in the room.

How could he have been such a fool? How could he ever have given her up?

"Do you know what he said to me?" Elizabeth's voice rang with disbelief.

"I am almost afraid to ask." Jonathon's gaze slid to Nick, then back to his sister. "But I really should tell you—"

"He said it would be a conflict of conscience to represent me in this matter given his relationship with Sir Nicholas. *A conflict of conscience?*" She snorted in disdain. "While it is exceedingly pleasant to hear a solicitor use the concept of conscience in so honorable a manner, at the moment I would prefer someone of less conscience and greater cunning." She blew a frustrated breath. "Although, as a courtesy to Father and you, he did look over the pertinent section of the will that you had provided me."

"And?" Jonathon prompted.

"And," Elizabeth sighed and dropped into the chair, "I am—oh, I have no idea how to say it politely."

"Do go on, Lizzie," Jonathon said, "it can't be that bad."

"Let us just say I am no less trapped than if I were a fox surrounded by snarling hounds." She shook her head. "I have no options whatsoever save your idea of flinging myself on Collingsworth's mercy."

"Yes, well, that was my idea." Jonathon glanced at Nick and looked very much like a man who wasn't entirely sure if he should laugh or simply flee. "And I'm certain you'll find him more than reasonable."

"Hah! I have yet to find a reasonable man today, and I am not willing to wager that Collingsworth is unique in that regard." She smacked her glove against her palm rhythmically, the dull slaps echoing in the large room, her brow furrowed with thought.

Nick had seen any number of men do something similar: tapping a pen or drumming their fingers on a tabletop. It always indicated a fervent search for an answer to whatever dilemma confronted them. Usually said dilemma was contingent upon Nick himself, which, then as now, gave him something of an upper hand.

"I must think of something, Jonathon, some way out of this nasty predicament my husband has placed me in. Aside from the fact that Charles's actions were neither fair nor necessary, I cannot simply trust a man I scarcely know with my finances. Indeed, with my life and those of my children." Her voice hardened. "Trusting a man I thought I knew quite well is what got me into this. I shall not put my fate, and the fate of my sons, in the hands of another."

In ten years, Nick had achieved every goal he had set for himself.

"You can tell him yourself." Jonathon's tone was deceptively casual. "He's here, Lizzie."

Winning back this woman's heart would be the most difficult task of all.

"I know he's here." She waved off her brother's comment. "I heard you earlier. You said he arrived yesterday."

"I don't mean here in London."

And the most important.

"Well, what do you mean?" She huffed. "Honestly, Jonathon, I have no time for guessing games. If I am to get the best of a man like Collingsworth, I must focus my efforts on that and nothing else. Now, what are you trying to say?"

Nick drew a deep breath and stepped around the sofa. "What your brother is trying to say, Lady Langley, is that I am not merely in London, I am in this very room."

Nicholas Collingsworth?

Elizabeth sucked in a sharp breath, her eyes widened with disbelief, and her stomach plummeted, very much as if she had just been physically hit. Hard.

"Jonathon?" Her voice was little more than a croak.

"I told you he was here," Jonathon said idly, as if the fact that Nicholas Collingsworth was in this very room listening to every word she'd just said was of no significance whatsoever.

"Lady Langley, it's delightful to see you again." Nicholas strode toward her as if he were a ghost stepping out of the past.

She rose to her feet and struggled for words. Something, anything, no matter how inane or foolish. She had never in her life swooned, nor had she ever wished to, but she knew any number of women who had the ability to swoon on command. At the moment, she envied them. Perhaps if she did indeed crumple to the floor in an unconscious heap, the perfect words would be on her lips when she awoke.

Nicholas reached her, took her ungloved hand, and drew it to his lips. "And, might I add, you are looking as lovely as I remember."

His lips, warm and firm, brushed across her skin, and his gaze bored into hers. "Indeed, you have not changed at all."

Nor had he. His eyes were as dark and smoldering, his face as handsome, the touch of his skin to hers every bit as electric as she'd remembered in the dark recesses of her most secret dreams. Without warning, she was swept back through the years to a moment before she had married or borne two sons or discovered even the most secure of lives was not secure at all.

She was once again Lizzie Effington, and she was gazing into the eyes of the man she might or might not have loved. Whose kisses had curled her toes. Who had spoken with her as though she were his equal.

The man who had humiliated and embarrassed her.

The very man who absolutely had not broken her heart.

She snatched her hand from his. "What are you doing here?"

Jonathon groaned.

Nicholas raised a brow. "What a charming greeting. I see the years have not dampened your penchant for speaking before due consideration. And yes, I am well, thank you."

"I don't care if you're well or not." She grit her teeth. "I don't particularly care if you're breathing or long since dead and buried. What are you doing here?"

"Why, I am reacquainting myself with my old friend." He cast Jonathon a friendly smile.

Jonathon grinned. "We have had a great deal to talk about."

"Ten years is a very long time." Nicholas picked up a glass of brandy from the desk and took a sip. His gaze lingered on her even as he drank. As if she were a butterfly pinned to a board and he were a student of such things. It was most disconcerting. And no doubt the reason, the only reason, why her heart thudded in her chest.

Worse still was the thought that rose unbidden in her mind. What was the result of his assessment? Did he find that the years and childbearing and life itself had taken its toll? She'd never considered herself especially vain, but at the moment she couldn't help but wish that she had worn the emerald walking dress that brightened the color of her eyes or that she'd cinched in her corset a bit tighter. Not that she cared one bit if he found her attractive, but she'd long known a woman's beauty was as great a weapon as her intelligence. Greater, perhaps, because few men looked beyond beauty.

Of course, there had been a time when he and he alone had.

Or rather she'd thought he had. Still, that was a very, very long time ago and much had changed. She certainly had.

Elizabeth squared her shoulders slightly. Confidence gathered in the last years, forged from self-reliance and accomplishment, had well prepared her for such a task. No matter how clever or powerful or wealthy Nicholas might be, now that he was here in the flesh, she hadn't a doubt in the world that she could handle him. She'd simply needed a moment to recover from the shock of his unexpected appearance. There was nothing more to her reaction than that.

She drew a deep breath and forced a pleasant smile. "Do forgive my rudeness, Sir Nicholas, it has been a long, trying day thus far."

Nicholas chuckled. "So I gather."

Heat flushed up her face. She hadn't blushed in years, and the fact that she did so now was almost as infuriating as everything else that had happened today.

"Yes, well, that's neither here nor there," she said in an offhand manner. "May I be so bold as to ask what the two of you have been discussing?"

"All sorts of things, Lizzie," Jonathon said quickly. "Nicholas has done and seen a great deal during his travels. You can't begin to imagine the—"

"You, my lady," Nicholas said coolly. "We have been discussing you."

"Well, not really you, exactly, or not you exclusively," Jonathon cut in. "That is to say—"

Elizabeth ignored him. "Do go on, Sir Nicholas. Exactly what about me were you discussing?"

"Exactly?" The corners of his lips quirked upward.

"Exactly." She narrowed her gaze, but her smile never wavered.

"I can see I'm probably not needed," Jonathon murmured and edged his way toward the door.

"Don't take another step, Jonathon." She addressed her brother, but her gaze never left Nicholas. Her cool tone matched his. "You are very much a part of this."

"More's the pity," her brother muttered.

"Let me see if I remember *exactly*." Nicholas furrowed his brow in apparent thought, although she didn't doubt for a moment it was some sort of ploy simply to heighten her annoyance. It worked exceedingly well. "I inquired as to the health of your sons. Christopher and Adam, I believe."

"They are quite well, thank you for asking." Her voice carried just the right shade of politeness.

"I imagine they are eager for Christmas?"

"They are eight and six years of age, Sir Nicholas. They can think of little else."

He chuckled. "I look forward to meeting them."

"Oh?" She raised a brow. "Then you are planning to stay as long as Christmas?" She tried to stop herself, but the words came of their own accord. "This year."

"Dear Lord, take me now," Jonathon muttered.

Nicholas stared for a moment, then laughed. "Well said, my lady. I daresay I deserve it. Between my earlier travels with my uncle and my own pursuits, I have missed—what? Thirteen Christmases in London? Far too many."

"Too many indeed," Jonathon said firmly.

"I confess I have missed it greatly. Perhaps it is the sentimentality in the air or the spirit of goodwill toward all, but at this time of year, my thoughts tend to dwell on past Christmases and on those persons I cannot be with yet have a deep affection for nonetheless. I find a measure of comfort in those memories and in the various occurrences of the season that remind me of home. In particular, I find nothing brings my thoughts, and indeed my heart, home quite like a reading of," Nicholas's gaze met hers, *"A Christmas Carol."*

Her breath caught.

Nicholas smiled in a far too innocent manner. "Don't you agree, Lady Langley?"

She ignored the racing of her pulse at his mention of the book. After all, thousands upon thousands of people had read the story since its publication. It had become the quintessential depiction of Christmas, particularly in England. The fact that it had provided Nicholas comfort during his travels had nothing to do with her.

"It's a wonderful story," she said, her tone a bit harder than she had intended.

"Indeed it is, and while I am grateful to Mr. Dickens for bringing a measure of home to me during my years in America, I daresay, despite his remarkable work, there is nothing that can replace being in London for Christmas." He smiled in a wry manner. "As I said, I have missed it."

There was something truly genuine in his manner and his smile, and if it had come from any other man, Elizabeth would have been quite moved by it. That no doubt was his plan, to work his way past her defenses with charm and sincerity. Well, she was having none of it.

"I'm sure Lord Thornecroft has missed you," Elizabeth said.

"As have we all." Jonathon nodded.

"But I shall not miss another Christmas." Nicholas's tone was firm. "This is not a mere visit. My days of travel are at an end. I fully intend to make England my home for the rest of my days."

"Excellent." Jonathon beamed.

"How very nice. For your uncle," she said pointedly, her stomach lurching at the thought of Nicholas Collingsworth being back in her world, apparently for good.

"He is quite pleased, and I see now I was remiss in my responsibilities as his nephew not to have returned some years ago." Nicholas nodded thoughtfully. "Indeed, my uncle's pleasure is such that he has decided to host a small dinner to celebrate my return."

"Like the proverbial prodigal son," she said in an overly sweet manner. "Will he be sacrificing a fatted calf as well?"

Jonathon muttered something she was rather glad she didn't hear. She knew full well her reaction to Nicholas's presence was perhaps a bit unreasonable, but she couldn't seem to help herself. The man was a threat to the security of her family, her life, and possibly, if she allowed it, even her heart.

"I don't think he's all that fond of fatted calf." Nicholas's voice was matter-of-fact, but an annoying twinkle gleamed in his eye. "Still, I shall suggest it. One never knows. You should be receiving invitations in the next day or so. Jonathon."

Nicholas's words were directed at her brother, but his gaze never left her. "I do hope your family will be able to attend."

"We shall make a point of it," Jonathon said firmly.

"I, however, fear I am otherwise occupied." Elizabeth shrugged apologetically. "Christmas is but a few weeks away, and my social obligations are rather more extensive than usual." She forced a light laugh. "The days surrounding Christmas have become more and more popular for merrymaking. Why, there are dinners and musicales and routs and all manner of entertainments. I do apologize, but there you have it."

"That is awkward." He narrowed his gaze. "Especially as I have not mentioned specifically what evening my uncle has proposed his celebration to mark my homecoming."

"I'm certain whatever evening is chosen I shall be unable to attend. I couldn't possibly fit one more thing onto my calendar." Her gaze met his directly, and she couldn't resist a smug smile.

"We shall see," Nicholas said softly.

"Indeed, we shall." She turned to her brother. "Have you and Sir Nicholas discussed anything else I should be aware of?"

"We talked about your finances, Lizzie." Jonathon glanced at her account books stacked on the desk. "You'll be pleased to know, Nicholas has found everything in order and has decided—"

"I have decided, as competent a job as you have done up to now, it's past time I lived up to the responsibilities assigned to me by your late husband," Nicholas said smoothly.

"What?" Jonathon's brow furrowed.

"Competent?" She stared in disbelief, and her voice rose. "*Competent?*"

"Competent." Nicholas's tone was firm.

"My dear Sir Nicholas, my handling of my family's finances has been substantially more than," she nearly choked on the word, "*competent*. The value of virtually everything from Charles's investments to the estate has increased."

"So it would appear. However—"

She waved at the ledgers on the desk. "Haven't you looked at my accounts?"

Nicholas shrugged. "I have glanced at them, but I have yet to do an exhaustive study, which is, frankly, of utmost importance before I can make any decisions regarding your financial state and my administration of it."

"Then take them." She grabbed the heavy pile of oversized books and thrust them toward him. "Study them. Read every line entered for the past three years. Peruse every figure, every decimal, every erasure if you will. And then tell me my handling of my money has been merely *competent*."

Nicholas set his glass on the desk in an annoyingly unhurried manner and accepted the books. "I shall do precisely that. And, as I am certain I will have any number of questions regarding my findings, I shall present myself at your residence this evening."

"This evening?" She glared. The arrogance of the man. "I can't possibly—"

"The sooner we deal with these matters, the sooner we can establish how we are to proceed from this point forth," he said with an irritatingly pleasant smile.

She crossed her arms over her chest. "Am I to understand that your *living up to the responsibilities assigned to you by my late husband* means you intend to take over the active administration of my financial affairs?"

He nodded. "You may indeed assume that. For the time being at least."

"I must say I am somewhat confused," Jonathon murmured.

"It's quite clear to me," Elizabeth said sharply. "Sir Nicholas has the conceit typical of his gender in that he cannot conceive of the idea that a mere female can handle something as complicated as finances."

"I say, Lizzie, that's not entirely fair," Jonathon said.

"No, Jonathon, it's entirely fair, if not entirely accurate," Nicholas said. His gaze met hers. "Most men of my acquaintance, and I should include the late Lord Langley among their number, do not consider the fairer sex to be intellectually equipped to deal even adequately with the complicated matters surrounding the management of money. It is admittedly something of a far-fetched idea, yet I am one of those rare specimens who believe there may well be the rare woman who can do precisely that."

"As I have," she snapped.

"Prove it to me." A distinct challenge sounded in his voice.

"And if I do?"

"Then we shall see."

She stared at him for a long moment. "Very well, it seems that you, the solicitors I have spoken to, even Charles himself have left me with little choice." She drew a deep breath. "I shall expect you this evening."

"Excellent." Nicholas smiled that enigmatic half smile she had never quite forgotten, and she ignored the odd things it did to the pit of her stomach. "I shall take my leave then."

"Allow me to see you out." Jonathon cast a quick glance at his sister, then escorted Nicholas from the room.

The moment the door closed behind the men, Elizabeth crumpled into the nearest chair and rubbed her hand across her forehead.

Dear Lord, she'd known there was every possibility her path would cross Nicholas's again some day, but she'd always rather hoped it would be when they were both very, very old. Old enough that her knees would no longer weaken at the mere look in his eye, or her hand tremble at the briefest touch of his, or her heart speed up when he smiled.

In spite of her words and her confidence in her own abilities, she had to admit, at least to herself, the mere presence of Nicholas unnerved her. What she wasn't willing to admit was why. She certainly didn't want him, or anyone for that matter, managing her accounts, but now that Nicholas had actually returned it was obvious her apprehension was not limited merely to the control of her finances.

She'd spent ten years telling herself that what she'd felt for Nicholas had not been significant. A youthful moment of confusion brought on by nothing more lasting than innocent friendship and a kiss or two. If anything it had been a young girl's first taste of, well, desire. Even, perhaps, lust.

Lust that had obviously not passed with the years.

She sank back and absently drummed her fingernails on the arm of the chair.

As difficult as it was to admit, even after all this time the man did, well, *something* to her. Something no other man, even her own husband, had ever done to her. Something that would obviously be difficult to handle with any sort of usual method. Still, she was nine-and-twenty and a widow. By her own standards, she was an intelligent woman and, by anyone else's, an experienced one. She had been married for seven years, after all, and had given birth to two children. Surely she could cope with lust. Her own, and—if the look in his eyes was any indication—his as well.

A tremor of excitement tripped up her spine.

Oh, she could certainly handle lust. And Nicholas Collingsworth. Both might be rather enjoyable and the kind of adventure she'd never actually had.

What she couldn't handle with Nicholas was love.

And if she was even half as clever as she thought she was, she wouldn't have to.

Chapter 7

It was a damnably good thing Nick had already gone over Elizabeth's account books once today. Now, sitting across the table from her in the small library in her home, he found it impossible to concentrate on the neatly written rows of numbers.

Indeed, what male in his right mind could? Only a dead man could sit in the same room with her and fail to notice the way the light from the gas lamps fell on her blond hair and tinted it the color of spun gold. Or ignore the graceful curve of her neck as she bent over the books. Or disregard the manner in which her eminently proper gown molded to her bosom like a caress.

Or the way her green eyes shot sparks each and every time their gazes met.

In spite of the veneer of politeness she'd adopted, there was no doubt in his mind that she was still angry with him. On the one hand, that was something of a problem. Just getting her to accept him back into her life would be a challenge. On the other, the fact that she had obviously not, after ten long years, forgiven him struck him as possibly a good sign. If she had not forgiven him after all this time, perhaps she had not lost whatever feelings she'd once had for him. Indeed, at the moment she appeared to truly despise him. And wasn't there little more than a fine line between love and hate? Right now, hate was a very good sign indeed.

They'd been in the room for hours, and together they had indeed gone over every entry and every figure in each and every accounting book. He'd had her explain every notation and every action she'd taken. Not that it was truly necessary. Her ledgers were efficient and self-explanatory. In the beginning he'd feared he'd sounded like something of a simpleton, then he'd realized that she took his questioning not as a result of his own lack of intelligence but as a sign of his opinion of hers. Still, she'd been nothing but businesslike and relatively cordial, if distinctly remote, throughout the evening. It must have taken a great deal of self-control on her part.

Elizabeth leaned back in her chair and studied him. "Well?"

"Well what?" He drew his brows together in confusion.

"You've seen everything there is to see, Sir Nicholas." She brushed an errant strand of hair away from her face with a weary hand in a gesture she probably didn't realize was exceptionally charming. "Have you come to any conclusions?"

"I have come to any number of conclusions."

"And?"

"And I have an apology to make."

"Oh?" She raised a brow.

"Your management of your finances has indeed been brilliant." He waved at the account books spread across the desk. "I must commend you. You have done as good a job as any man could have and far better than many I have known."

"I'm surprised that you would admit such a thing," she said slowly.

"Are you? Now I'm surprised. Why?"

"You are a man of business, and it has been my experience that most men, men in general, but especially men of business, do not consider women capable of adequacy, let alone brilliance, in the handling of accounts."

"You will find I am not like men in general." He leaned back in his chair. "I have not managed to achieve what I have by being like most men, particularly most men of business."

"Perhaps," she murmured, then drew a deep breath. "Then will you give me leave to continue to handle my money?"

He considered her for a long moment. From a strictly business standpoint, it was exceedingly foolish to remove a man from a position which he not only liked but excelled at. Yet if he relinquished his duties as administrator, he would have no excuse to see Elizabeth. And the very moment he'd seen her again he'd known that would never do.

"I will give it due consideration," he said in his most businesslike way.

" 'Due consideration'?" She blew a frustrated breath. "That's it? You admit I have performed in an outstanding manner, yet 'due consideration' is the best you will offer me?"

"I will, however, propose a compromise you may find to your liking."

"I doubt it. I can't imagine that any compromise you propose would be to my liking save that of your washing your hands of all of this and leaving me in peace."

"Would that I could." He shook his head forlornly. "But I have responsibilities—"

"Yes, yes, I am well aware of your responsibilities." Elizabeth rolled her gaze toward the ceiling. "What kind of compromise?"

"You shall continue to manage your accounts much as you always have. I shall go over them on a daily basis until such time as I am confident it is no longer necessary."

"How utterly ridiculous." She crossed her arms over her chest. "I have been doing exactly that without anyone looking over my shoulder for three years."

"Then this shall not be at all difficult for you."

"And if I refuse?"

He shrugged. "I shall remove all financial activity from your control. You shall have an allowance, of course. A set amount for your personal needs and a separate amount for your household. And I should think—"

"Fine," she snapped. "I accept your proposal, but only as the lesser of two evils. Just how long do you anticipate this *compromise* to continue?"

"Until Christmas Eve. The Effington Christmas Ball," he said without thinking, then winced to himself.

It was the first thing that popped into his head, and it had been a very long time since he'd said the first thing that came into his head in regards to any kind of negotiations whatsoever. Of course, she was a far cry from the men he usually negotiated with, and this was far more important than business. Besides, it would be ten years ago this very Christmas Eve that they had last been together. What better time than Christmas Eve and what better place than the Christmas ball to begin anew? He rather liked the irony of it.

"Christmas Eve?" Her eyes widened with disbelief. Apparently Elizabeth did not appreciate irony. "The Christmas ball?"

"Unless that does not meet with your approval." He forced a casual note to his voice, as if there were nothing of note about that particular date.

"It scarcely matters to me," she said with a shrug that belied the flash of annoyance in her eyes. "There are still a few weeks until Christmas." She paused, and he could almost see the gears and wheels of her mind in motion. "Very well." She nodded slowly. "I can agree to that."

"There are conditions, however," he said quickly.

"I should have known there would be." Her voice was wry. "What kind of conditions?"

"First," he braced himself, "you must allow me to escort you to my uncle's party."

"I scarcely think—"

"You are obviously not still in mourning. Lovely dress, by the way." His gaze drifted over the most becoming peach-colored gown she wore this evening. The silk complemented the creamy tones of her skin, and the color brought out the blush in her cheeks. It was at once a pity and completely beneficial to his frame of mind that it was not the least bit revealing. "It quite suits you."

"I know." She smiled sweetly. "Everything I wear suits me. It is one of the benefits of having adequate funds, thanks to the brilliant management of my money."

He refused to take the bait and change the topic at hand. "Surely I will not be the first gentleman to serve as your escort since your widowhood?"

"No, you will most certainly not be the first." She laughed softly in an altogether too knowing manner that he didn't like in the least. "I am widowed, Sir Nicholas, and, as you well know, have been for some time. However, my life did not cease upon my husband's death." She raised a shoulder in a graceful shrug. "I have always enjoyed the numerous entertainments offered by London society, indeed I have always believed in having a bit of fun and, while I mourned my husband for the requisite period, I see no need to spend the rest of my days doing so. Lord Langley is dead, but I am very much alive."

"Indeed you are," he murmured.

"In the past two years, I have found it most beneficial to be escorted to various events by suitable gentlemen." She studied him for a moment as if trying to ascertain if he was suitable or not.

"Well?"

She rose to her feet and crossed the room to a side table bearing a decanter and glasses. "It has been a very long evening, and I believe it is past time for a brandy."

"Brandy is an excellent idea." He followed her without pause. "But you are avoiding the issue at hand."

"Am I?"

"You have not agreed to my condition."

"Haven't I?" She poured two glasses and handed him one. "Is it necessary, then, for me to agree?"

"Yes," he said firmly.

"Although, in truth, once again, I have no choice." She shrugged. "Very well then, I shall allow you to escort me to your uncle's dinner."

"And any other occasions that arise in the next few weeks," he said quickly. If he were to win Elizabeth's heart by Christmas Eve he needed to be with her as much as possible. "Most particularly the Effington Christmas Ball."

"Oh, dear. That might be rather awkward." She took a sip

of her brandy. "While I am willing to agree to that as a deadline, I may well have already accepted an offer for an escort to the Christmas ball."

His hand tightened on the glass. "Then change your plans."

"That would be unforgivably rude." She shook her head in feigned regret. "And I do try not to be unforgivably rude."

He snorted. "This afternoon you—"

"My apologies, Sir Nicholas," she said in her most composed manner. "I was simply caught unawares. Your appearance was something of a shock in a day already full of shocking and most unpleasant surprises."

His gaze met hers. "And was I an unpleasant surprise?"

She smiled. "Yes."

"I see." He drew a deep swallow of the liquor. Nick wasn't certain if she was baiting him or flirting in an odd, challenging sort of way or simply trying to drive him mad. Probably all three. "Have you recovered from your shock?"

"Most certainly." She gazed up at him in an innocent manner he didn't believe for a moment. He'd give much of his fortune at the moment to be able to read her mind.

"Dare I ask if there is one escort in particular out of those gentlemen you find suitable that you especially favor?" The words were out of his mouth before he could stop them.

If indeed there was another man who had already claimed her affections, his own efforts would be futile. No, not futile, only more difficult. He had learned through the years that it was always best to know what the possible obstacles were in any proposed venture.

"I suspect you would dare to ask or do almost anything," she said mildly.

He stared at her for a long, frustrating moment. What on earth had happened here? He had the upper hand, held all the cards as it were, yet she was firmly in control of this exchange between them. Worse yet, he could tell by the look in her eyes that she well knew it.

He drew a deep, calming breath. "And do you dare to answer?"

She laughed, a genuine laugh for the first time today, and

the sound and the memories rippled through his blood. "I do indeed, Sir Nicholas. And even though your query is completely improper, highly personal, and really none of your concern, I will confess there is no one gentleman that I especially favor at the moment, although admittedly there are a few who would wish to take up that position in my life."

Relief flooded through him. "I can understand that."

"Oh?" She sipped her drink and considered him over the rim of her glass.

"You are a wealthy widow with formidable family and social connections. In addition, you are extremely clever, and the years have been most kind. I myself find you even lovelier, if possible, than when you were a girl."

"You flatter me, Sir Nicholas." She tilted her head and studied him as if he were a puzzle she could not quite figure out. "I do not recall that you were especially free with flattery in your youth. I don't remember you as being quite this charming."

He laughed. "Have I changed that much then?"

"Yes," she said without hesitation and narrowed her eyes thoughtfully. "Granted, it has been a very long time, but I remember you being far more serious in manner than you are now. It may be simply the passage of years and a maturity of character perhaps, but you strike me as a man very much in command of his world and at ease with your place in it. There is an air of confidence about you now that did not exist before. I do not remember you being as—I don't know exactly." She thought for a moment. "Content perhaps?"

He nodded. "Perhaps. I have accomplished much of what I set out to do in life, reconciled my past, or rather my family's past, and I find I am indeed at peace, if you will."

"How lovely for you," she murmured and moved away.

"And are you at peace?"

"What an odd question to ask."

"Not really. If you would prefer not to answer, I can certainly—"

"I am content with my life." Her words were measured, as though she was puzzling them out even as she answered.

"Though I did not exactly choose this path, one never expects to find oneself a widow with two children after a mere seven years of marriage—"

"No, of course not."

She turned to him and her gaze met his. "But I must admit that now I quite cherish my independence and my freedom."

"And you resent me for taking them away." It was as much a question as a statement.

She arched a brow. "Wouldn't you in my position?"

"Without question." He chuckled. "And I would probably be doing exactly as you are now."

"That is?"

He grinned. "Devising a means of escape."

She stared at him for a moment, then laughed. "Excellent, Sir Nicholas, most perceptive. But I have already thought of a means of escape, as you put it." She swirled the brandy in her glass and met his gaze directly. "According to my brother, my finances would no longer be under your management, or his for that matter, if I marry someone," amusement sparkled in her eye, "*suitable.*"

"Rather an extreme measure when you could well be free of me entirely by Christmas," he said wryly.

"Indeed it is, especially as I have no desire to marry again."

"Why not?" He forced a casual note to his voice. "I had understood you and Charles were quite happy together."

"We were," she said a shade too quickly. Was she trying to convince him? Or herself?

At once Nick wondered if Jonathon was wrong; if indeed Elizabeth knew of her husband's indiscretions. His stomach twisted for her. Surely not. She would not keep such a thing to herself. Or maybe her pride dictated that that's exactly what she would have done. His uncle was right. One never knew what transpired in the privacy of a marriage.

"Quite happy indeed." She caught his gaze, and there was a look of challenge in her eye, as if she dared him to think otherwise. "Nonetheless, I am not looking for a husband."

He drew his brows together. "Why not?"

Her tone was light, but she obviously chose her words with

care. "I have had one husband and I'm not entirely sure one is not more than enough. I have experienced marriage and, even as perfect as it was, I see no need to do so again."

"I see."

"Do you?" She raised her chin and her eyes flashed. "I like the freedom afforded a widow in this world, Sir Nicholas. I like being able to do as I please with whomever I please. You may well control my finances for a time or forever, but you shall not control my life."

"I have no desire to do so."

"What do you desire, Sir Nicholas? What do you want from me?"

The question hung in the air between them.

I desire you. I want the life we should have had. I wish to have you in my bed for the rest of my days. And in my heart forever.

He drew a deep breath. Now was not the time to tell her that the years had changed nothing for him. That he had lied when he had pushed her away so long ago. That the moment he'd seen her again he'd realized that losing her—no—giving her up had been the greatest mistake of his life.

He set his glass down and forced a light note to his voice. "At the moment, I want you to call me Nicholas."

She shook her head. "That would be most inappropriate."

"Why?" His restraint snapped, and he stepped closer to her. "Blast it all, Elizabeth, why won't you call me Nicholas?"

She narrowed her eyes. "Does it bother you that I don't?"

"Yes, damn it all, it does." He glared at her.

"Excellent." She smiled sweetly. "Calling you by your given name would be most improper and would imply a relationship we do not share."

He clenched his jaw. "You used to call me Nicholas."

"I used to be nineteen and very, very foolish."

"I don't remember you as foolish."

"Memories are selective, *Sir Nicholas*. I remember myself as being foolish enough to think . . . to feel . . ." She waved impatiently. "That's neither here nor there. It's not the least bit important now."

"I think it is." He moved nearer.

"Well, you are wrong." She was within arm's reach, and she glared up at him.

What would she do if he pulled her into his arms? "Everything that passes between us is important."

"Once, perhaps, but not now. Now it is simply an insignificant moment in a long-forgotten past."

"And have you forgotten?" If he pressed his lips to hers and kissed her with the pent-up passion of a decade?

"Yes," she snapped, but she made no effort to move away.

"All of it?" His gaze shifted to her lips, full and firm and irresistible. "Everything?"

"There was nothing of significance to forget and nothing important enough to remember," she said staunchly. "You are standing entirely too close, Sir Nicholas."

"I am not standing nearly close enough."

"Do you intend to kiss me?" Her voice was firm but sounded a shade breathless nonetheless.

"I'm not entirely sure what my intentions are, Elizabeth." Her scent wafted around him, subtle with a touch of spice and vaguely reminiscent of Christmas.

"Lady Langley, if you please."

"I do please," he murmured, "or so I've been told."

"*Sir Nicholas*, I am shocked." Even so, she seemed to lean ever so slightly toward him.

"Do you remember the last time we kissed?" Or was it that everything about Christmas was vaguely reminiscent of Elizabeth?

She drew her brows together. "Have we kissed?"

"Once or twice."

"You must have me confused with someone else. I don't remember kissing you at all." He could read the lie in her eyes.

"You don't remember your lips meeting mine?" His gaze shifted to her lips. "Your life's breath mingling with my own?"

"No." Her voice was firm, but she wet her lips in a nervous manner, as if his words had sapped the moisture from them. His stomach tightened.

"Or the way in which I took you in my arms?" He noted the rise and fall of her chest with her quickened breath. "And how you fit against me as if we were made one for the other?"

"No." Her gaze never wavered from his and he stared into her green eyes, now shadowed with memories she could deny but could not forget.

"Or the way a current of desire surged between us so strong we were left weak and breathless." The same desire that surged between them now like an arc of endless electricity. Dangerous and exciting and irresistible.

"No." Her voice was little more than a whisper.

"I remember, Elizabeth." It took every modicum of self-control he possessed not to reach out now and pull her into his arms. "I remember it all."

"Well I do not, because there is nothing of significance to remember." She swallowed hard. "And I warn you, if you attempt to kiss me now, I shall—"

"You shall kiss me back."

"I most certainly will not."

"That would be a very great shame. I remember the way you kissed me back. The way you clung to me as if to life itself. The way you—"

"Stop it at once." She drew a shuddered breath and stepped out of his reach. She turned away and gripped the back of a chair as if needing support merely to stand. "Why are you doing this to me?"

He willed a note of cool reserve to his voice. "Doing what, Elizabeth?"

"You know full well what you're doing. You're trying to force me to recall something that it serves no purpose to remember. Something that really exists," she shook her head, "only in your imagination."

"My imagination is not that good." He stepped to the table, picked up his glass, ignored the slight tremor in his hand, and downed the rest of his liquor. "I know I hurt you once, and for that you have my apologies."

She whirled around to face him. "A bit late for apologies, don't you think?"

"Perhaps." He refilled his glass. "I had reasons for doing what I did."

"Yes, I know. How was that again?" She narrowed her eyes. "Ah yes, you said my money and my family connections were tempting but that I was far too frivolous for you. You also said I would be amusing in the manner of such things between men and women. Most amusing, I believe."

"I see you remember that," he said mildly.

"Vaguely!"

"It sounded quite specific to me."

"What I do remember *specifically* is being very silly and very young and being intrigued by the idea of the life of adventures you were about to embark upon. And . . . and . . . throwing myself at you in a most absurd and pathetic manner." She wrapped her arms around herself, anger etched in every line of her body. "I was a complete and utter fool, and I do remember that quite clearly. And nothing more than that."

"There was a great deal more than that. A great deal more to us than that."

She jerked her chin up and glared. "There was no *us*."

"There would have been and indeed should have been. You were not the fool." His gaze trapped hers. "I was."

She sucked in a sharp breath.

"I should never have let you go. I made a mistake, Elizabeth, one I did not fully realize the enormity of until I saw you again." He stared at her for a long moment and wondered, as he had over and over today, how he could ever have let her go. He wanted nothing more than to sweep her into his arms and make everything between them right. And never let her go again. But at this moment, that too would be a mistake. "I shall not make another."

"What exactly do you mean by that?"

"I mean that I have spent the last ten years achieving everything I set out to achieve. I acquired everything I have ever wanted in life with one notable exception." He drained the rest of his drink, placed the glass firmly on the table, then looked at her. "You."

"You seek to acquire me? *Me*?" She stared in disbelief. "Like a ship or a company?"

"I would not put it so crudely as that."

"You just did!"

He shrugged. "My apologies. Again."

"They are not accepted! Not for your behavior tonight. Not for ten years ago. Not today, not ever. Now." She jerked her head toward the door. "Do be so kind as to leave my house. Immediately."

"You're quite right. The hour is late and our business for the moment is completed. Indeed, I still have a few other matters to attend to this evening."

"What other matters?" Suspicion sounded in her voice.

"Correspondence, for the most part. I have long found my mind clearest for such work late at night after the"—he cleared his throat—"temptations of the day are laid to rest."

"Good evening, Sir Nicholas," she said through clenched teeth.

"Good evening, Lady Langley." He turned toward the door, then turned back. "Oh, I would like to establish a regular schedule for the inspection of your daily accounts. I should think half-past-two would be an agreeable time."

"Do you actually intend to inspect my accounts on a daily basis?"

"I most certainly do." He cast her a pleasant smile. "And I should very much like to meet your sons tomorrow as well."

"Why?"

"I have been charged with the responsibility of the management of their inheritance even if, at the moment, you are serving in that capacity."

"Only under your watchful eye." Disgust sounded in her voice.

"Be that as it may, an introduction seems only proper."

"They are children, Sir Nicholas."

"One is a viscount and the other is his heir. Regardless of their youth, they deserve to meet those to whom their financial futures are entrusted."

"They have met me." She fairly spit the words at him. "I am their mother."

"And you will be their mother always. However," he shook his head in a regretful manner, "whether you will always administer their affairs remains to be seen."

"Is that a threat, Sir Nicholas?"

"Probably not, but," he flashed her a wicked smile, "one never knows. Until tomorrow then." Once more he started for the door.

This evening hadn't gone at all as he'd expected. Up until the very moment the words had fallen from his lips he'd had no plan to confess his revelation about their past, nor had he intended to declare his intentions. Not that he had done any of that especially well. Still, if he knew nothing else at this point, he was certain she still detested him, which was far better than indifference, and certain as well that the spark that had once simmered between them still burned. Both discoveries boosted his confidence. It would not be easy to win Elizabeth's heart and hand, but nothing he had achieved thus far in his life had been easy.

He reached the door, pulled it open, stepped over the threshold, then glanced back at her. "One more matter before I take my leave, Lady Langley."

"What is it now?" she snapped.

"You should know I have accomplished everything I have set my mind to in the last decade. I have never failed and do not intend to do so now."

"Your intentions are of no particular concern to me." She shrugged in an offhand manner.

"I would be disappointed if they were. However, I would be remiss if I failed to mention one last thing." Nick cast his gaze over her in a forward and most appreciative manner, then grinned. "You would indeed have kissed me back."

He pulled the door closed behind him and waited no more than a fraction of a second. A crash sounded in the library and he stifled a grin.

No, this evening hadn't gone at all as he'd expected.

It may have gone much, much better.

Chapter 8

"I have never felt so blasted helpless in my life." Elizabeth paced across the width of her breakfast room, barely avoiding her sister, who paced in the opposite direction.

"I cannot believe Charles would do something like this to you." Indignation colored Jules's voice. "If my husband dared to put such stipulations on my life after his passing, I vow I would dig him up for the simple pleasure of wringing his neck."

"As he would be dead, that would be rather pointless," Elizabeth murmured even if the satisfaction of such a symbolic act certainly held a great deal of appeal.

"Although I daresay I would never find myself in such a situation," Jules said firmly.

Elizabeth stopped in mid-step and stared at her sister. "This is not something I brought about myself. Nor did Charles feel it necessary to discuss the matter with me. How on earth do you think you could avoid all this?"

"For one thing," Jules paused and leveled her sister a pointed look, "I have never felt it necessary to hide my intelligence. Therefore no one, but particularly not the man I chose to marry, has ever underestimated my abilities. For another, I have learned from your mistakes."

Elizabeth raised a brow. "Oh?"

Jules nodded. "Since Charles's death, I have made it my purpose to be well versed on the state of my own family's finances, investments, estate management and so forth. Oddly enough, my husband has been rather pleased by my interest."

"How wonderful for you both," Elizabeth said wryly. "Why have you never mentioned this before now?"

Jules shrugged. "There was no need. Besides, it seemed rather smug of me to say anything."

"That has never stopped you before."

"Perhaps I have at long last conquered at least one flaw in my character." Jules grinned.

In spite of Elizabeth's foul mood, her sister's grin was infectious, and she grudgingly returned her smile.

"Now then, to the matter before us." Jules clasped her hands behind her back and resumed her pacing. "What are we—or rather you—going to do about Sir Nicholas?"

"I don't know that there is anything I can do." A weary note sounded in Elizabeth's voice, and she again took up her own trek to and fro across the small room. "Believe me, I have thought of nothing else since last night."

It had been a very long night with very little sleep. Elizabeth had gone over and over her meeting with Nicholas and had come to no conclusions whatsoever. There was, of course, a fair amount of satisfaction in his admission that leaving her was a mistake and more than a bit of shock in realizing the truth of his parting comment. She would indeed have kissed him back.

Her fury at the revelation of Charles's actions and Nicholas's subsequent arrogance had sustained her through much of the evening. But when Nicholas had left, and she'd thrown a particularly valuable vase that she was exceedingly fond of against the wall and not felt much better for it, her anger had mellowed to a state of utter confusion. Feelings she'd thought were long past had arisen with a vengeance.

Nicholas wanted her?

He wanted her now, and it was apparent he had indeed wanted her ten years ago. Why then had he chosen to toss her aside in so callous a manner? Surely he had realized his words would wound her deeply. So deeply she might never forgive him. He'd said he'd had his reasons, but still it made no sense to her at all and simply added to the confusion that muddled her mind.

"It seems to me," Jules began thoughtfully, "that Sir Nicholas has indeed offered you a means of escape. You simply have to continue to manage your money in the manner in which you have and you will be free of him by Christmas. It's not a terribly long time, and certainly you can be civil to him until then."

"It's rather more complicated than that." Elizabeth sighed. "He seems to want to control my finances not nearly as much as he seems to want, well, me."

"You?" Jules stopped and stared at her sister. "What do you mean he wants you?"

"What do you think I mean?" Elizabeth blew a long breath. "Unless I am sadly mistaken, and I think the look in his eye eliminated any misunderstanding on my part, he wants me in the manner in which a man wants a woman."

"Good Lord, the sheer nerve of the man." Jules's eyes widened in utter disbelief. "The fact that he has the right to manage your money does not give him the right to anything of a more personal nature. How can he possibly think he can walk into your life and propose such liberties, especially as, while he was Jonathon's friend, he was never more than a mere acquaintence of yours in the first place?"

"He may not recall it exactly that way," Elizabeth murmured.

Jules narrowed her eyes. "He *was* never more than a mere acquaintance, was he?"

"Well." Elizabeth wrung her hands together. "Perhaps a bit more."

"Lizzie!"

"Have I never mentioned that?" Elizabeth said innocently.

"No, never, not a single word." Jules crossed her arms over her chest. "Do feel free to tell me now. And tell me everything."

"It was all very long ago, ten years to be exact and before I married Charles." Although it no longer seemed very long ago at all. Indeed, it seemed as recent as yesterday. "Nicholas and I . . . we . . . that is to say . . ."

"You what?" Jules's voice rose.

"It's not as bad as all that." Elizabeth waved an impatient hand. "We shared a certain . . . *friendship,* I suppose I would call it. We used to seek each other out at parties or gatherings to meet privately—"

"Privately? Alone, you mean?"

"Private does generally mean alone, yes."

"Dear Lord," Jules said under her breath. "No one ever knew about these clandestine meetings of yours?"

"I wouldn't call them clandestine exactly."

"If no one knows, then they are secret, which generally does mean—"

"Very well then, *clandestine,* but to talk, Jules, only to talk. We had long, fascinating discussions on any number of interesting topics. Art and politics and hopes for the future." Elizabeth shrugged. "That sort of thing."

"You had long talks with a man about politics? You?" Jules shook her head in a skeptical manner. "Such a thing would not surprise me today, but a decade ago you rarely talked to a man about anything that was not—"

"Frivolous?" Elizabeth wrinkled her nose. "I know. I was firmly convinced that a woman should not display her intelligence if she wished to be attractive to men."

Jules snorted. "Yet another mistake of yours that I learned from."

"Yes, well, in that regard, you're probably smarter than I was," Elizabeth snapped. "I fully admit it was a rather dim-witted attitude, and in many ways it's precisely what has placed me in the predicament I'm in today."

"Not entirely, Lizzie." Jules sighed. "To give credit where credit is due, Charles, of all people, should have known you better."

"I should have known him better as well." Elizabeth's gaze met her sister's. Jules was the only one in the world Elizabeth had told about Charles's indiscretions.

Elizabeth had discovered the existence of Charles's mistress a scant two days before he'd died. For the first time in her life, she had not known what to do and had delayed confronting him until it was too late. She'd been furious, of course, her anger coupled with a deep sense of betrayal, as well as a surprising amount of guilt and the uneasy feeling that somehow this was her fault. That she had not been a good enough wife. Or she had not loved him enough. But she had loved him, had always loved him, even if it had not been the grand passion her brother had described. And perhaps in that had lain her failure.

Up until the moment she'd found the letters written by the woman Charles had been involved with, she'd not had a doubt in the world about the perfect nature of their marriage. Certainly, in many respects, they went their own way and lived their own lives. He was busy with matters of finance and the types of things gentlemen of his station in life typically occupied themselves with, and she was concerned with family and charitable endeavors and social obligations. And if they did not always attend a particular dinner or party or play together, why, what married couple did? It didn't mean that they were not happy with one another. She'd never suspected for a moment that hers was not the only bed he frequented. Up until the very end, she'd thought that too, like every other aspect of their marriage, was relatively perfect.

Perhaps the comfortable, warm, pleasant type of love they'd shared had simply not been enough for him. Perhaps what Charles had needed was a grand passion, and possibly he had found it with someone else.

Was it past time she found it as well?

"I suppose that's neither here nor there at the moment. To my way of thinking, Charles betrayed you in life and now has done so again in death." Jules's voice was hard. "I would give serious consideration to my suggestion of digging him up if I were you."

"As appealing as that sounds, I have other matters on my mind at the moment."

"Ah, yes," Jules grinned wickedly. "Sir Nicholas. Mr. Collingsworth. *Nicholas.*" Jules seated herself at the table and refilled her teacup. "You have not finished telling me about the two of you."

"There is little more to tell." Elizabeth sat down and poured a cup of her own.

"Did he kiss you?"

Elizabeth nodded. "Twice."

"And?"

"And . . ." And he'd curled her toes and made her ache with newly discovered desire and touched her soul. And in spite of her denial last night, she hadn't forgotten so much as a single word they'd spoken or a moment they'd shared. She had simply stored the memories of him in a disused portion of her mind as one would pack away summer linens or winter blankets in the bottom of a chest.

"And," Elizabeth shrugged, "and that was it. There was nothing more to it than that."

Jules gasped. "You're lying. I can see it on your face."

"I am not," Elizabeth said quickly and met her sister's gaze defiantly. "I'd been kissed before, you know," she sighed in surrender. "But not like that. Never like that."

"Not even by Charles?"

Elizabeth blew a long breath. "Not even by Charles."

Jules's eyes widened. "My, my, this is a revelation. And juicy enough that I shall forgive you for taking a decade to tell me about it."

"I do appreciate that."

"So," Jules took a sip of tea and adopted a casual tone. "How is Nicholas after all these years? Still as grim and serious as I recall?"

"Not at all. He's actually rather charming when he's not being terribly arrogant or annoyingly high-handed. He was quite gracious, especially given as I was not particularly pleasant to him." She picked absently at the lace table covering. "I did not expect to encounter him yesterday or ever again really. His appearance came as something of a shock."

"As well it would." Jules studied her sister curiously. "Is he as handsome as ever?"

"Handsomer I think. He has aged nicely."

The smoldering quality of his dark eyes was as intense as she'd remembered, perhaps more so. Indeed, in nearly every aspect Nicholas was more than she'd remembered. The moment he entered a room it seemed entirely too small for his presence.

The brooding nature she recalled had vanished, and the confident manner that had replaced it was compelling, even perhaps irresistible. This was a man who enjoyed life. A man one wanted to be in the company of. A man who could weaken her knees with a single look and, as much as she was confident she had not let him know, had done just that last night.

"He's still the heir to a respectable title and he's become terribly rich as well, hasn't he?"

Elizabeth nodded. "Terribly."

Jules pulled her brows together. "Does he have a wife?"

"I don't think so."

"A mistress then?"

"He's barely arrived back in London. I daresay he hasn't had the opportunity to acquire a mistress."

Jules snorted. Charles's infidelity had affected his sister-in-law as deeply as it had affected his wife. Jules was now firmly convinced that no man, with the possible exception of her own husband, was completely trustworthy.

"Are his intentions honorable?"

"I don't know."

"Does it matter?"

"Certainly. I—" Elizabeth stared at her sister. "I don't know that either."

"How very interesting," Jules murmured. "Let's see then. Nicholas is rich, handsome, charming, and interested in you with intentions that might or might not be honorable." Jules ran her finger around the edge of her teacup. "Aside from that annoying problem of his involvement in your financial affairs, which may not last especially long, I fear I don't understand your problem."

"Jules!"

"Unless, of course," Jules raised a brow, "there's more you haven't told me."

"There might be a little more." Elizabeth got to her feet and meandered aimlessly around the room. "The night before he left—"

"The night of the Christmas ball?"

Elizabeth nodded.

"Ten years ago this upcoming Christmas ball?"

"Yes."

"My, that is an interesting twist," Jules murmured.

"I offered to go with him and," Elizabeth looked at her sister, "he didn't want me."

"I see."

"You're not shocked?" Elizabeth sank back down in her chair and studied her sister nervously.

"I should be, I suppose, and I would have been at the time, but no, I'm not especially shocked. As you've said, it was years ago and nothing really came of it." Jules thought for a moment. "So Nicholas rejected your offer and you proceeded to marry Charles."

"I loved Charles," Elizabeth said simply.

"Everyone loved Charles." Jules's tone was wry. "I believe that was his problem." She paused and considered her sister. "Did you love Nicholas as well?"

"No. What an absurd thought," Elizabeth said quickly. "How could I have married Charles if I loved someone else?"

"I'm not saying you didn't love Charles. You had loved Charles in some fashion for much of your life," Jules said slowly. "But I wonder if what you felt for Nicholas wasn't love as well. You did offer to run off with him."

"It wasn't love." Elizabeth shook her head firmly. "It was nothing more than, I don't know, lust, I suppose. A desire for adventure and excitement. That sort of thing."

"Then he didn't break your heart?"

"Absolutely not. My pride, perhaps, but not my heart."

"Well, if you didn't love him—"

"I didn't."

"And he didn't break your heart—"

"He didn't."

"Then again, dear sister, I simply don't understand." Jules leaned forward and stared into her sister's eyes. "Do you still have feelings for him?"

Elizabeth raised her chin. "I detest him."

Jules scoffed.

"Perhaps I don't detest him exactly, but I certainly don't trust him."

"Then don't marry him."

"Marry him?" Elizabeth started. "The question of marriage is not an issue. He certainly did not mention marriage, nor have I any intention of marrying him. I have agreed to do no more than accompany him to his uncle's party, and that only because I had no real choice. Why, the thought of marriage to Nicholas, to any man for that matter, has not so much as crossed my mind."

"What has crossed your mind?"

"Nothing of any consequence. Not a thing, really." She smiled weakly and acknowledged the lie to herself. In spite of her confusion, the one thing she had realized in the long, sleepless hours of the night was that she would like to do considerably more than return Nicholas's kiss.

Jules studied her in a considering manner but didn't say a word.

Elizabeth heaved a resigned sigh. "I may possibly want him as well."

"Then I see no reason why you should not have him." Jules smiled and sipped at her tea as if she were suggesting an excursion to Bond Street for perfumed soaps and not something scandalous and improper and immoral.

"I couldn't possibly." Even to her own ears, Elizabeth's denial did not quite ring true.

"Why not?"

"It would be wrong. I have certain principles, after all. There is a question of propriety. Certain rules of behavior that onc is expected—"

"Men have liaisons of an amorous nature all the time," Jules said in a matter-of-fact manner.

"I am not a man."

"No, but you see no reason why you should not be given the same consideration as a man when it comes to your abilities with your finances." Jules sipped her tea and widened her eyes in an innocent manner Elizabeth didn't believe for a moment. "Why is this any different?"

"I don't know, but it seems completely different." Was it really? Charles, and any number of other men she could name, married men at that, apparently had no qualms about taking a lover. Why should she?

"After all, Lizzie, you are a widow, not a wife. You quite enjoy the freedom your status affords you. Why should that freedom not extend to your bed?"

"Jules! How can you say such a thing? I had no idea you were so . . . so . . ." Elizabeth searched for the right word, "free thinking!"

Jules laughed. "Not at all. I am simply happy with my life, and I wish you to be happy as well."

"I was happy."

"No, my dear, misguided sister. You were content." Jules leaned back in her chair and considered her sister. "When you married Charles, I thought your life would be perfect. Indeed, I thought he was perfect. It wasn't until I met and married that I saw what true happiness was. My husband is the other half of my soul."

"A grand passion," Elizabeth murmured.

Jules nodded. "Exactly. I don't think Charles was a grand passion."

Elizabeth stared. "You think my marriage was a mistake?"

"I'm not sure I would call it a mistake." Jules paused to choose her words. "Indeed, if we were to turn back the clock and live those days once more, I'm certain I would encourage you to marry Charles again. It's only hindsight and experience that now make me think otherwise. Although it scarcely matters anymore." She adopted a brisk tone. "You have an entire life ahead of you, and you have earned the right to live it exactly as you please." Jules grinned in a most suggestive manner. "And it seems to me there is one thing that is virtually guaranteed to please. A special Christmas gift, to yourself, if you will."

"Nicholas Collingsworth," Elizabeth murmured.

"You said you wanted him."

"It's exceptionally difficult to admit such a thing."

Whether she was willing to admit it aloud or not, she did indeed want Nicholas now, as she had ten years ago. As she might well have wanted him somewhere in the back of her mind every day between then and now. But lust was a far cry from love.

"You should have him then."

"I should, shouldn't I?"

"Think of him like a sweet that you have denied yourself for a very long time."

"Ten years," Elizabeth said under her breath. Ten long years.

Why not indeed?

It had been her experience that the desire for sweets long denied simply grows with the passage of time, the sweet itself becoming more and more irresistible. A simple sampling, nothing more than a taste really, might serve to ease the desire.

Ten very long years.

But gorging on said sweet might well satisfy the craving forever.

Of course, it would never do at all if she'd truly been in love with him. But as it had been simply lust then and simply lust now there was certainly no risk to her heart. Certainly, there was the possibility of hurting him if indeed he truly cared for her. His admission of having made a mistake notwithstanding, if he had loved her, how could he ever have left her? And left her in a manner that virtually assured she would turn to Charles.

Excitement brought Elizabeth to her feet. "I'll do it."

"Excellent!" Jules beamed at her sister and stood. "And you may count on me to assist in whatever way you deem necessary."

Elizabeth raised a brow. "I do appreciate the offer, but I doubt that I will need any assistance. I have never seduced a man, but how difficult can it be? I can't imagine there will be a great deal of resistance. I know I have not had any, shall we say, *practice,* in this particular area since Charles's death, but I daresay I remember how."

"It's like riding a horse," Jules said confidentially. "Once you know how, you never—"

"Jules." Elizabeth laughed. "That's quite enough, thank you." She sobered. "I have no intention of marrying him, however."

"Nor should you. You cherish your independence far too much."

"And while I expect to feel a certain fondness for him, love will not enter into this."

"Not that I disagree, mind you, but why not?"

"The one thing I have learned in handling my own finances is that one should never risk more than one can afford to lose," Elizabeth said simply.

"I see." Jules paused, then nodded. "Love is neither required nor expected."

"At the end, he shall go his way and I shall go mine."

"No need to do otherwise."

"It's settled then. I shall embark upon a relationship with Nicholas based on nothing more than prurient desire and unbridled lust."

"Here, here." Jules raised her cup. "To prurient desire and unbridled lust."

"I have no intention of changing my mind, but," Elizabeth drew a deep breath and grinned, "I can't believe I am planning such a thing."

"Neither can I." Jules laughed. "But it should be an extraordinarily merry Christmas."

Chapter 9

"It is an honor to meet you, my lord." Nick adopted his best formal manner and nodded his head in a polite bow.

"And you as well, Sir Nicholas." The eight-year-old Viscount Langley, Christopher, gazed up at Nick and acknowledged his greeting with a tone that matched the older man's in formality even if it was considerably higher in pitch and his stance substantially shorter. It was apparent the boy was exceedingly conscious of his position as viscount.

"And what of me, Sir Nicholas?" six-year-old Adam interrupted, as Nick suspected he was prone to do. "Is it an honor to meet me as well?"

"Most certainly, Mr. Langley." Nick extended his hand. "A very great honor."

Adam shot his mother a grin. "I thought it would be."

Elizabeth smiled a sort of long-suffering smile, but pride in her sons showed in the looks she cast them and the smile on her lovely face. The two fair-haired, blue-eyed boys resembled her greatly in coloring and appearance. Nick wondered if they would be tall like their father.

They should have been mine.

He ignored the thought. Now was not the time for such regrets.

"I understand you were a friend of our father's," Christopher said.

"Indeed I was." Nick nodded solemnly. "Your father and your uncle Jonathon were my closest friends in our youth."

"And Mummy as well?" Adam asked.

"Mummy as well." Nick cast her a quick smile, and she returned it politely.

"Mummy needs friends, I should think," Adam said in a confidential manner.

"That's quite enough, Adam." Elizabeth leveled him a stern glance.

Adam's eyes widened innocently. "Well, you do. Uncle Jonathon says one can never have too many friends."

"Your uncle is exceptionally wise," Nick cut in smoothly. "I count myself fortunate to be among his friends, and yours, too, now, I hope."

Adam gave his mother a smug smile.

"Are you just visiting London, Sir Nicholas?" Christopher considered Nick curiously. "I had heard you lived in America."

"I did for many years, but England is my home and I have now returned for good."

"Just in time for Christmas." Adam glanced at his mother, then leaned toward Nick and lowered his voice. "One can never have too many friends at Christmas, you know, better than any other time of year. What with the giving of gifts and all. I am always happy to have a new friend who might understand that a train is an excellent gift at Christmas—"

"Adam." A distinct threat sounded in Elizabeth's voice.

"Or any time at all," Adam said quickly, then clamped his mouth closed tight, as if to prevent any further suggestions of Christmas gifts from springing from his lips of their own accord.

"I can certainly see where a train would indeed be an excellent gift." Nick nodded in his most somber manner and tried not to laugh. "At Christmas and all year round."

"Did you have grand adventures in America, Sir Nicholas?" A light shone in Christopher's eye. "Did you see Indians?"

"And pirates?" Adam added eagerly.

Nick bit back a grin. "I might have seen an Indian or two. Possibly even a pirate. I should be delighted to tell you of my adventures someday."

Suspicion washed over Adam's face. "Someday?"

"Someday soon." Nick placed his hand over his heart. "You have my word."

"Aunt Jules says you have made a great fortune in steamships and other interesting things. She came this morning to talk to Mother. She says you are obscenely wealthy." Christopher studied Nick as if obscenely wealthy could be noted somewhere on his person. "Are you?"

Elizabeth winced. If Nick remembered correctly, Elizabeth's sister had never been especially fond of him. He wondered what else she might have said to the boys.

Nick thought for a moment. "Yes, I believe I am."

Adam's brows pulled together, and he looked at his mother. "Are we obscenely wealthy, Mummy?"

"No, dearest, we are not," Elizabeth said firmly.

"Are we poor then?" Worry creased the child's forehead.

"Don't be silly." Christopher snorted. "Grandfather is a duke, and dukes are never poor."

Adam breathed a sigh of relief. "Good. I should hate to be poor and live on a shovel and have to eat gruel all the time."

Nick narrowed his eyes in confusion. "A shovel?"

The boys' governess stood off to the side and cleared her throat. "I believe that's a hovel, sir."

"Of course," Nick murmured.

"No, Adam, we are neither poor nor obscenely wealthy. However, the state of our finances is not a topic for discussion." Elizabeth's voice rang with motherly chastisement. "And one does not discuss money in polite conversation."

"You do." Christopher frowned. "So does Aunt Jules and Grandmother and, well, nearly everyone else in the family. Who has money and who doesn't and all sorts of things like that. It seems to me there is always a lot of talk about people who have acquired a great deal of money or people who have gambled away their money or squandered it irresponsibly on poor investments or women of a questionable nature—"

"Christopher!" Elizabeth signaled to the governess. "I believe it's time for your studies."

"It's always time for our studies when the conversation gets the least bit interesting," Christopher said in an aside to Nick, one man confiding in another.

"Do you think it's impolite to discuss money?" Adam gazed up at Nick.

Nick chose his words carefully. "I think there is a time and a place for such discussions."

The boys exchanged triumphant grins.

"However," Nick continued, "I also think young gentlemen should always do as their mother requests."

At once triumph turned to disgust at the defection of the only other male in the room as evidenced by the look on their faces and a bit of muttering. The governess stepped forward to usher them from the library.

Christopher stopped in the doorway and glanced back. "I shall look forward to hearing of your adventures, Sir Nicholas."

"And soon," Adam added. "You promised."

"And I never break a promise." Nick grinned. "Especially not a promise made to friends."

"Friends who like sailboats almost as well as trains," Adam called over his shoulder, then vanished through the doorway with his brother. Whoops and laughter echoed in the hall behind them.

"They are rather precocious, aren't they?" Nick said mildly.

"They remind me very much of Jonathon at that age." Elizabeth smiled wryly. "I thank God every day for Miss Otis. She grew up with six brothers and is not overly upset by even the most vile of boyhood pranks. Most of which tend to follow a visit from my brother."

Nick chuckled. "I can well imagine."

"I'm certain you can."

"Will Adam be receiving a train for Christmas then? From St. Nicholas perhaps?"

"We shall see. A train is just one of many items on a rather impressive list the boys have compiled, and they will not receive it all. I do not wish them spoiled. Still." She smiled apologetically. "I find it difficult to refuse them much of anything."

"It is Christmas, after all." And Sir Nicholas could definitely be depended upon even if St. Nicholas failed. Surely it wouldn't be all that difficult to find a toymaker and purchase a train and a sailboat for good measure. For both boys. "And exceptions should be made. For Christmas."

"Perhaps for Christmas. Now then." She adopted a brisk manner, no doubt to hide her nerves, and moved to the table they'd sat at last night.

Elizabeth had been distinctly on edge and noticeably restless since the moment he'd arrived. He'd caught any number of odd, speculative glances thrown in his direction. She could have simply been nervous about this introduction of her sons, but he doubted it. They were fine young men, and she was obviously well pleased with them.

No, he'd wager a great deal that her demeanor had little to do with her children and everything to do with last night. It was an excellent beginning.

She waved at the table. "The account books are here, but there is little new since yesterday. A few household bills that I have already dealt with. I daresay, it should take you no more than a minute or two to peruse them."

"We shall see," he said in his most businesslike manner, trying not to cringe at the pompous note in his voice, and moved to the table.

"Yes, we shall," she said under her breath and clasped her hands together. The woman was most definitely nervous. "I have been giving a great deal of thought to our conversation of last night."

He stifled a grin, leaned back against the table, and crossed his arms over his chest. "Have you?"

"To be honest, I have thought of little else and," she paused, for courage perhaps, "I have a confession to make."

"I cannot wait to hear it."

She met his gaze directly. "I would have kissed you back."

He grinned. "That's scarcely a confession."

"Yes, well, perhaps you will appreciate this more. I . . . I . . . I misspoke last night."

"Misspoke?" This was excellent.

She drew a deep breath. "I do remember everything that passed between us ten years ago."

"Do you?" Excellent indeed.

"I do. And furthermore, given that," she squared her shoulders, "I don't think simply kissing you back would have sufficed."

"I scarcely thought it would," he said with a smug grin, then realized the import of her words. His smile faded. "You don't?"

"I do not. Not last night and not today."

"Today?" He straightened and stared, any previous sense of satisfaction swept away by confusion. She couldn't possibly be saying what he thought she was saying. "What do you mean, *'today'?*"

"Today, this very moment, right now." She stepped toward him. "I think my meaning is perfectly clear."

He stepped back. "Not to me."

"Come now, *Nicholas.*" She moved toward him and again he moved away. A slight smile played across her lips. A smile of, well, *seduction.* "You said you wanted me. Like a ship."

"Not like a ship." This was ridiculous. "Not like a ship at all."

"A company then. Or a stock. It scarcely matters." Her voice was low and inviting. "In point of fact, you want me. I'm the only thing you ever wanted that you didn't get. After a great deal of thought—'due consideration,' that is—I've decided you can have me. Or perhaps it is I who can have you."

She moved closer, and he sprinted out of reach to put the table strategically between them.

Nick glared at her. "What exactly are your intentions, Lady Langley?"

"My intentions?" She laughed with sheer delight. It would have been most contagious under other circumstances. As it was, it sent a distinct chill up his spine. "My dear Nicholas, I should think my intentions are terribly obvious. And not terribly honorable."

"Perhaps you should spell them out for me," he said slowly.

"Honestly, Nicholas." She crossed her arms over her chest. "One would think you've never been seduced before."

"I've never been seduced by you before, and therein lies the problem."

"Oh, dear. Am I doing it all wrong then?"

"Yes! No!" He huffed. "I don't know."

"How could you possibly not know?" She studied him curiously. "Surely, you've been seduced before?"

"Generally, I have been the seducer." He narrowed his gaze. "However, there have certainly been . . . on occasion . . . a particular lady might . . . blast it all, Elizabeth, this is highly improper and most embarrassing."

"Why?"

"Because you're you!"

"Now who is being unclear? Unless I completely misunderstood you last night, and I daresay that was difficult to do, this is exactly what you want. Therefore I cannot understand your hesitation. Unless . . . of course. I should have realized." She smacked her forehead with the palm of her hand. "You're concerned about my lack of experience."

He stared in shocked disbelief. "Not at all."

"I was married for seven years, you know, and we were not celibate by any means."

He groaned. "Elizabeth, I do not wish to hear—"

"You shall find me most enthusiastic. Granted, I have not had the same variety of experiences as you probably have with the opposite gender—"

"Elizabeth!"

"Goodness, Nicholas, you needn't look so outraged. I simply meant that Charles is the only man who has ever shared my bed, whereas I have no doubt you have sampled the charms of countless numbers of women."

He had never in his life denied any of his amorous liaisons, but Elizabeth made him sound very much like, well, a tart. "I would hardly term them countless."

"How many then?"

"I have no idea." Indignation rang in his voice and struck

him as somewhat absurd. Of course, what about this entire conversation was not absurd?

She scoffed. "Surely you have some idea? An educated guess, perhaps?"

"I don't know," he said staunchly.

"Thousands?"

"I don't know! Although," he muttered more to himself than to her, "thousands does seem like rather a lot."

"We'll settle on hundreds then." She nodded firmly.

He frowned. "I don't see what concern it is of yours anyway."

"If I am about to fling myself into your bed, I should like to know beforehand that it shall be worth the flinging." She winced. "So to speak."

He drew himself up indignantly. "I have never had any complaints before about the flinging." He paused. "So to speak."

"Excellent." She beamed at him. "I have never had any complaints either, although I have certainly not had the vast experience you have and—did I mention my enthusiasm?"

"Good God, yes."

"You also should know I am more than willing to learn. I distinctly remember you once mentioned having learned a lot on your travels about men and women and the very good times they could have together." She braced her hands on the table and leaned forward. "I should very much like to have a very good time."

He backed up and shook his head. "Why are you doing this?"

"Why?" She shrugged. "The more appropriate question should be why not."

"Very well then." He eyed her suspiciously. "Why not?"

She straightened and ticked the points off on her fingers. "We are both adults, well past the age of consent. Neither of us is currently married or otherwise encumbered." She paused. "You aren't married, are you?"

"No," he snapped.

Her eyes narrowed. "Have you a mistress?"

"Not at the moment."

"Good." She nodded with a hint of what might have been relief. "In addition, while one of us is obviously better versed in the subject matter, neither of us are virgins, which means there should be no moments of intense awkwardness." She cast him a brilliant smile and started around the table toward him.

"Elizabeth!" He started backwards, caught his foot in the leg of a chair, and fell into it.

"I must admit to a great deal of surprise, Nicholas." Elizabeth moved to stand in front of him and smiled down at him. "I never thought you of all people would be so stuffy about matters like this."

"I'm not stuffy. I'm simply confused. And shocked."

"It's quite simple really." She rolled her eyes toward the ceiling as if praying for patience, although surely heavenly guidance played no role in this. "I have spent ten years with you lingering in the back of my mind. Oh certainly, I didn't realize it or perhaps I didn't accept it until I saw you again. You want me and I want you. There's nothing more to it than that."

He struggled to sit upright. "There's a great deal more to it than that."

She shrugged. "Not at all."

"I thought you had no desire for marriage." He would have gotten to his feet, but she would have had to move for that—or he would have had to move her. Being that close to Elizabeth or, God forbid, touching her in any way at this particular moment was not an action that would encourage rational thinking. And he definitely needed all his wits about him.

She smiled in a most wicked manner. "I am not suggesting marriage."

Relief battled with disappointment. The relief was expected. The disappointment came as yet another surprise in an afternoon full of surprises. His thoughts hadn't turned toward marriage, but why shouldn't they?

He chose his words carefully. "What are you suggesting?"

"What I am suggesting, or rather what I am proposing, is a temporary . . . *arrangement* I suppose is the best word. Consider it something of a counteroffer to your own compromise. Very businesslike, really."

He stared up at her. "And this counteroffer consists of what?"

She hesitated for no more than a fraction of a second. "For the next few weeks, the length of time you originally proposed for the management of my finances, perhaps scheduled promptly at half past two before you look at my accounts or possibly after, it scarcely matters, I suppose, until Christmas at any rate, I shall share your bed willingly and with enthusiasm—"

"Yes, I believe you've mentioned enthusiasm," he muttered.

"At the end of that time you will return, in a legal fashion I should think, all control of my finances to me. We will have furthermore laid to rest this undeniable attraction between us, lust if you will. We will each be satisfied and can therefore go our separate ways."

"Our separate ways?"

"Absolutely. There shall be no encumbrances, no binding ties, no permanence whatsoever. Furthermore, I do not expect love or anything of that nature, nor should you, although a certain amount of friendly affection between the two of us would certainly be welcome."

"Friendly affection?"

She nodded in a pleasant manner, as if what she was suggesting had no more significance than an afternoon carriage ride.

"But not love?"

She shook her head. "The goal is to deal with lust. Love has nothing whatsoever to do with it."

"Just out of idle curiosity and because I prefer to have all the facts before I agree to any kind of contractual agreement—"

"As well you should."

"Why eliminate the possibility of love?"

Her green eyes were cool and unreadable. "I have my reasons, just as you had your reasons for casting me aside ten years ago."

"I see," he said slowly. "And at the end of this period, we go our separate ways?"

"Indeed. I should prefer never to see you again."

He shook his head. "I'm afraid I still don't quite understand."

"For a man who is reputed to be so brilliant in business,

you're really rather dim when it comes to a simple businesslike agreement." She huffed. "Very well, think of it this way. I am a ship and you are a sweet."

"What?"

"Chocolates, toffee, candied nuts, plum puddings, fruit tarts—something of that nature. Quite wonderful really, but when one has had enough, the desire has vanished. And one might never wish for plum pudding again."

"Are you insane?" He glared up at her.

She smiled. "Probably."

He narrowed his gaze. "Why would you agree to such a thing?"

"Why?" Her voice lowered and she braced one hand on each arm of the chair, effectively trapping him. A lovely trap, but a trap nonetheless.

He swallowed hard. "Why."

She leaned closer. "Because I remember how you took me in your arms and the way your lips met mine and the way your body was warm against my own."

Her lips were a scant breath from his own.

"I remember the longing that welled up deep inside me when you walked into a room and the palatable tension in the air when we were together, so thick I could scarcely breathe. And the way your kiss curled my toes."

Her lips whispered against his and he jumped, jerking backwards with a force born of shock and desire. His head smacked the back of the chair and the front legs rose. Elizabeth straightened in surprise, and for a fraction of a second he balanced precariously, then he and the chair tumbled backwards. The upholstery absorbed most of the fall, saving him from serious injury, but his pride was most definitely wounded.

Elizabeth tried and failed to smother a laugh.

Nick lay face up on the floor in a most annoying and distinctly humiliating fashion. "I am glad you found that amusing."

She grinned. "Most amusing."

"Enjoy it, Elizabeth." He scrambled up from the floor and brushed off the sleeves of his jacket, his voice polite and cool.

"As it is the only amusing thing that has been said in this room today."

"Not at all. Why, your very attitude is most amusing. I should have thought you would have jumped at my offer." She choked back a laugh. "Or rather fallen for it."

"I have never accepted a proposition, be it business or personal, without due consideration, and I shall not do so now."

He nodded and headed toward the door. What he needed was a moment, or a lifetime, to consider all the ramifications of Elizabeth's offer and what it truly meant. He simply couldn't think rationally with those serene green eyes assessing him. "I shall give your proposal serious thought and let you know my decision."

"What about my accounts?"

"I shall pass on the perusal of them today," he said over his shoulder. Her accounts were the last thing he wanted to think about.

"And your uncle's dinner? I received his invitation this morning."

"As per our arrangement, I shall escort you." The dinner he had prompted his uncle to give was supposed to have been the first step toward working his way back into Elizabeth's affection. Sharing her bed was not supposed to have been so much as a possibility. Yet.

"As that is a full week from today, I assume I shall be seeing you before then?" She waved at the ledgers. "For my accounts if for no other reason."

"I really cannot say at the moment, Elizabeth. I'm not entirely sure what my plans are or exactly how I feel about your proposition." He'd never expected anything like this. Certainly, he had hoped to rekindle the feelings that Elizabeth had once had for him, and desire was among them, but he wanted much more from her.

"If it helps your offended sensibilities, you may think of it as a Christmas gift. For both of us."

"A rose by any other name and all that. We may call it a Christmas gift or whatever we wish, but that does not change the fact of the matter." He grabbed the door handle.

"Nicholas." A firm note sounded in Elizabeth's voice, and he turned back to her.

Her gaze met his directly. "I threw myself at you once before and I warn you I shall never do so again. If you truly wish for this particular ship, you need to either set sail or disembark."

"I see." He studied her for a long moment. "You shall have my answer soon, then." He nodded and again started to open the door, muttering to himself. "Christmas gift."

She laughed softly behind him.

Perhaps it was her laugh or the subtle shade of triumph that colored her voice or the simple fact that he'd never coveted a ship he hadn't eventually acquired, but abruptly his confusion vanished and his mind cleared. Realization struck him like a nasty blow to the head.

The blasted woman had turned the tables on him once again. She'd done it to him last night and was doing it to him today. He had all the bargaining chips, yet she had him backing away like a frightened fawn from a huntsman. What on earth was wrong with him?

Only an idiot would leave this particular woman at this particular moment.

Nicholas Collingsworth was no idiot.

He turned on his heel, stalked across the room, and before she could utter a word, wrapped one arm around her and pulled her tight against him.

"I am willing to accept your proposal, Lady Langley." He kissed her hard and fast. "But I have some conditions of my own."

"I thought you might," she said breathlessly and stared up at him.

"And I cannot agree to your conditions."

She shook her head. "They are not negotiable."

"Everything is negotiable. It's the first rule of business."

"Then I take it back." She pushed against him, but he refused to release her. "All of it."

"You can't. We have an oral agreement. And I have accepted." He kissed her again, slower this time, and longer, until she sagged almost imperceptibly against him. He felt the resistance in her body diminish and his own desire swell. She tasted as he remembered, as she'd tasted in his dreams, faintly of cinnamon and ginger and long-ignored desire. If he continued for so much as a moment longer he'd accept her conditions, damn the consequences, and take her right here on her library carpet.

He drew his lips from hers and stared down at her. He wanted her heart, he knew now he always had, and all she offered was her body. Very well then. He would take exactly what she offered. For now.

Her eyes were glazed with the resurgence of a passion far too long denied, and she struggled to keep her voice steady. "What are your conditions, Nicholas?"

"Due consideration, Elizabeth, I told you I have never accepted a proposition without due consideration." He pulled her closer and brushed his lips across hers. "I shall give our arrangement the thoughtful consideration it deserves and inform you of my terms when next we meet."

"When will that be?" She rested her hand lightly on the front of his shirt, and the muscles of his chest tightened.

He grabbed her hand, pulled it to his lips, and kissed her palm. She shivered against him.

The carpet was looking better and better in spite of the time of day and the distinct possibility that children and servants were liable to appear at any moment. Still, there were doors with locks for that sort of thing.

He blew a long breath and released her, contenting himself with the fact that she appeared more than a bit unsteady on her feet. Excellent. He was rather unsteady himself.

It had been his experience with women, countless or otherwise, that for a female like Elizabeth, the physical act of lovemaking went hand in hand with love. She could resist it all she wished, but it was part of her very nature. He just had to convince her of that.

Of course, he could not mandate love. He could not make it a condition of their arrangement. For now, he would take what she offered, but he would not rest until he had her heart as well.

"When I escort you to my uncle's dinner."

"But that's not for a week."

"I shall see you in a week's time then."

"But what about," she waved feebly at the ledgers, "the accounts? You did say promptly, every day at half-past-two?"

"I shall simply leave you to your own very competent devices for the time being." He stepped to the door and pulled it open. "Oh, and I must tell you Elizabeth, I have never missed a sailing before, and I do not intend to miss one now."

He shut the door and paused. A moment later a crash sounded and he grinned.

It was amazing how a vase broken in anger and another broken out of frustration had distinctly different sounds. And one was infinitely more satisfying.

Chapter 10

"I have no idea what I'm going to do now," Elizabeth said out of the corner of her mouth even as she kept a pleasant smile firmly on her face.

She and Jules stood in the parlor at Lord Thornecroft's house and surveyed the guests milling about for Nicholas's welcome home dinner.

"I can't imagine Lord Thornecroft—indeed, anyone, and certainly not a bachelor at that—being able to organize a gathering of this size in such a short amount of time," Jules said thoughtfully. "There must be more than forty people here."

Elizabeth watched Nicholas work his way through the crowd, kissing a feminine hand here and greeting a gentleman there. He moved with a masculine grace, enhanced by the breadth of his shoulders and the surety of his stride.

"I had thought Nicholas would have made an appearance at my house by this point," Elizabeth said, as much to herself as to her sister.

Nicholas was completely at ease and wore confidence as if it were a coat tailored for him and him alone.

"Someone must have assisted his lordship, with the invitations at the very least." Jules nodded at the bunches of mistletoe and holly hanging conspicuously in the entryways, the swags of greenery festooning every doorway and window, the silk ribbons and berries tied with joyous abandon on stair rails and sconces. "Someone who has begun the celebration of the season far earlier than usual. Quite festive really, although whoever saw to the decorations is overly fond of mistletoe."

And when he laughed the sound caught at Elizabeth's heart.

"To check on my expenditures if nothing else."

"Perhaps Lord Thornecroft has a secretary? Or Mother might have had one of her staff assist him."

"How long could *due consideration* possibly take anyway?" Elizabeth had expected Nicholas yesterday and the day before and each and every day since their talk in her library. "Why, the man isn't even checking on my accounts, which begs the question of exactly what he is doing."

Jules's gaze skimmed the group. "We do know nearly everyone here, however. Indeed, many of the guests are relations of ours, which stands to reason as this is a party to welcome Nicholas home and both he and his uncle have long been thought of fondly by everyone in the family, especially Mother. As for the others, friends and acquaintances, no doubt, of Lord Thornecroft. Nicholas never struck me as being especially convivial."

"He's probably letting me simmer in my own sauce," Elizabeth muttered. "Wondering when he'll decide to begin this arrangement of ours."

"Still, I may have misjudged him," Jules murmured.

When Nicholas had arrived precisely at the appointed time at Elizabeth's door to escort her to his uncle's house, he hadn't said a word that could have been construed as anything other than polite. He'd made no mention of her proposal or her accounts and had not said so much as a single word about his absence. He'd been pleasant but no more than that. Even when he'd helped her into his carriage, his hand had not lingered overly long on hers. Furthermore, he had positioned himself in the confines of the vehicle neither too close nor too far away.

"No doubt he's intentionally trying to drive me mad. And doing an excellent job of it."

It was most annoying, especially since, now that she had acknowledged to herself and to him how very much she wanted him, it was increasingly difficult to be in his presence and not press her lips to his or run her hands over his chest or drag him bodily to a secluded spot where she could let him have his way with her. Or have her way with him.

It had been hard enough to say everything she'd said at their last meeting. While she'd never been particularly shy, she'd never been anywhere near that bold, either. Her cheeks warmed at the very thought. And now a lifetime of proper behavior, coupled with a fair amount of pride, held her in check. She had meant it when she'd told him she would not throw herself at him again even if waiting for him to give her proposal *due consideration* was indeed driving her mad.

"He always was a handsome devil," Jules said under her breath. "But there's something distinctly different about him now."

There wasn't the tiniest doubt in Elizabeth's mind that he wanted her every bit as much as she wanted him. But the blasted man's behavior was nothing short of impeccable. She didn't trust him for a moment.

"I have no idea what his conditions might be, but regardless, I have no intentions of agreeing to them." Elizabeth might not be able to do anything about his management of her finances, but in this, at least, she still had a choice.

"Engaging and most provocative. Practically irresistible," Jules said softly.

Certainly he had accepted her proposal, but it had been contingent on her conditions and her conditions alone. Not only did he not understand that fact, but he had refused to agree to her conditions. It seemed only logical therefore that her offer was null and void even if Nicholas had not seen it that way at all. It was increasingly clear that Nicholas Collingsworth was used to getting his own way in virtually everything.

"I have run my life as I have seen fit for the last three years. I have no intention of letting a man control it now," Elizabeth said firmly.

"He makes you want to run your fingers through his hair," Jules murmured at precisely the same moment.

"What?" the sisters said in unison.

Elizabeth huffed with annoyance. "Were you listening to me?"

"No more than you were listening to me, dear sister." Jules's gaze drifted back to Nicholas. "Although I can certainly see how your thoughts might be otherwise occupied."

Elizabeth followed her sister's gaze. Nicholas was across the room at his uncle's side, and, at the moment, was raising the hand of a startlingly lovely and vaguely familiar woman to his lips in a far too attentive and entirely too charming manner. Jealousy stabbed at her and she brushed it aside. It was absurd to feel so much as a twinge of jealousy. After all, whatever she might or might not soon have with Nicholas would be temporary.

The lady leaned closer to Nicholas and murmured something in his ear. A startled expression crossed his face and he laughed. The woman favored him with an all too inviting smile. Elizabeth's jaw tightened. Still, temporary or not, she would add fidelity to her list of conditions.

"I should do something about that if I were you," Jules said.

"He does not belong to me, Jules." Elizabeth shrugged. "I have no claim on him."

"I should do something about that too." Jules studied Nicholas for a moment. "He is rather a catch."

"If one were seeking a salmon. I, however, am not in the mood for a fish course." She flashed her sister a wicked grin. "Only dessert."

"Pity," Jules said pointedly.

It wasn't a pity, though. Jules might well never understand, as she had never submitted to anything in her life. But until her husband's death, Elizabeth had spent much of her life letting other people, primarily Charles, make her decisions for her. Not simply about finances but about everything. Even Nicholas had had more of a hand in deciding her fate on that night ten years ago than she had. Worse still, it had never especially bothered her.

Now, she quite liked being an independent woman. She liked choosing the direction her life took and being responsible for herself and her sons. Indeed, she liked who and what she was, who and what she had become. She would not allow Nicholas or anyone else to take that from her.

And there was absolutely nothing to prevent an independent woman from engaging in an arrangement based on no more than prurient desire and unbridled lust. Oh, certainly, there were the endless rules of proper behavior even a widow was expected to adhere to, but she had no intention of publicly flaunting her arrangement with Nicholas. Still, she had better add discretion to her conditions.

The woman speaking to Nicholas laid a hand lightly on his arm and leaned closer in a manner entirely too intimate to be completely innocent. Elizabeth narrowed her gaze. Certainly, she had no actual claim on Nicholas, even if she fully intended to occupy him until Christmas, but neither was she inclined to share.

"Do you know who she is?" Elizabeth said to her sister.

"No, but I'm certain I have seen her before." Jules pulled her brows together. "I simply can't place her at the moment."

"I think I should like to place her at a far distance from here," Elizabeth said under her breath. "And I think it's past time I chatted with Lord Thornecroft. Would you care to join me?"

"I would prefer to find my husband and flirt with him in a provocative manner." Jules grinned. "He quite likes that."

Elizabeth laughed and started across the room toward Lord Thornecroft, standing beside Nicholas. Had she ever flirted with Charles? Certainly she couldn't remember having done so after they were married. In truth, she couldn't remember having flirted with him before, either. He'd always been there and had always loved her just as she'd always loved him. As she looked back, there had been no real effort on either side to make one another happy. They had simply expected and assumed happiness. Still, they *had* been happy—or at least content.

Or had their marriage possibly been a well-intentioned mistake? Simply because everyone, including themselves, had believed they'd been meant for each other, neither of them had ever truly questioned it. Even when Elizabeth had thought she might love Nicholas, it had been in addition to Charles, not instead of him. What if she, what if everyone, had been wrong?

"Ah, Elizabeth, I cannot possibly get everything I want. Some things were not meant to be."

What if her true fate, the future she was always supposed to have, was even now flirting with an all too beautiful woman?

It was an intriguing idea and one that should be given further consideration at another time. Sometime after Christmas, perhaps when she had sated her desire for Nicholas and could consider what they might once have shared in a rational, logical manner. Besides, the days when she'd had any interest in permanence were long behind her. Her only interest now was in this particular man and only at this particular Christmas.

"Lord Thornecroft, what a delightful gathering." She extended her hand to the older man.

"The delight lies fully in the charm of my guests." He lifted her hand to his lips, his gaze never leaving hers.

"I cannot recall ever attending a party of yours before, but I do hope I shall be included again in the future."

"My dear Lady Langley, you have not been invited in the past only because I have not had a fete like this before." A twinkle sparked in Lord Thornecroft's eye. "I live an exceptionally dull life dedicated primarily to the study of ancient flora and fauna."

Nicholas choked back a laugh.

His uncle ignored him. "However, I should have parties each and every evening if you would promise to grace us with your lovely presence."

"I would consider it an honor," Elizabeth said with a smile.

Odd, she had never considered the older gentleman in any manner other than as a friend of her parents and, as such, a figure of parental guidance. The slightly wicked gleam in his eye now was anything but fatherly. Nor had she ever noted how attractive his lordship was or how very much his nephew resembled him. While she had never quite believed it before now, at once she realized Lord Thornecroft's reputation with women was obviously well founded.

She pulled her hand from his and turned to the woman beside Nicholas. "Please forgive me. I seem to have forgotten your name, although I am certain we have met before. You look remarkably familiar."

"I rather hope I am, Lady Langley." The woman smiled a genuine kind of smile, and Elizabeth couldn't help but like her immediately. "While our paths have crossed at an occasional ball, we have never actually met."

Elizabeth shook her head. "I'm afraid I don't—"

"Do allow me to introduce you both," Nicholas cut in smoothly. "Elizabeth, Lady Langley, may I present Miss Theodora Godwin."

"The actress?" Elizabeth's eyes widened with recognition. "Of course. I have seen you perform any number of times. You're quite good."

"So I have been told," Miss Godwin said with a light laugh. "But I dearly love hearing it again."

Theodora Godwin was well known in London for her skills on the stage, and, unlike many other actresses, she was considered something of a private person. While many actresses were as famous for their reputations off stage as for their acting abilities, Elizabeth had rarely heard more than the occasional rumor about Miss Godwin. Either the woman was remarkably chaste or remarkably discreet.

She was also remarkably beautiful, with dark, nearly black hair, porcelain skin, rather lush lips, and clear blue eyes. While Elizabeth had seen her on the stage for years, she must have started at an early age. The woman couldn't possibly be more than a few years older than Elizabeth herself.

"Teddy is quite extraordinary, in my opinion." Lord Thornecroft cast the actress an affectionate smile. "And exceedingly generous with her time."

"Teddy helped my uncle with this evening's festivities," Nicholas said. "And did an excellent job of it, given the speed with which the task was undertaken."

"Not at all, Nicky." Miss Godwin smiled up at Nicholas. *Nicky?* "The credit for this evening belongs to Frederick's staff." She leaned toward Elizabeth in a confidential manner. "His housekeeper, butler, and cook are true wonders, and I daresay he has never taken the tiniest advantage of their skills. It is the Christmas season after all, and the poor dears were simply dying to do something of a festive nature in this stuffy old house."

"Nonsense," Lord Thornecroft said staunchly. "This is your doing. Why, you penned the invitations, selected the menu, directed the decorations—"

"The mistletoe," Elizabeth murmured.

"Christmas wouldn't be Christmas without mistletoe." Miss Godwin glanced around the room with a satisfied smile. "It has always seemed rather a shame to me that we hesitate to decorate in the fashion of the season until the very day or so before Christmas. I know it's considered bad luck, but, as Frederick gave me free rein for everything surrounding Nicky's coming-home party, I thought why shouldn't we start the celebration of Christmas with the celebration of his return?"

"Why not indeed?" Elizabeth said pleasantly. *Nicky?* "It is lovely, Miss Godwin. Quite in the spirit of Christmas. And I agree. It is never too early to begin the celebration."

"Oh, do call me Teddy." Miss Godwin—Teddy—laid her hand on Elizabeth's arm and met her gaze directly. "I much prefer it to Miss Godwin. There is something rather dreary about the title of Miss at my age. It simply serves as a reminder that I have failed in that most illustrious of female pursuits, that of marriage."

"Come now, Teddy, I know for a fact you have had numerous proposals and ample opportunity to acquire a husband," Nicholas—*Nicky*—said.

Teddy laughed. "I have indeed had numerous proposals, few of which were for marriage, and ample opportunities for the acquisition of a husband. Unfortunately, none of them my own."

The comment hovered in the air.

"How very interesting." Elizabeth stared at the other woman, not quite sure if she should be offended or rather envious. Everything in her upbringing dictated shock, yet Teddy was obviously a woman who had always run her own life, apparently on her own terms. Elizabeth drew a deep breath and smiled. "And you must call me Elizabeth. My friends do."

"Excellent." Lord Thornecroft breathed a sigh of relief, beamed at Elizabeth, then turned to Teddy. "I don't believe you've met Elizabeth's parents, the Duke and Duchess of Roxborough, and you really should. Remarkable couple, I've always thought." He offered Teddy his arm. "Shall we?"

"Of course." Teddy studied Elizabeth for a moment. "It was very nice to meet you at last." She nodded at Nicholas. "Nicky, we shall have to have a long chat later."

"I shall look forward to it." *Nicky* grinned.

Elizabeth watched the couple cross the room to greet her parents. Her mother would no doubt be delighted by Teddy's straightforward nature. The Duchess of Roxborough was rather unique among her peers in that respect. As for her father, Elizabeth doubted there was a male alive who would not appreciate the actress's more obvious charms, including the man beside her.

She turned to Nicholas and raised a brow. "Nicky?"

He grinned. "Are you jealous?"

"That she called you by a pet name? Not in the least." She shrugged. "But Nicky? Come now, Nicholas, it's the name one would use for a little boy."

He laughed. "I used to be a little boy."

"Yes, well, you have grown some." She tried and failed to stifle her curiosity. "Have you known her for very long?"

"Ah." He nodded in an annoyingly smug manner. "You are jealous."

"I most certainly am not." She narrowed her eyes. "But if I was, not that I am, mind you, but if I was, would I be justified?"

"If you were," he tucked her arm in the crook of his elbow and steered her toward the entry, "you would not be justified. Teddy and I are simply very old friends."

"How old?"

"I knew you were jealous." He chuckled. "Very well then. We met once, years and years ago, before my uncle and I left on our travels. She was in a rather dreadful play called *The Bandit's Bride,* or something like that, although she was quite good. We renewed our acquaintance when she toured America. I had no idea she knew my uncle until he reintroduced us last week." He glanced down at her. "Does that ease your mind?"

Last week? Before or after she had issued her proposal? She brushed aside the question.

"I am merely curious, therefore my mind does not need easing, thank you. However, if it did, you have not precisely answered my question, and furthermore . . ." She realized they had moved into the foyer, and she stopped in midstride. "Where are you taking me?"

He continued to steer her forward. "There is something I wish to show you."

"What?"

"In here."

He pushed open a door and allowed her to pass by him into what looked very much like a gentleman's library and smelled very much like a place where said gentlemen indulged in brandy and cigars. Not an offensive odor, more of an essence really, a memory of past times, and not at all unpleasant.

She stepped into the room and turned toward him. "Well?"

He closed the door behind him and leaned against it. "I wanted to thank you. Privately."

"Oh?"

"For being so kind to Teddy."

Her heart sank. "I see."

"You were most gracious, and I am most appreciative."

A leaden weight settled in the pit of her stomach. That was that then. She certainly was not about to have any relationship whatsoever, let alone a temporary arrangement based on nothing more than lust and desire, with a man who was already involved with another woman. Whether that involvement was of a legal nature or something substantially less official, she would not be in the position of destroying another woman's happiness. She was disappointed of course, but there was nothing more to it than that.

Elizabeth shrugged in an offhand manner. "It wasn't at all difficult. She is quite charming."

"She is an excellent actress, but she has been extremely apprehensive about tonight."

"Why?"

"Why?" His brow rose. "This is a rather intimidating gathering. You and I may not realize it because these are people we have known much of our lives, but Teddy is the only one in the entire room without a title or, barring that, great wealth. The only guest here who was not born to rank and privilege is Mr. Cadwallender, and even he is now Sir Ephraim."

Elizabeth pulled her brows together. "I am not intimidating."

"No?" He stepped toward her. "Do you have any idea what kind of reputation you have today, Elizabeth?"

"No," she said sharply. "But as long as it is not frivolous and featherbrained, I don't know that I particularly care."

"You should." He clasped his hands behind his back and circled her slowly. "I have been back for little more than a week and I have already heard comments about Lady Langley, who not only carried on bravely after her husband's death but has brilliantly managed his affairs, continued her charitable works, and is considered well versed in matters ranging from architecture to politics."

"Really?" She stared in disbelief. "They say that?"

"Indeed they do." He nodded and continued his circle. "In point of fact, the gentlemen at my uncle's club consider you intelligent, charming, quite lovely, and eminently eligible. In spite of the fact that there is not the slightest hint of impropriety about you, you have no end of suitable, as well as optimistic, escorts. Am I right?"

"Perhaps." She tried and failed to hide a grin. "Probably."

"You have social status, wealth, and independence, and your beauty has only improved with age." He stopped in front of her. "So you see why, through no intentions of your own, you could be somewhat intimidating."

"I suppose I could. I had never thought of it that way, and I'm not entirely sure if the idea of being intimidating to anyone, let alone Theodora Godwin, is flattering or rather upsetting." She shook her head. "Although one wouldn't think a woman like Miss Godwin—Teddy—used to performing in front of vast numbers of people would be intimidated by much of anything at all."

Nicholas gazed down at her, his dark eyes thoughtful. "People have all sorts of fears one would never suspect simply by looking at them."

"Perhaps." She drew a deep breath. "As I said, I found her charming, and I can certainly see why you're taken with her."

"I am not taken with her." His lips curved upward. "But my uncle may well be."

"It wouldn't matter to me if you were, you know." Even as she said the words she realized it would matter. And realized as well it wasn't simply a question of fidelity.

"I never for a moment thought it would." His expression sobered. "Teddy and I met in America at a time when I was longing for home and she was torn over a love affair. She is my friend, Elizabeth, and has never been more than that."

"I see." She felt like a complete and utter fool. A jealous fool at that.

"You feel a bit foolish now, don't you?" A superior note sounded in his voice. The man was right and he knew it.

She wanted to smack him. Or break a vase.

"For jumping to conclusions?"

Perhaps over his head.

"I did a moment ago." She narrowed her gaze. "But now I don't feel the least bit foolish. If I did not know better, and quite frankly I don't, I would think that everything you've said this evening to or about *Teddy* has been for the express purpose of trying to make me jealous."

His eyes widened, and he gasped in an overly dramatic manner. "I would never do such a thing."

"You would do anything that gets you what you want." She aimed her finger at him. "It won't work, you know."

He frowned. "It won't?"

"It most certainly will not." She poked her finger at his chest and glared up at him. *"Nicky."*

"I thought it was working rather well."

"You cannot have everything your own way."

"Oh, but I can." He reached out and pulled her into his arms. "Everything."

His mouth met hers in a gentle kiss, his lips warm and firm against her own. A kiss of discovery perhaps, or recognition. Tender and sweet and not nearly enough.

She slipped her arms around his neck, and he pulled her

tighter against him, and all restraint between them vanished. She pressed her lips harder against his in a kiss fueled by the denial of a decade. His mouth was demanding, insistent, plundering, and she met him in kind. Her lips parted, and her tongue met his in a frenzy of taste and passion, and still it was not enough.

She wanted to touch him, taste him, run her fingers over his naked body. His hands splayed across her back and she wanted to feel those hands on her body without layers of clothing between them. She wanted his mouth on her breasts and his bare legs entwined with her own and the sensation of him buried deep inside her.

Her blood pounded in her ears and she could feel the thud of his own heart racing in tempo with hers.

He wrenched his lips from hers and stared down at her, his dark eyes a smoldering reflection of her own need. "This is neither the time nor the place."

"Absolutely not." She swallowed hard.

"We are about to go in to dinner."

"I know I am especially hungry."

He stared at her, indecision warring with desire on his face. "Damnation, Elizabeth."

"Damnation indeed." She sighed and pulled his head back to hers. He tasted of champagne and desire and never-forgotten memories. And merely kissing him was at once wonderful and completely insufficient.

He drew his lips from hers and trailed kisses along the line of her jaw. His voice was low and labored. "We really should return to the others."

"Someone will certainly miss us otherwise." She gasped and tilted her head, concerned with nothing more than the feel of his lips on her neck. "But you wished to show me something."

"The mistletoe," he murmured against her skin.

She glanced upward, his lips drifting to the base of her throat, and she moaned. "I . . . I see no mistletoe."

"No? My mistake." His one hand was still wrapped around her waist. "And my apologies." His other hand skimmed her side, then lightly cupped her breast. Her nipple tightened beneath the layers of silk and corset.

She gasped. "Accepted."

He ran his mouth along the curve of her neck and nibbled on her shoulder, which was left exposed by the low cut of her fashionable gown, and she sent a quick prayer heavenward in thanks for the dictates of fashion.

"Do I take this to mean that you have given my proposal due consideration?" Not that she cared at this particular moment.

"I have thought of very little else." His fingers toyed with the neckline of her bodice.

She sucked in a sharp breath. "What of my conditions?"

"We shall discuss them later."

"Very well." She wanted nothing more than to melt into a small, hot puddle at his feet and pull him down with her. "I should wish to add fidelity."

"Fidelity, yes." His lips replaced his fingers, and she thought she would surely die of sheer sensation at any moment.

"I would prefer that we remain discreet as well." She could barely get the words out. "I should hate to ruin my reputation."

"I wouldn't mind at all if you ruined my reputation," he murmured.

"And honesty." Even through the layers of her skirt and crinolines she could feel his arousal, and she pressed herself hard against him. "I should like honesty between us."

"Honesty . . . yes . . . very good . . . without a doubt."

"Nicholas, could we not . . . here . . . now?"

He stilled against her and drew a deep, shuddering breath. "No."

"No?" Her voice rose. "Why not?"

He raised his head and looked at her. His voice was wry. "I shall not allow you to have your way with me here. As if I were a common tart."

"But I've always liked tarts," she said without thinking. "Jam tarts and fruit tarts and—" She stared at him. "And toffee and plum pudding as well."

He snorted.

She grinned. A moment later laughter bubbled through her. He joined her and pulled her close against him once again.

Nicholas rested his chin on the top of her head and blew a long breath. "What are we going to do about that craving for sweets of yours?"

"Indulge," she said with a sigh and reluctantly pushed out of his arms.

He chuckled. "I've always been fond of indulgences."

"And ships as well." She smoothed her skirts, patted her hair, and struggled to return her breathing to a semblance of normal. Although she suspected that with Nicholas around, her breathing, and everything else, would rarely be normal again.

"Ships are simply an indulgence on a grander scale." He laughed, took her elbow, and started toward the door.

The last thing Elizabeth wanted right now was to return to the others and pretend nothing whatsoever had just happened between them. Pretend there was not this aching need building inside her to have this man in her bed. Regardless, it could not be helped. In spite of the desire triggered by his kiss, Nicholas was right. Again. This was not the proper place or time to consummate their bargain. She had waited ten years for this man, she could certainly wait a few hours more. Surely, when he escorted her home after dinner . . .

"Tell me, Sir Nicholas, did we just reach an accord as to our arrangement."

"Absolutely not, Lady Langley." He grinned down at her. "Absolutely not."

"In many ways I think Scrooge was nothing more than an astute businessman," Jonathon said in an idle manner. He glanced across the table at Nick, and a wicked spark shone in his eye.

"Lord Helmsley, how can you possibly say such a thing?" The debutante sitting beside Jonathon gasped in shocked dismay. She was pleasant enough in a very young, very sweet, very naïve way, and for the life of him, Nick could not remember her name.

Juliana, seated next to Nick, turned away from an animated discussion with her husband and another guest, a gleam similar to her brother's in her eye. "His lordship says something along the very same lines every year as Christmas approaches." Anticipation sounded in her voice. "Usually when he judges the dinner conversation at his end of the table to be not as amusing as he thinks it should."

Jonathon chuckled and took a sip of his wine.

"Still, it is, as always, an interesting question." Elizabeth studied Nick from her place beside her brother. "What do you think, Sir Nicholas?"

Nick chose his words with care. "I think Scrooge was extraordinarily lucky."

"Really?" Elizabeth studied him. "Why?"

"He had the opportunity few of us do in this life," Nick said thoughtfully. "To make amends for his mistakes. For a second chance at happiness, as it were."

"Very good," Jonathon murmured.

"How lovely." Miss Sweet Young Debutante sighed.

"Yet he could have simply avoided his mistakes in the first place," Juliana said pointedly.

"Indeed he could have, but how many of us do? I know of any number of people, myself included, who have made serious mistakes in judgment in their youth. Mistakes that have affected their entire lives." His gaze met Elizabeth's. "Even if the reasons behind their actions seemed at that particular point in time to be not only wise but indeed noble."

Elizabeth raised a brow. "Noble?"

"Sometimes it's necessary to sacrifice one's own desires in the best interest of someone else."

"I don't think Scrooge sacrificed anything in the best interest of anyone else. I think his only concern was his own interests." Juliana shook her head firmly. "He gave up Belle, the one love of his life if one reads beyond Mr. Dickens's words, for the sake of his own pursuits and nothing more than that."

"Although, according to the story," Nick said smoothly, "it could well be argued he gave her up because, however right or wrong he may have been in the matter, he did not feel he was financially able to wed. Many consider that position wise in this day and age. If you look at it that way, sacrificing his own desires for her welfare," he shrugged, "could indeed be viewed as noble."

"Rubbish." Juliana huffed. "He sacrificed her for the sake of his own ambition."

"Ambition is a demanding mistress," Nick said in an offhand manner.

"Even so." Elizabeth leaned forward slightly. "Couldn't he have pursued his ambition without losing his soul?"

"Did he lose his soul, I wonder?" Jonathon said.

"Yes, I think he did." Elizabeth nodded thoughtfully. "In spite of his success in business, he was not a happy man. Mr. Dickens makes that perfectly clear. Scrooge did not even indulge"—a blush warmed her cheeks at the word, and Nicholas bit back a grin—"himself with his wealth. His supper on Christmas Eve was taken in a tavern followed by gruel before a meager fire. His rooms were cheap and shabby, his furnishings mean and sparse."

"Surely you're not saying happiness can be purchased?" Jonathon raised a brow.

"Don't be ridiculous. Of course she isn't," Juliana scoffed. "But comfort can, and it's far easier to be happy if one is comfortable than if one is miserable."

"Still, that's not the point of it." Elizabeth thought for a moment. "What he had or didn't have or the manner in which he spent, or rather hoarded, his money, his material assets as such are not significant. Why, the Cratchits had nothing yet were obviously happy in spite of their poverty."

"Poor, dear, dear Tiny Tim." Miss Sweet Young Debutante sighed.

"The point is," Elizabeth continued, "that there was no joy in Scrooge's life. He was alone. He had no family save his nephew, and he was not overly cordial to him, no friends, indeed no one to mourn at his passing. I think a man like Scrooge, completely alone, with no affection, has no joy. No raison d'etre, as it were. So yes," Elizabeth settled back in her chair, "I do think he lost his soul. Or more accurately, tossed it away."

"And the ghosts of Christmas returned it to him," Juliana

said firmly. "Or rather gave him the opportunity to reclaim it by understanding and accepting the true meaning and spirit of Christmas. Generosity towards others being paramount."

"Generosity not simply of material goods," Elizabeth added. "Not only sending the prize turkey to the Cratchits or raising Mr. Cratchits's salary, but a generosity of spirit. Opening his heart. Keeping Christmas all year long. And in that regained his soul."

"Excellent, Lizzie." Jonathon grinned.

"Very good," Nick murmured.

A satisfied smile tugged at the corners of Elizabeth's mouth. Her gaze met his and lingered, and there was far more than simple triumph in her eyes. There was a distinct invitation and a definite promise. It was all Nick could do to keep from leaping to his feet and reaching across the table to take her in his arms. Drag her onto the table and press his lips to hers, mold her body against his. Sweep aside the candles and crystal and food-laden plates to feel the satin heat of her skin against his and the thud of her heart against his own. Tear the clothes from her body and make her his own here and now in the midst of poached fish and roasted meat. Lick the wines splashed across her hard, delicate nipples and savor the sauces spilled upon—

"What of you, Sir Nicholas?"

Nick started. "What?"

"I was asking if you have celebrated Christmas these past ten years?" Juliana said.

"Christmas?" Nick said slowly.

Christmas was the last thing on his mind at this particular moment, although the idea of sugarplums and toffee and tarts and other Christmas treats was tempting. He drew a calming breath and glanced at Elizabeth. An altogether too knowing look sparked in her eyes. She couldn't possibly know what he had been thinking, could she?

He forced a pleasant smile. "It seems the height of sacrilege to admit it among this festive assembly, but I have not particularly celebrated Christmas at all. I confess it has often been simply another day for me."

"Just like Scrooge," Miss Sweet Young Debutante murmured.

"And what of your employees?" Elizabeth narrowed her eyes. "Is it simply another day for them too?"

"No, my lady, it is not." Nick met her gaze with the solid, resolute stare that had made grown men quiver and immediately reconsider their positions. He was oddly pleased that she didn't so much as twitch. "Only those men in my employ whose jobs require a continuous presence work on Christmas Day, and they are compensated extremely well. Each and every employee receives a bonus at Christmas as well. A practice, I might add, that is not widespread among employers, but I have found that workers who are well treated are more productive and are extremely loyal. In many ways, they are my responsibility, a sort of family, if you will. I consider them such and treat them accordingly.

"Furthermore, I have certain moral standards I adhere to. I do not permit the hiring of children. The widow of any man killed while in my employ receives a substantial pension. And I donate generously to charities here and in America." He turned toward Miss Sweet Young Debutante. "So you see, my dear, there is really little comparison between myself and Scrooge."

Miss Sweet Young Debutante's eyes widened. "But he didn't mark Christmas in any way, and neither do you."

Juliana snorted.

"I have marked it in benefits to my employees and goodwill toward those less fortunate. As for myself, I have not celebrated in the past, but I anticipate that will change now that I have returned home." Nick glanced around the table. "Christmas is a time to gather with family and friends, and it is at this time of year that being apart from them is especially difficult. My only real family is my uncle, and he resides here in London, as do those I count as friends. And I confess, I do regret the long years spent away."

"You had no friends in America?" Juliana studied him curiously.

"I had any number of acquaintances, primarily of a business nature. But those I consider true friends have always been here." He chuckled wryly. "Most in this very room."

"And what of women, Sir Nicholas?" Juliana said. "You have not married?"

Elizabeth smiled politely. He wouldn't be at all surprised if the sisters were in league with one another. Indeed, Juliana's questions might well be retaliation for letting Elizabeth think, if only for a moment, that there was something beyond friendship between Teddy and himself. Not that he had actually done that, of course, but he perhaps hadn't discouraged that impression quickly enough.

Jonathon raised a brow. "Which has to do with Scrooge, the topic of discussion, in what manner?"

"You have obviously failed to notice, Jonathon, but we've long since exhausted discussions of a literary nature and have proceeded to far more interesting things." Juliana shot her brother a quelling glance. If Nick didn't know better, he would swear they were all children again. She cast Nick a brilliant smile. "We have turned to Sir Nicholas."

Nick laughed. "Am I more interesting then than Mr. Dickens's characters?"

"Oh, infinitely." Juliana nodded. "One knows nearly everything about the characters in a book, at least by the final page. But in reality, it's difficult, if not impossible, to know everything about anyone. Particularly when they don't answer your questions."

"Perhaps they do not answer because those questions are overly personal," Jonathon said mildly.

Juliana ignored her brother. "Now, then, Sir Nicholas, are you going to answer mine?"

"It is good to know the years have not diminished your forthright nature." Nick chuckled. "Very well then, no, I have never married. And to forestall your next question as to why, I really cannot say."

"You are obviously financially able to wed," Juliana pressed. "So the reason you proffered for Scrooge does not hold true for you."

"Perhaps Sir Nicholas is of a romantic nature," Miss Sweet Young Debutante said with enthusiasm, obviously no longer equating him with Scrooge. "Perhaps he has never found a lady who could capture his heart?"

"Or a woman he would wish to tie himself to for the rest of his days," Elizabeth said.

Nick glanced at Elizabeth.

"Or perhaps any woman who might well capture his heart had already been spoken for." Juliana met his gaze firmly.

"Or possibly . . ." He took Juliana's hand and drew it to his lips. Her eyes were a deeper shade than her sister's, more blue than green, and held a look of amusement and possibly even appreciation. ". . . she was entirely too young and far and away too outspoken to be a suitable wife and he missed his opportunity." He brushed a kiss across her hand. "To his everlasting regret."

Juliana burst into laughter and pulled her hand from his. "Well said, Sir Nicholas." She nodded with definite approval. Nick had the distinct impression she was approving him for something far more important than his way with words, and he wondered exactly how much she knew about the relationship between her sister and himself. "Well said, indeed."

Juliana turned away in response to a comment from her husband at her side. Jonathon cast Nick a curious grin, then directed his attention to another guest, and a moment later, the others took up various conversations.

Across the table Elizabeth toyed with her wineglass and spoke absently to the gentleman seated beside her.

For years Nick had refused to admit to himself the depth of his feelings for Elizabeth. Feelings that had been ignored but had never faltered.

Juliana was right. He had never married because the one woman who had indeed captured his heart had already been spoken for. He had never married because no other woman had come close to touching his soul the way Elizabeth did. No, she didn't merely touch it, she owned it. Possessed it. For better or ill, he was hers, he had always been hers, for now and forever.

Now he just had to convince her of that.

Tonight, thanks to the outrageous bargain she had proposed, he would finally make her his. He intended to take full advantage of her scandalous decision to at long last give in to the desire that had lingered between them for a decade. But her conditions were absurd, and, aside from fidelity and discretion, he had no intention of abiding by them. He had spent the past seven days considering her proposition and making arrangements of his own.

Nick had let her go once in the guise of a noble mistake but a mistake nonetheless. He would not let her go again. Not after Christmas, not ever. He sipped his wine and watched her thoughtfully. He had a great deal of time to make up for.

Getting into her bed would be the easy part. Working his way into her heart would require a great deal of effort. He wasn't sure why she resisted the idea of love, but he had never let an obstacle stand in his path before and he would not start now.

Nicholas Collingsworth had never failed to acquire a ship he had wanted, and he would not fail now to gain the love, the heart, of the one woman in the world who owned his soul.

Elizabeth glanced at him, and her gaze met his. He raised his glass in a private, discreet toast.

And he intended to have a great deal of fun in the process.

Chapter 11

Nicholas helped Elizabeth out of the carriage, and they started toward the front door. All in all, the dinner to welcome Nicholas home had been lovely. Rather it *would* have been lovely if not for the anticipation that quivered deep inside her, fluttering in her stomach and catching at her breath. And the evening had stretched on forever.

This would be it, then. Tonight, probably within the hour, Nicholas would be in her bed. She wanted this, wanted him, more than she'd ever imagined possible. And almost as much as she wanted him, she wanted to know the *why* of it all.

Was it indeed the denial of a sweet long craved, or was it something more? Something ignored for a decade? Something lasting? Something forever?

She wanted to know, and at the same time, she feared the knowledge and what it said about her and the life she had led and the decisions she had made.

Elizabeth glanced up at the house before her and stopped in midstride. "Nicholas, your driver has made a mistake."

"Are you sure?" he said coolly. "My driver never makes mistakes."

"He has this time. This is not my house." She stepped back and shook her head. "Mine is one door down."

"Indeed it is, but it is no mistake." He took her arm and led her up the steps. The door swung open at their approach. He stepped aside to allow her to enter before him. "This is *my* house."

She swiveled to face him. "Your house? What do you mean, your house?"

"I mean it belongs to me." He shrugged off his greatcoat into the waiting hands of a discreetly nondescript servant, no doubt a butler. "I purchased it."

"What do you mean, you purchased it?" She unfastened her cloak and handed it to the butler with a nod of thanks. He accepted the garment and promptly vanished into the shadows of the foyer.

Nicholas raised a brow. "I thought I was being quite clear. I mean precisely what I just said. This house belongs to me because I purchased it."

Elizabeth stared at him suspiciously. "Why?"

He smiled in an enigmatic manner and strolled into the parlor. The man was as annoying as he was cryptic. And this latest action of his, like virtually everything else he'd done thus far, did not bode well.

Elizabeth grit her teeth and followed. "I don't believe you."

"Believe as you wish, but it's true."

"It couldn't possibly be true. Lord Halstrom has lived in this house forever." She narrowed her gaze. "What have you done with him then?"

"Lord Halstrom?"

"Yes, of course, Lord Halstrom, the poor dear man." Elizabeth pushed aside a tiny twinge of guilt.

She had lived in the house next door since Charles had purchased it shortly after their marriage, and Lord Halstrom had lived here for years before that. But admittedly, she wasn't at all sure she'd recognize the older gentleman if she ran into him in her own parlor. He was a widower and not overly social. Indeed, it was her understanding that he spent most of his time in the country.

"I bashed him over the head and left him for dead," Nicholas said mildly and crossed the room to where a decanter and glasses sat waiting on a table. "Ah, I see Edwards is efficient as always. He's working out extremely well. I'm quite pleased with him."

"Oh?" She crossed her arms over her chest. "Did he help you bury the body?"

He glanced at her with an amused smile. "I assume you would like a brandy."

"Yes, of course, although it won't do you any good, you know."

He chuckled. "I don't expect it to."

"Then your expectations will be met." She accepted the glass. "Well?"

"Well."

"You haven't answered my question."

"I thought I did."

"Nicholas!"

"Very well, I confess." He shrugged. "I did not bash him over the head. Indeed if anyone was the injured party in our transaction, it was myself."

She snorted.

Nicholas sipped his drink. "Even though his lordship was eager to sell and retire to his estate in the country, he wanted an exorbitant amount of money for this place. Fortunately, I was willing and able to spend an exorbitant amount."

"Why?" she said sharply, although she was fairly certain she already knew the answer.

"Property is always a good investment."

"And?"

"And I am always looking for good investments. I could scarcely go wrong with this one." He swirled the brandy in his glass. "It is an excellent location in a fine neighborhood."

"It is one door away from my house," she snapped.

He grinned. "I said it was an excellent location."

A horrible thought struck her, and she stared. "Surely you aren't planning on living here after Christmas?"

"Oh, but I am. Indeed, I have been living here for the past several days. I'm rather surprised you hadn't noticed."

She hadn't noticed, but then she probably wouldn't have

unless they had left their respective houses at the same moment. "Why aren't you living with your uncle?"

"I value my privacy and my independence, as does my uncle. Surely you can understand that."

"Go on."

"I thought, and he agreed, that having separate residences would suit us both best."

"I daresay the two of you could live in Thornecroft House for years and scarcely cross one another's path. The place is enormous."

"And this house is not." He glanced around the room and smiled. "Still, it's a good size and quite to my liking."

Elizabeth had scarcely noticed anything since she'd walked through the door. Now, she scanned the parlor curiously. The proportions were pleasant enough but not easy to discern given the vast amount of furnishings the room contained. The word that came to mind was *full.* Or rather *stuffed.* There were no less than a half dozen chairs and at least two sofas, plus tables, desks, several clocks, all manner of bric-a-brac, and a great deal of statuary. The mantel was lined with porcelain pots and vases, Chinese in appearance, and similar pieces perched on available space around the room. If she could have imagined a setting for Nicholas, this would not have been it.

"I purchased the place fully furnished. Halstrom apparently never saw an item of questionable interest that he could resist acquiring. He fancied himself something of a collector, I believe, although there is no rhyme nor reason in the varied assortment of articles to be found anywhere in the house. Indeed, he was as eager to rid himself of this stuff as he was to rid himself of the house. I can well understand why." He grimaced. "It is not to my taste, and I anticipate making a great number of changes, but it will suit for now." He nodded at the vases on the mantel. "The porcelain, however, is mine."

She raised a brow. "You collect pottery?"

"No. I collect fifteenth- and sixteenth-century Ming dynasty porcelain." He set down his glass and made his way to the fireplace, dodging a fainting couch, two antique French chairs, and a very large bronze Mercury. "Aside from its age, it's really quite unique." He picked up a small, long-necked vase with a blue-on-white design. "It's made from a special clay found in only one region of China. It took a dozen or so people simply to produce one individual jar or vase. Blue and white is more common than the colored pieces, although I do have a few of those. Most of mine have imperial markings, that is they were destined only for use at the imperial palace."

He turned the vase over in his hands. "Regardless of the effort of the craftsmen or the rarity of the clay, if a piece had so much as the tiniest imperfection, it would be shattered and discarded."

She stared. "I never imagined you would collect *pottery*."

"Imperial Ming dynasty porcelain," he said firmly. "And I did not set out to collect it. A small collection came into my possession as payment for a debt, and I found the history and the beauty of it fascinating and quite compelling." He shrugged. "And it's a valuable investment."

"As is this house."

"Exactly."

"Investment." She snorted in disbelief. "I don't believe you for a moment. I believe you bought this house for one reason and one reason only."

"Location?"

"Exactly. It's located directly next to my house."

"You live in a very nice neighborhood."

"It was a very nice neighborhood," she snapped.

He studied her curiously. "Did you mean it when you said honesty was a condition of your proposal?"

"Absolutely."

"Very well then. Let me be honest. In the next few minutes I fully intend to take you in my arms and carry you up the stairs and into my bedchamber."

"I don't want to be taken in your arms and carried up the stairs and into your bedchamber. I want to talk about why you've purchased the house next to mine. I want to know exactly what your intentions are in doing so."

He continued as if she hadn't said a word. "Once there I intend to disrobe you in a very slow and methodical manner."

"Nicholas." The man was impossible to ignore.

"I shall begin with your dress, of course." He sipped at his brandy, his gaze intense. "Lovely gown, by the way. It flatters the green of your eyes."

"Thank you," she murmured, pushing away the images his words produced. "That's all very well and good, but—"

"While in the process, I shall run my mouth lightly over your bare shoulders. Kiss the curve of your neck and that charming spot at the top of your spine."

His voice was low, and she could almost feel his hands upon her. "You intend to do that, do you?"

"Indeed I do. You will scarcely note that your dress is now a puddle of silk around your feet. Next, I shall peel your petticoats slowly down the length of your legs."

"Nicholas." In spite of her resolve, the word was more a sigh than a protest. "Stop."

He ignored her. "Then I shall turn my attentions to your corset. Blasted nuisances, to my mind. I don't know why women put up with them. Although there is little I find more attractive than a woman clad in only a corset. In addition, there is something quite intoxicating about loosening the laces of a woman's corset—your corset—and feeling your body relax with relief against my hands, your skin through the thin fabric of your chemise warm against my fingers."

"Good Lord, Nicholas." She downed the rest of her brandy, knowing, even as its liquid burn slid down her throat, that the liquor was not to blame for the heat washing through her body. And it was exceedingly warm in here.

"Your corset will drop discarded to the floor, and you shall scarcely notice, far too intent on the feel of my hands over the delicate material of your chemise and your drawers. Caressing your breasts, sliding down the curve of your waist, over your hips and across the swell of your stomach to the point where your thighs meet and—"

The glass slipped from her hands, bounced on the carpet, and settled at her feet.

He tossed back the remainder of his drink and set his glass on the closest available empty spot.

She swallowed hard.

His gaze shifted downward to her toes, then back up, in a slow, deliberate manner, as if she were already unclothed, as if he were already running his hands over her naked body.

"Nicholas." Her voice was as unsteady as her insides. "In the interest of honesty, I must say I have never heard such things spoken aloud, and, in spite of my forward manner last week, I am thoroughly shocked, and furthermore, as it has been rather a long time since I have been with a man, I don't think," her voice faltered, "I can possibly bear to hear about your plans for another moment without flinging myself at you."

"Then let the flinging begin." His voice was as low and as intense as his dark eyes.

Any doubts she might have had, any second thoughts, any considerations as to her conditions or the future vanished not merely with his words but with the look in his eyes. Smoldering with desire exactly as she remembered from years past and from her dreams, but there was more, something deeper, a yearning that went beyond simple passion. A need of the soul that matched her own.

She stared at him for a moment and then was in his arms. His lips crushed hers with a need too long denied. Her mouth opened to his in a welcome born of urgency and desire. He wrenched his lips from hers and kissed the corners of her mouth, her closed eyelids, her temples, as if he needed to taste every bit of her. She gasped and clutched at his shoulders. Her head fell back and his mouth explored the length of her neck and her throat. His tongue trailed a path to the valley between her breasts, and she cursed the voluminous skirts and petticoats that kept her body from his.

She wrapped her arms around his neck and pulled his mouth back to hers. To pillage and ravage and claim him as her own. His hands caressed her shoulders, and she shivered at his touch on her bare skin. His hands moved greedily over her back, and he fumbled without discernable success with the fastenings on her bodice.

She wanted to feel his naked flesh hot against her own and she had already waited far too long. Impatience and unrelenting need seized her, and she yanked his neckcloth free. She pushed his jacket over his shoulders and he shrugged it off. She tore at the buttons of his waistcoat until it opened and tugged his shirt free from his trousers. He pulled both over his head in one fell move and tossed them aside.

For a moment she could do nothing more than stare at his naked chest, firmly muscled with a triangle of dark hair trailing downward over his abdomen to disappear into his trousers. His shoulders were broader than she'd realized, his waist nicely narrow. All in all the man was certainly not a creation of his tailor. She drew a deep breath and rested her hands on his bared chest. His muscles tightened beneath her touch and he groaned.

"Damnation, Elizabeth."

Without warning, he whirled her around and deftly unfastened the tiny hooks at the back of her dress with a speed and efficiency unknown to even the most skillful maid. Precisely as he had promised, it dropped to her feet in a puddle of green silk. He tugged at the ties of her petticoats, and one by one they slid to the floor. His hands wrapped around her corseted waist and he pulled her against him and nibbled at the crook of her neck. She felt his arousal hard against her buttocks, separated from him only by the thin fabric of her drawers. His hands slipped upward to cup breasts supported by stays, and she marveled at the way they seemed to be a perfect fit in his hands. He moved to loosen the ties of her corset, and her patience snapped.

"Good Lord, Nicholas." She twisted to face him. "If we wait until we're rid of all of these blasted clothes it will be another ten years."

"Not while there's breath in my body," he muttered and pulled her back to him.

She met his lips once more and reveled in the taste of him. His hands caressed her derriere and she pushed her hips tighter against his. She could feel his desire and his heat, solid and straining against the material that still separated them. She shifted to slide her hand between his body and hers and fumbled with the buttons of his trousers. He groaned and pushed her hand aside. He unfastened his trousers and let them fall to the floor. His manhood sprung free against her, and without thinking, she ran her fingers over it. He slipped his hand between the legs of her drawers and found that part of her that was wet and wanting and aching with need. She jerked at his touch, then pushed against his fingers. His hand explored and fondled and stroked, and she moaned with the exquisite sensations his touch produced. Her hand tightened on his member, and it throbbed beneath her touch. And his moans matched hers.

Without warning, he shifted, grabbed the top of her leg, and lifted it to wrap around his, opening her up to him. She guided him between her legs and he slid over her in a teasing, enticing fashion that heightened her arousal. She sucked in a hard breath and flung her arms around him as she pressed herself tighter to him. He was hard and hot and she was wet and slick against him. He slid back and forth between her legs, and with every movement she rocked against him.

He wrapped one arm around her waist and supported her buttocks with the other, then skillfully lowered himself to sit on the sofa. She straddled his lap, her knees on either side of his hips. Her gaze locked with his. His eyes were dark with need and promise and something more than mere prurient desire and unbridled lust.

"Nicholas." She reached forward and brushed her lips against his. "You do realize I have not done this for a very long time?"

"Yes, I know," his lips murmured softly against hers. "And you do realize I have wanted you for a very long time?"

She brushed aside any tinge of hesitation. "As I have wanted you."

She straightened and poised above him, her gaze never leaving his, then slowly lowered herself onto him.

She was tight and he was larger than she'd thought: still, she slid down the long length of his shaft with an ease wrought by her own excitement and a yearning far too long ignored until at last her curls meshed with his. For a long moment she savored the feel of him inside her, a physical fullness she only vaguely recalled and a sense of completion she remembered only from her dreams.

He grasped her waist and guided her up and down, moving his hips in rhythm with hers. Her head dropped back and her eyes closed. She grabbed his shoulders, her fingers tightening on his flesh with every stroke, with the tension that swelled within her. The sofa beneath them creaked in protest. Or celebration.

They moved in measure with one another as though they had moved together always like this. As if their bodies were matched, made one for the other. In perfect rhythm, perfect harmony. As if their joining was inevitable. Fated. Meant to be.

Her fervor matched his with an aching sweetness that spread from her very soul and fired her blood and throbbed in her veins. She'd never known, had never suspected such passion. Pure and elemental and raw. Building within her, tighter and tighter, a spring coiling to a breaking point. Frightening in its intensity. Glorious in its power.

Nicholas groaned and heaved beneath her, thrusting upward in a powerful stroke. His body shuddered against hers and his heat spread through her. Her nails bit into his shoulders and her own body convulsed in an altogether unexpected and extraordinary manner that caught at her breath and stole her soul.

And she screamed his name.

She collapsed against him and clung to him and buried her face in his neck. He held her tight as if he could not bear yet to let her go.

It struck her in some oddly rational part of her mind that while she had always rather enjoyed relations with Charles and had always considered that part of marriage quite pleasant, it had been nothing like this. Perhaps it was the illicit, forbidden aspect of being with Nicholas that heightened the pleasure. Or the desire they'd both ignored for a decade that deepened the experience. Or perhaps it had more to do with the fact that she'd never straddled her husband's naked lap. Indeed, she could count on one hand the number of times she'd actually seen Charles completely unclothed, and they'd never made love anywhere but their bed.

"Elizabeth?" Nicholas stroked her back in an idle manner, but a note of concern sounded in his voice. "Are you all right?"

Was she? She wasn't entirely certain. She was somewhat shocked by her own wanton behavior as well as her body's response to his, and perhaps a little embarrassed by it all. And oddly enough, rather pleased with herself.

"Elizabeth?"

She raised her head and smiled into his eyes. "That was really . . . quite . . ."

"Indeed it was." He grinned. "Extraordinary."

"And it seems I am still . . . that is . . . well, you are . . ." Heat flushed up her face.

His grin widened. "Indeed I am."

She scrambled off of him and got to her feet, at once grateful that her drawers and her corset, loosened but still on her, provided a measure of modesty.

He stood slowly. She had never thought of him as overly tall, and the impression of great height might well have been exacerbated by his lack of clothing. Nonetheless, it was rather daunting to be staring up at a man who looked very much like an ancient classical statue come to life. A naked ancient classical statue.

He caught her hands and drew them to his lips. His gaze met hers, his dark eyes simmered. "You are everything I have ever imagined. Everything I have ever wanted."

Her breath caught. "As are you."

A smile lifted the corner of his mouth. "I think my bed would be a much better place to continue."

She tilted her head and studied him. "What makes you think I wish to continue?"

"Do you?" His voice was low and inviting, and a tremor of sheer anticipation shivered through her.

She stepped away, hid a smile, and gathered up her clothes.

"Does this mean you do not?"

"This means I would prefer to have my clothes near at hand, as eventually I shall have to dress." She glanced at him and raised a wicked brow. "Your bed is upstairs, I presume?"

"Allow me."

He scooped her into his arms, bundle of clothes and all, and started toward the stairs.

"My slippers?" She clutched her clothes with one hand and waved absently with the other.

"Of course," he said gallantly, tossed her over his shoulder, scooped up the shoes, repositioned her, and continued as if nothing whatsoever had occurred.

Elizabeth stared at him. "That was quite impressive."

He smiled in an overly smug manner and started up the stairs. "I know."

"Do you think the servants will see us?"

"I don't particularly care."

"They're probably well used to seeing you stark naked carrying a half-clothed woman up the stairs."

"Not at all, as they are all new to my employ. However," he grinned, "I expect they will grow used to it in time."

"Nicholas!"

The man was most arrogant and she shouldn't find him the least bit amusing, but he was. She laughed and snuggled closer against him. She realized she was, at the moment, rather unreasonably happy. Possibly even blissful. The thought occurred to her that she would prefer there being only one half-clothed woman he ever carried up the stairs stark naked, but she pushed it aside. This was supposed to last no longer than Christmas. That was her plan, after all.

They reached his bedchamber, and he shoved the door open with his foot, stepped into the room, and kicked the door closed. The gaslight on the table by the side of his bed was lit but turned low. He set her on her feet, then took her clothes and placed them on a chair. She glanced about the room curiously.

The furniture was very dark and rather heavy and obviously quite old. But aside from a few pieces of his Chinese pottery, the room was relatively bare. Indeed, it was positively stark when compared with the rest of the house.

"Didn't Lord Halstrom's collections extend to the bedrooms?"

"Lord Halstrom's collections filled every room in the house." He moved to stand at her back and put his arms around her. "I simply could not bear to sleep amidst the displays of Japanese armor and stuffed heads of exotic beasts, so I had everything save the furniture moved to another room." He chuckled. "You can scarcely open the door in that room now."

"I see," she murmured, her gaze sliding to the bed. It was far and away too big for one person but nicely spacious for two. Even if one was wanton and enthusiastic and the other skilled and well-practiced.

He ran his fingers along the front opening of her corset and murmured in her ear. "Damnation, Elizabeth, you wear a great many clothes."

She unhooked her corset and tossed it in the direction of the chair. "It didn't seem to bother you earlier."

"It didn't bother me earlier." He turned her around to face him. His gaze roamed over her in a decidedly hungry manner, as if she were the sweet and he long deprived of sugar.

Elizabeth quite liked it.

She caught his gaze, reached behind her to unbutton her drawers, and let them fall. She gathered the hem of her chemise, pulled it over her head, held it out by two fingers in a manner as provocative as she could muster, and dropped it to the floor. She had never before stood in front of a man naked, and she marveled that she wasn't especially nervous. Apparently, there was something to be said for wantonness.

He stared at her for a long moment, then opened his arms, and she stepped into his embrace.

His body was warm and strong against her own. Her breasts flattened against his chest, his growing arousal nudged against her stomach. His hands roamed lightly over her back and lower to her buttocks, and she shivered with his touch and her rising desire.

He gathered her closer, picked her up, and deposited her on the bed. His gaze swept over her, and he smiled, then climbed on the bed to lie by her side.

Nicholas cupped her breast in his hand and bent close to take the hardened nipple in his mouth, his manner undemanding and gentle and as intoxicating as brandy. The frantic nature of their earlier coupling had vanished, replaced by a lovely, languorous enjoyment. Pure pleasure. He shifted his attention to the other breast, caught her nipple carefully in his teeth, and flicked it with his tongue. She sighed and her eyes drifted closed. He trailed his hand lightly between her breasts and over her stomach in a slow, easy exploration. A promise of passion to come. His fingers traced lazy circles and dropped ever lower.

She arched her back slightly to urge his touch lower still. His fingers toyed with the curls between her thighs and her legs fell open. She held her breath and waited. Her existence narrowed, the world itself faded, and she knew only the touch of his hands, the heat of his body beside hers. His hand teased the top of her legs and the inner flesh of her thighs. And still she waited. For a moment or an eternity.

At last, he slipped his hand between her legs and stroked her. A shock of exquisite pleasure shot from his touch and rushed through every part of her. She gasped and arched upward and she wanted more. He slid his fingers faster over her and she struggled to breathe against the extraordinary tension once again building within her. And more was not enough.

"Nicholas." She moaned and clutched at him and pulled him toward her. "I want . . ."

"As do I," he murmured, his voice harsh with need. He shifted to position himself above her, then guided himself into her.

For a moment he didn't move, and she reveled in the simple joy of their joining, of being one with him. Then he withdrew, his manner measured and restrained, and she could feel every inch of him within her. He slid forward slowly. She wrapped her leg around his and he rocked to and fro, his tempo increasing with the beat of her heart. She met his thrusts with hers, boldly and eagerly and with a frenzied need that spiraled ever tighter in the very core of her being.

Until her body arched upward seemingly of its own accord and wave after wave of release and unimagined pleasure rushed through her. He thrust hard and deep and shook with his own release until he lay spent and exhausted. His heart pounded in his chest against her and matched and meshed with the beat of her own.

And she wondered at the feeling she could not ignore that being in Nicholas's bed, in his arms, even in his life was right and true.

And wondered as well if he was a craving she would ever be able to satisfy.

Chapter 12

The first rays of morning light streamed in the tall windows of Nicholas's bedchamber.

Elizabeth lay straddling one of his legs with hers, her chin resting on her hands on his chest, the beat of his heart thrumming beneath her fingertips. She was at once utterly exhausted and wonderfully satisfied and surprisingly content. All in all, she'd never felt quite so cherished. Or so loved, even if love had nothing whatsoever to do with this.

"I should be going home," she murmured.

"Yes, you probably should." He idly stroked her naked back.

"The children won't be up for hours, but even at this late hour—or rather this early hour—there will be servants about."

"We wouldn't want to ruin your reputation."

"I confess your purchase of this house may prove to be most convenient."

"Location," he said sagely.

"We should also discuss my conditions for our arrangement."

"There is nothing to discuss."

"Nonsense, just because I allowed you to seduce me—"

"You allowed *me*? To seduce *you?*"

"You must admit, the seducing was firmly in your hands. All that *'I shall start with your dress'* nonsense."

"You didn't think it was nonsense." He chuckled and kissed the tip of her nose. "Indeed, I daresay you did not allow me as much as encourage me."

"That's neither here nor there," she said in a prim manner that belied the fact that her naked body was still draped over his.

"I think it's very here." He kissed the curve of her shoulder. "And there." His mouth murmured against the base of her throat. "And perhaps here again."

It would be easy to allow him to continue. Easy to close her eyes and allow herself to slide back into the sensual state of sheer sensation he was so very good at producing. She pushed away the thought that he might not be a simple craving after all but a serious addiction.

"Nonetheless." She shifted away from him and propped herself up on her elbow. "As we have obviously begun our arrangement, I shall expect you to abide by my conditions."

He ran the tip of his finger around her nipple, and she caught her breath. He smiled at her wickedly. "No."

"No?" She batted his hand away. "What do you mean, no?"

"I mean, my dear Elizabeth, exactly what I said. I have no intentions of abiding by your conditions."

"You must." She smirked. "I have already begun to fulfill my end of the agreement. And you gave your word."

"I most certainly did not." His smirk matched her own. "I said only that I would give your proposal due consideration. Which I have now done."

"Yes, but given all that has passed between us . . ." She pulled her brows together and searched her mind. Indeed, he hadn't agreed to anything whatsoever. She sat up and glared at him. "You tricked me."

"I did nothing of the sort." He reached out and trailed his fingers between her breasts.

She slapped his hand away again, hard. "You led me to believe that this," she waved impatiently at the bed, "was the beginning of our arrangement."

He grinned. "Not that I recall."

"You led me to assume—"

"I may well have led you any number of places in the past few hours but not to the assumption that I accepted your conditions." He shook her head. "If indeed you assumed that, then you are mistaken."

She scrambled off the bed, yanked off the sheet in as vicious a manner as she could muster, and wrapped it around herself. "Of course I assumed that. You know full well I assumed that. I certainly never would have—"

He raised a disbelieving brow.

"Very well, perhaps I would have," she snapped. "But not with the same *enthusiasm!*"

He snorted. "I could not have curbed your enthusiasm with a bucket of cold water."

She gasped but could scarcely dispute his claim. "You are a vile, vile man, Nicholas Collingsworth."

"No, I'm not." He sat up, arranged the pillows, laced his fingers behind his head, sank back on the pillows, and studied her. "I used to be overly somber and serious, but now I am really rather charming. Everyone says so."

"Then everyone is wrong."

"Everyone can't be wrong." He grinned at her, looking not unlike an arrogant Greek god who has just satisfied himself with an entire village of swooning peasant girls. Certainly he had a body worthy of being depicted in marble, yet, at the moment, a strategically placed fig leaf would not be out of order. The man had absolutely no shame.

"In this case, they are." She gathered her sheet tighter with one hand and clapped the other over her eyes. "And do cover yourself."

"I don't see why. It's rather warm in here, and I am exceedingly comfortable precisely the way I am."

"Well, I am exceedingly *uncomfortable* with the way you are."

"You didn't seem exceedingly uncomfortable last night," he said mildly. "Or this morning. Or just a few moments ago, for that matter."

"Regardless, I am now." She grit her teeth. "I am not used

to having discussions of a serious nature with an unclothed man."

"What kinds of discussions are you used to having with unclothed men?"

"Nicholas!"

He chuckled, and she heard the rustling of covers.

"Are you decent?"

"That is an exceptionally difficult question to answer. I do consider myself a fairly moral person, although I will admit there may have been an occasional business deal in the past in which my scruples have not been entirely—"

"Damnation, Nicholas, I'm not asking if you are an upstanding member of society! I want to know if you've covered those portions of your anatomy that should be covered."

"I knew precisely what you were asking, however I did think I should take the opportunity, given our relationship, to advise you on some of the more sterling aspects of my character."

"Yes, yes, you're a blasted saint," she said impatiently.

"I do have my good points. You may uncover your eyes now if you wish."

She dropped her hand and glared.

He studied her calmly. "One of said good points is that I consider myself an honorable man. Furthermore I am a man who knows what he wants, and I do not abandon the pursuit of what I want until I have achieved it. Determination is another of my good points."

"I would not call it a good point but most annoying. However, I will concede that in certain circles determination is considered an asset. Very well, then." She narrowed her gaze. "What do you want?"

"You."

"Then you have already achieved success. You have had me. Several times, in fact."

He shook his head. "It's not enough."

"I have proposed that we continue—"

"I will not join you in your bed at half-past-two in the afternoon in conjunction with the examination of your accounts until Christmas and then vanish from your life." He shrugged. "I want more than that."

She stared at him. "But that is my offer, and it is all I am willing to offer."

"Then you shall have to reconsider."

She snorted. "I think not."

"I want you, Elizabeth," his gaze bored into hers. "Always and for the rest of my days. I want your heart, your love, and I want you as my wife."

Her breath caught and she said the first thing that came into her head. "No."

"What do you mean, no?"

"I mean no. Absolutely not. I told you I am not interested in marriage."

"I am not proposing marriage in general. I am proposing marriage to me."

"It scarcely matters. I have no desire to turn my life over to someone else, let alone you. I like managing my own affairs."

"You will marry me, Elizabeth."

"Have you heard a word I've said?"

"Every one."

"Yet you ignore what I want in the face of what you want. You may well be the most arrogant man I have ever met and the most conceited."

He flashed a grin. "Yet another of my good points."

"Yet another reason to shoot you in your sleep," she snapped.

He was outrageous and annoying, and at once she understood he quite enjoyed this battle of wills between them that had started with their first conversation. And was shocked to realize she rather liked it as well. Quite simply, Nicholas Collingsworth made her blood race and her heart pound, and fired her veins with passion. Within the confines of bed and without. A grand sort of passion, perhaps? The abrupt realization bore further consideration, but right now there were more pressing matters to attend to.

She stared at him for a long moment, then laughed. "You

are far too sure of yourself, Nicholas. And this time, you shall be disappointed."

"I told you I have never failed to achieve what I have wanted, and I shall not fail now. Mark my words, Elizabeth, you will marry me."

He smiled that smug, self-satisfied smile, and for once she didn't wish to smack it off his face. That would be entirely too easy and he'd probably like it. But she would find a way to remove it nonetheless.

"We shall see." It might well be that the only way to play this little game of his was to play it with his rules. An overwhelming sense of calm and assurance filled her. Very well. She smiled back, a slow, knowing smile, and for just a moment, the confidence in his eyes faltered.

"Now." She adopted a brisk manner, turned away from him, and plucked her undergarments from the floor. "Do help me get dressed. I cannot manage it by myself, and it would be most inappropriate to call one of your staff. And I certainly can't return home wearing only a sheet with my clothes bundled in my hands."

Behind her, she heard him get up from the bed with a rustling of fabric that hopefully indicated he was covering his delightful, but distracting, naked state.

"I am not a lady's maid," he said with a distinct note of indignation. "I haven't the vaguest idea what to do."

"You managed to take everything off." She pulled on her drawers and buttoned them, then tossed her chemise on over her head. "Simply reverse the process."

She turned toward him, grateful to see he had pulled on his trousers. She never noted before how terribly, well, tempting a man clothed in only trousers was. And while Nicholas might well look like a Grecian god completely nude, he was even more appealing partially clothed. The image of a pirate from a romantic novel popped into her head.

He plucked her corset from the floor and stared at it ruefully. "I don't think I can."

"Honestly, Nicholas." She snatched the corset from his hands, wrapped it around her midsection, then fastened the front. She held the garment firmly against her sides and glanced at him over her shoulder. "All you have to do is tighten the laces in the back."

He took the laces and pulled tentatively, muttering all the while. "I can't believe you would rather be my mistress than my wife."

"Tighter. I do need to get back into my dress, you know. Oh, and I have no intention of being your mistress."

"Then what will you be?" He yanked harder on the laces.

She gasped. "I don't know, but a mistress usually receives some sort of recompense or financial support or something of that nature. I want nothing from you."

"Save that I should vanish from your life after Christmas as if I was never here," he said under his breath.

Something rather sharp and painful stabbed at her that had nothing to do with the corset. Guilt, perhaps? Doubt? Regret? "You're pulling the laces entirely too tight."

"A minute ago I wasn't pulling them tight enough," he muttered.

"I can't believe you've never helped a woman into a corset before. Do they all go home with their undergarments in hand?"

"Yes," he snapped and blew a short breath. "If you refuse to be my wife and don't wish to be my mistress, how do you view your position in my life?"

"I don't know. Your," she bit back a grin, "your friend perhaps?"

"My very good friend." He tied the laces snugly.

"If you wish."

"My very good, *special* friend." Nicholas kissed her shoulder and she shivered. Would he always have that effect on her?

"Stop it." She shrugged him off and stepped away. She found her stockings and shoes and slipped them on, noting that she could not recall having removed them in the first place. "However," she scanned the room for her discarded gown, "if that's what you prefer, I shall be happy to be your very good special friend."

"Dear God, Elizabeth." He crossed his arms over his chest

and glared. "You make it sound like you're the invisible playmate of a small child."

"Rather appropriate then, as you act very much like a small child insisting on his own way. I am used to dealing with small children, you know, and I shall not permit it." She located her dress, arranged it on the floor, stepped into it, then pulled it up over her arms. "Fasten the back, if you please."

He fumbled with the fastenings. "This is impossible. There are hundreds of these hooks. I can unhook them but fastening them again is a different matter. My fingers are entirely too big for this."

"I thought your fingers were extremely dexterous," she murmured.

He paused, then continued in an irritated silence. "There," he said at last. "That shall have to do."

"Your efforts are most appreciated." She turned toward him and smiled pleasantly. "Now then, if you have no intention of abiding by my conditions, I take back my proposal. You may put it completely out of your head." She waved at him as if she could magically erase all memory. "Forget all about it."

He glared. "And I suppose I should forget the last few hours as well?"

"That would be best." She nodded firmly even while realizing she would never be able to put the last few hours from her mind if she should live to be a hundred years. "Although you may cherish them as a fond memory if you wish. I know I had a delightful time."

"A delightful time?" He sputtered. "That's it? A delightful time?"

She nodded. "Most delightful."

"As you wish, Elizabeth." He crossed his arms over his chest and studied her. "If your proposal is withdrawn, I withdraw mine as well."

"And which proposal is that?" she said lightly. "If you're referring to your offer of marriage, then I suppose I would be willing to reconsider my proposition."

"Oh no, my dear, my proposal of marriage stands."

"Then—"

"I am speaking of my original offer to simply oversee your accounts until Christmas and then turn them back into your capable hands."

She stared in disbelief, although she should have expected as much. "You wouldn't dare."

"I most certainly would." He shook his head in feigned regret. "Upon reconsideration, I have decided to fully undertake the responsibilities placed in my hands by your late husband. Starting today, my dear Lady Langley, I shall handle every aspect of your finances. Every expenditure, every penny, every shilling, every pound."

He was baiting her, waiting for her to fly into a rage. Well, she would not give him the satisfaction. She drew a deep breath and chose her words with care. "Am I to assume if I agree to marry you, my finances would be placed back into my hands?"

"You do jump to assumptions rather easily, but in this case you are essentially correct. As your husband, of course, I would expect to have some say, and legally your assets would be mine. However, you have proven yourself to be more than capable—"

"Brilliant," she said firmly.

He ignored her. "—in regards to finances."

"Then I would go on as I have? Managing the estate, my investments, and the boys' inheritance?"

"Not exactly." He clasped his hands behind his back and paced the room. He would have been most imposing had it not been for his naked chest and bare feet. "Until my return to London I had not seriously considered exactly what I wished for in marriage. I admit, the very idea of marriage had never more than fleetingly crossed my mind, but now I understand I do not wish for such a union to be a dictatorship but more a partnership."

She raised a brow. "Oh?"

"You are competent and capable and clever and amusing. And something of a challenge as well, which I find both stimulating and exciting. In short, you have everything I would wish for in a partner, and I wish to be partners with you, Elizabeth. In finances and in life."

"Equal partners?"

"Don't be absurd." He scoffed. "I am a man after all. In spite of the enlightened age we live in, even with a woman on the throne of England, no one in their right mind would propose being equal partners with a wife. I'm thinking more of a," he thought for a moment, "seventy percent to thirty percent partnership."

"And I would be the thirty percent partner," she said wryly.

He nodded. "It is an excellent offer."

"Perhaps in the business of steamships or other investments, but it does not strike me as being especially advantageous." She shook her head. "At the moment, I am one hundred percent in control of my finances and my life. My decisions are my own and not dependent on the approval of anyone else."

"That's not entirely true, as I will be in control of your finances."

"And I admit that will be both awkward and most annoying. However, the rest of my life is still entirely in my own hands."

"I shall not be unreasonable as to your expenditures."

"How magnanimous of you."

"However, I shall draw the line at frivolous expenses."

"I'm certain of that." She struggled to remain calm. "This is blackmail, Nicholas."

"Nasty word, blackmail, but yes, I suppose it is."

"You leave me no choice."

"I thought you would see it that way." He grinned. "I vow that I shall make you happy, Elizabeth. Every day for the rest of your life."

"No, Nicholas, you would drive me mad every day for the rest of my life and I would have to cope with that." She started toward the door. "Now, if you would escort me downstairs, I can certainly make my way home by myself."

"Elizabeth?" For the first time uncertainty sounded in his voice.

She ignored him, strode down the hall to the stairs, and did not lessen her pace until she reached the front door. Her cloak and gloves were conveniently, and discreetly, placed on a bench by the front door. Edwards was indeed efficient.

"Shall I make the arrangements then?" Nicholas said, as he helped her on with her cloak. "For the wedding?"

She scoffed. "Don't be ridiculous."

"Of course. You should probably do it. I have no idea how much trouble is entailed in the arranging of a wedding."

"No trouble at all really, as I have no intention of marrying you," she said coolly.

"But you just said I gave you no choice."

"Now who is making assumptions?"

He stared in utter disbelief. "You'd rather give up total and complete control of your finances than marry me? Do you dislike me so much?"

"I don't dislike you at all." She slid her arms around his neck and pressed herself close against him. "In fact, I find I am really somewhat fond of you. And I am more than willing to be your very special friend."

He glared down at her but wrapped his arms around her nonetheless. "Then why won't you marry me?"

"Women marry for security, social and financial. I already have that. As for marriage itself," she smiled, "I don't trust it as an institution and I don't trust you."

His brows drew together. "Why not?"

"Ah, Nicholas." She brushed her lips across his. "You very nearly broke my heart ten years ago and I shall not let that happen again." She pulled out of his arms and put on her gloves. "However, I really should thank you."

"For what?" he said suspiciously.

"As much as I value my independence, and while I have enjoyed managing my own financial affairs, it has not been easy." She favored him with her brightest smile. "I shall send over my accounting books and files this very morning and forward all bills and any other pertinent papers the moment they arrive."

"There's no need—"

"There's every need, especially as we will not be sharing a bed after all." She glanced down at his bare toes and slowly raised her gaze in a long perusal of his various attributes, precisely the way he had cast his gaze over her last night, until her eyes met his. Clearly he was most discomfited being on the receiving end of such a study. Good.

She heaved an exaggerated sigh. "It is something of a pity but it cannot be helped, I suppose, although I confess, I will never be able to face half-past-two again without a rather warm feeling of—"

"Elizabeth!" His eyes widened in shock.

"—affection, Nicholas." She widened her eyes innocently. "I was simply going to say affection. The type of affection one feels for a friend. A very special friend." She fluttered her lashes in a wicked manner.

"Elizabeth!"

"The more I think about it, the more I think it shall really be something of a relief not having to worry about accounts and tenants and crops and everything else. I might well enjoy being a lady of more leisurely pursuits again. Indeed, I might even revert to some of my more frivolous ways." She pulled open the door.

"What do you mean?" he said slowly.

"This does seem to be a continuing problem between us. Neither of us quite understanding what the other has said. I thought I was clear, but perhaps not." She stepped through the open door and glanced back at him. "Dear Nicholas, as it's more than likely impossible to beat you in this game you do seem to so enjoy playing, I shall join you."

"What?" His brow furrowed in confusion.

"And I shall have a great deal of fun in the process." She flashed him a brilliant smile and shut the door firmly in his face. And tried very hard not to laugh aloud.

Elizabeth sailed down the steps and walked briskly along the walk toward her own door. There was no one about at this hour, but even if there had been she didn't particularly care about her reputation at the moment.

She had quite turned the tables on Nicholas Collingsworth. Certainly he was in charge of her finances, but, in point of fact, there was nothing she could do to prevent that anyway. And perhaps he had given her the very weapon to use against him.

While her records were meticulous, and every transaction was documented on paper, she also kept a running calculation in her head of exactly what she had down to the very last penny. She had never doubted her own intelligence, but this was a gift she had not suspected until she'd started managing her own affairs, and it had thus far served her well. Right now she knew precisely what was available for the sole purpose of persuading Nicholas to abandon the idea of marriage, at least to her. Partnership. Hah!

Her door opened at her approach and she stepped inside. Although she had returned home late on occasion, she had never been out all night before. Still, her butler didn't so much as raise a brow at her untimely appearance. Hammond was exceptionally well trained. She murmured a greeting, handed him her cloak and gloves, and started up the stairs.

Nicholas, of all people, should well understand why she wasn't interested in marriage. He valued his independence, indeed he had always followed his own path. Why shouldn't she value hers as well? Simply because she was a woman? Nonsense. A woman ran the country. Why couldn't a woman run her own life?

Certainly, Elizabeth might be willing to give up the condition about not seeing him again after Christmas. Indeed following last night, she rather liked the idea of continuing their arrangement well into the future.

I want your heart, your love, and I want you as my wife.

Her step slowed. He wanted her love? Did he truly mean that, or was it just something to say that he thought might sway her position? Love was an entirely separate issue from marriage.

She had spent ten years firmly believing she hadn't loved Nicholas. Even now she refused to consider the possibility that she'd been wrong. If she'd been wrong about loving Nicholas, then perhaps she'd been wrong about loving Charles as well. And if she'd been wrong not to follow Nicholas in spite of his words, had her marriage been a mistake as well?

Had she married the wrong man? Married the man who probably should never have been more than a dear friend while she'd allowed the grand passion of her life to slip away?

No, of course not. She pushed the thought aside. It was an absurd idea. Why, it would mean much of her life had been based on a lie. A pleasant, comfortable lie, but a lie nonetheless. And that she could never accept.

This was precisely why she was willing to share Nicholas's bed for a time but not his life. Never his life. It would be best for all concerned and much, much easier if they simply had a passionate liaison, sated their respective desires, then went their separate ways. Prurient desire and unbridled lust and nothing more than that.

Elizabeth didn't love Nicholas then and she refused to love him now. Loving him would beg the question of whether she loved him again.

Or worse.

Loved him still.

Chapter 13

"Have you spoken to your sister of late?" Nick said, his gaze fixed firmly on the bills and receipts piled on the desk before him.

"What? No 'Good day to you, Jonathon'? No 'Felicitations of the season, your lordship'? No thank you for forgoing your own concerns and rushing over here in response to my urgent message?"

"Good day to you, Jonathon. Felicitations of the season, your lordship. Thank you for forgoing your own concerns and rushing over here in response to my urgent message." Nick glanced up. "Have you spoken to your sister?"

"My sister? The sister who lives one door down?" Jonathon grinned and lounged against the doorframe. "I suspect there is an interesting tale to tell about your acquisition of this house and the purpose behind the purchase."

"It's a good location and a good investment," Nick murmured.

"Yes, I thought that was it."

Nick ignored him. "Your sister is apparently avoiding me in hopes that I shall vanish from the face of the earth. However, if you have spoken—"

"I haven't seen Lizzie since your uncle's party, and that"—

Jonathon stopped in his tracks—"was four days ago." An odd sort of stunned expression appeared on his face.

In spite of his current foul mood, Nick grinned. He suspected that very same look had crossed his face upon stepping over the threshold to this room. "It's quite impressive, isn't it?"

"Impressive is not exactly the word I would use." Jonathon straightened and stared.

"I believe it was originally intended to be a library." Nick glanced around ruefully. "It has shelves at any rate and a fair amount of books."

"One almost feels sorry for the books. Being so outnumbered, that is." Jonathon stepped cautiously into the room, under an arch formed by the crossed spears of two larger-than-life Nubian statues.

Lord Halstrom's library was as packed as every other room in the house, perhaps more so. Indeed, the chamber seemed to have become a repository for all manner of bizarre items the old gentleman had not been able to squeeze into another room.

Jonathon made his way toward Nick, maneuvering around a large armillary mounted on a marble column and several ancient urns, to a nearly as ancient overstuffed armchair wedged in a clearing in front of Nick's desk. Jonathon settled gingerly in the chair and spotted a plate of fruit tarts perched on what appeared to serve as a table but looked suspiciously like the dried leg of an elephant. "May I?"

"Be my guest. Take them all if you'd like."

"I would, but that would be rude." Jonathon selected a tart. "I love tarts."

"It obviously runs in the family," Nick muttered.

Jonathon took a large bite, appreciation widening his eyes. "Nothing like a good tart to put a man right with the world, and these are superb. Your cook is to be commended."

"My cook had nothing to do with them. Your sister sent them."

"Lizzie?" Jonathon turned the tart suspiciously. "Are they poisoned?"

"We shall see, won't we?" Nick said wryly.

"Death by tarts?" Jonathon studied the tart, then shrugged

and took another bite. "It's not a bad way to go, I suppose. With sugar on your lips and the taste of cherry on your tongue. Rather thoughtful of Lizzie really, especially as she is ignoring you."

"It's a message." Nick narrowed his gaze at the tarts as if they truly were lethal. "It started with sugar plums. Next it was butterscotch. Yesterday, toffee, and now tarts."

"What precisely is she trying to say?" Jonathon popped the rest of the pastry in his mouth.

"She's trying to show me what I am missing."

"Well, you needn't miss anything," Jonathon said, taking another pastry. "There are plenty of tarts."

"Tarts are not the problem. These are the problem." Nick waved impatiently at the papers before him. "Bills run up by your sister in the past few days. Extravagant, silly purchases for the most part."

"Don't be absurd." Jonathon scoffed. "While she's not especially frugal, I have never known her to be the least bit extravagant or silly in her purchasing."

"She is now. Look at these." Nick rifled through the receipts. "There are charges here from jewelers, milliners, dressmakers, antiquities dealers, cabinet makers." He pawed through the papers. "It appears she's commissioned an entirely new wardrobe. And here." He picked up a paper and waved it. "She's ordered two new carriages as well. Two!"

"Perhaps she needed two new carriages?" Jonathon said helpfully.

Nick snorted. "One possibly, but not two."

"How very odd and completely unlike her. Even when Charles was alive she was never especially irresponsible in her spending. And since she's been managing her own affairs—" He paused and studied his friend. "She is still managing her own affairs, isn't she?"

"Not exactly."

"Then I am confused." Jonathon furrowed his brow. "It was my understanding that you had agreed to simply oversee her accounts."

"Yes, well, that didn't work out quite as I had expected."

Jonathon's gaze slid from Nick's to the tart in his hand to the papers on the desk. "I gather that is a message as well."

"Most definitely."

"Do you understand this one as well as you do the tarts?"

"I'm afraid so." Nick blew a long, frustrated breath. "Your sister is trying to convince me that she is not the woman I thought she was."

"And she's doing that by driving herself deeply into debt? How very clever of her," Jonathon murmured.

"It is clever. Even diabolical." Nick leaned back in his chair and stared at the papers before him. "As much as she has squandered thus far, it is no more than she can afford to spend, although it took me a bit of work with her figures to realize that. Indeed, her finances are so sound that she can continue on this way for months without serious consequences."

"That long?"

"Perhaps as long as a year," Nick said grimly.

"All in an effort to prove to you she is not the woman you thought she was?"

"Exactly." Nick blew a frustrated breath. "Not the kind of woman I wish to marry."

Jonathon narrowed his gaze. "You wish to marry her?"

"Yes."

"Why?"

"Why?" Nick drew his brows together. "I don't know, because I do." He shook his head. "She is intelligent and amusing. Every conversation with her is either a level exchange or a battle of wits, and all are most challenging. The blasted woman makes my blood flow. Did you hear her comments at dinner about Scrooge?"

Jonathon nodded.

"Elizabeth is the only person I have ever known that I feel a kindred spirit with. As if we were both not exactly alike, mind you, but rather perfectly matched. Two separate gears that mesh together to form a flawless union."

"Flawless?" Jonathon raised a brow.

"Flawless probably isn't the right word but," Nick thought for a moment, "*right* nonetheless."

"I see," Jonathon said slowly. "In many ways, however, she is exactly the same person she was ten years ago. She simply no longer hides her true nature."

Nick toyed absently with his pen. "Yes, I know."

"Of course, you knew her true nature then."

"Yes, I suppose I did."

"And, even today, you still love her."

"Of course, I still love her. I have never stopped loving her. I—" His gaze jerked to Jonathon's. "I've never said a word to you about loving your sister."

"I am exceptionally perceptive."

"Hardly." Nick scoffed. "Why did you say that?"

"I saw the look in your eye that first day when she walked in on us. Furthermore." Jonathon shrugged. "Ten years ago you turned Lizzie away in a manner that guaranteed she would marry Charles."

"How did you—"

Jonathon waved off the question. "How I know scarcely matters. Suffice it to say, I do." He met Nick's gaze directly. "I should have realized it long ago, but it takes a great deal of love to sacrifice your own desires for the good of someone else."

"Is that what I did? It seemed so at the time, but now I am no longer sure." Nick shook his head and leaned back in his chair. "I have tried, through the years, not to think of Elizabeth at all, and for the most part I have succeeded, but on those occasions when I could not push her from my mind I have wondered if I gave her up because it was best for her or because it was the easiest course for me. Maybe it wasn't love as much as it was the selfish action of a foolish young man." Nick smiled wryly. "It no longer sounds as noble as it did a moment ago, does it?"

"What it sounds like is that, with the passage of years, you have given your actions a motive they did not have at the time. Perhaps it eases any sense of regret to believe a mistake is the result of bad intentions rather than good. After all," Jonathon pointed his half-eaten tart at Nick, "if you gave up Lizzie for selfish reasons, why, you deserved to lose her."

Nick stared for a moment, then chuckled. "Convoluted logic, but it makes a certain amount of sense, I suppose."

"Thank you." Jonathon started to take another bite of his pastry, then apparently thought better of it and tossed the remainder of the tart back on the plate. "As it seems to be an afternoon of confession, let me make mine now. At the time, I too thought your actions were correct. I thought the best thing for my sister would be for her to marry Charles."

"And now?"

"Now I know how very much I don't know. Dreadful to admit and probably a sign of maturity, as I used to think I knew everything, but there you have it." Jonathon sighed. "Lizzie always appeared content with Charles, but then he always appeared content with her and we know that isn't entirely accurate. I wonder now if perhaps she would have been happier with you."

"Perhaps we might well have suited better then than now," Nick murmured, ignoring the sharp sense of regret that had engulfed him from the moment she'd stormed back into his life. Still, regret had its benefits. It fueled his determination to win her back. "It does not lessen my resolve, mind you, but now I fear we will drive one another mad."

"Ah, but what a grand madness it will be."

"A grand madness." Nick grinned. "I rather like the way that sounds."

"Good." Jonathon nodded firmly. "Then what is your plan?"

"My plan?"

"Surely you have a plan."

"I have no plan."

"Oh, you should definitely have a plan."

"Yes, I suppose I should."

What was wrong with him anyway? Of course he should have a plan. He'd never gone into any kind of negotiation without a plan. And he'd certainly never let anyone get the upper hand with him the way Elizabeth had, over and over again. Just when he would think he had her exactly where he wanted her, she'd turn the tables on him.

"You could cut off her credit, close her accounts—that sort of thing."

"It's really not necessary. As I said, she could continue in this manner for a long time without posing a serious threat to the solidity of her finances." Nick shrugged. "Closing her accounts would serve no real purpose save to annoy her."

Jonathon grinned wickedly. "And attract her attention. She could scarcely ignore you then."

Nick raised a brow. "You're very good at this."

Jonathon lifted a shoulder in a modest shrug. "She is my sister. I have been provoking her almost since the day she was born."

Nick laughed. "Very well then, I shall force her attention by cutting off her funds. Perhaps I will give her an allowance, what with Christmas coming and all that."

"You can afford to be gracious."

"However, simply getting her attention does not seem like much of a plan." Nick drummed his fingers on the table.

"The problem with Lizzie is that she spent so many years being less than who she really was, she now thoroughly enjoys being exactly who she is."

"Hence her keen desire to maintain her independence."

"Exactly." Jonathon thought for a moment. "It seems to me your best course is to show her the price for that independence. Show her how very much she is missing."

"I have made a few attempts in that direction," Nick murmured.

"I'm not sure I want to know precisely what you mean by that. I am her brother, after all."

"Yes, of course. So." Nick pulled his brows together. "What is she missing?"

"Excellent question. I'm not sure I have an excellent, or even an acceptable, answer." Jonathon fell silent for a long moment, then shook his head. "We shall have to consider that point further. However, in the meantime, you should court the boys, I think. She is exceptionally fond of them."

Nick snorted. "I don't know anything about children."

"You used to be a child."

"It's been a long time."

"Not that long." Jonathon shook his head. "Good Lord, Nicholas, have you really noticed nothing about this house beyond the fact that it is next door to my sister's?"

"Certainly. It's a respectable size." Nick glanced around the room. "It's an excellent investment and location."

Jonathon groaned.

"And it's exceptionally full."

"Look again."

Nick cast his gaze around the room and shrugged. "It's still exceptionally full. There's scarcely room to move."

"Although there are any number of places to hide."

Nick drew his brows together in confusion. "Probably."

"I can't believe you could have made all that money and still be this obtuse." Jonathon rolled his gaze toward the ceiling. "Look at this room again. This time through the eyes of a child. A boy child if you will."

Nick heaved a long-suffering sigh. "Very well."

He scanned the room slowly, trying to put himself in the place of Elizabeth's sons. Certainly, if one were only eight or six years of age the mounted heads of exotic beasts hanging on the walls would be intriguing if not downright frightening, the medieval suit of armor in the corner, one of many lingering throughout the house, might well be fascinating, the swords hanging on the walls, the miniature cannon, the models of ships in full sail . . .

"Good God." Nick's mouth dropped open. How could he have failed to notice? "The place is the proverbial boyhood dream come true."

Jonathon nodded sagely. "Exactly."

"All I really have to do is invite them over and set them free." Nick considered the possibilities. "Of course Elizabeth might not be overly pleased by the prospect of her children spending time with me."

"Yet, as you are in charge of the management of their inheritance, it only makes sense that you should wish to get to know them," Jonathon said mildly. "Besides, Lizzie's efforts to show how frivolous she is probably demand she spend a great deal of time away from the house. It has been my observation that women cannot shop to their full potential when confined within the walls of their own homes."

"You are suggesting I court these children without their

mother's knowledge? Earn their affections before she can protest?"

"Exactly."

"It seems rather underhanded to me."

"Oh, it most certainly is."

Nick grinned. "I like it though."

"I thought you would." Jonathon smiled smugly. "After the children, you need to get the support of the rest of the family. Indeed, you may already have it, as they've always thought highly of you."

"Still, the biggest obstacle to winning Elizabeth's hand remains Elizabeth herself."

"I can help with the children and the family, but I'm not sure I can help you with that." Jonathon blew a long breath. "However, I am confident my sister once cared for you, and I would wager a great deal she still does."

"Why do you say that?" Nick said slowly.

"The vehemence with which she denies that she felt anything whatsoever for you coupled with the way she defends what she had with Charles. I think she's very much afraid of admitting that she still cares for you, as well as admitting that her marriage was not as perfect as she'd always thought it was. Both admissions might lead one to the conclusion that she married the wrong man."

Nick shook his head. "I gave her no choice."

"We are talking about my sister." Jonathon raised a brow. "Even back then, high-spirited and frivolous did not equate with submissive and stupid. Elizabeth Effington Langley has always to my knowledge had a choice about everything."

Nick could still remember the look in her eyes. "Not this time."

"Nonsense." Jonathon snorted. "She could have insisted you take her with you instead of calmly accepting everything you said and pretending she didn't care. Indeed, she could have followed you. But she wasn't sure enough of her feelings so she chose the safe, and one might have argued at the time, wisest course for her life."

Nick narrowed his gaze. "You know a great deal about

what passed between Elizabeth and myself. I find it difficult to believe that she would have confided in you. Not about this."

"It's not important how I know what I know, only that I do know." Jonathon waved away Nick's comment. "As I was saying, it was Lizzie's choice as much as it was yours."

"Still, she was young and I broke her heart."

"She'll never admit to that. And therein lies your problem."

Nick scoffed. "Just one?"

"Perhaps she needs to accept the feelings of the past, and more, her own mistakes—"

"And mine."

Jonathon nodded. "Absolutely yours. Regardless of your intentions, you were a fool."

"Thank you for putting it so succinctly," Nick said wryly.

"My pleasure." Jonathon leaned forward. "You never stopped loving her, and I suspect there is every possibility she never stopped loving you as well. However, that admission changes everything in her life." He studied his friend. "Have you told her?"

"Told her what?"

"That you love her?"

"Not that I recall."

"What did you tell her when you said you wanted to marry her?"

"I said she would make a good," Nick winced, "partner."

"Partner?" Jonathon's brow rose.

"It seemed the thing to say at the moment."

"You would have been better off with the gear analogy. Halves of a whole and all that."

"No doubt, but I am new to this business of proposing marriage." Nick blew a frustrated breath. "I have never given it a great deal of thought, but I have always assumed the why of an offer of marriage was not as important as the offer itself."

"You know nothing about women, do you?" Jonathon cast him a pitying glance.

"On the contrary, I know a great deal about women," Nick said staunchly, then grimaced. "I simply know nothing about offers of marriage. And I don't know why I'm listening to you.

You've never been in this position." Nick narrowed his gaze. "And why haven't you? We are of a similar age. Why aren't you married?"

"Alas," Jonathon heaved an overly dramatic sigh. "I have yet to find the woman of my dreams." He grinned. "Or she has yet to find me."

Nick raised a brow.

"I come from a family of headstrong, clever women. Indeed the Effingtons are known for it. I long thought I wanted a wife who was completely different. A wife who would be biddable and complacent and would make my wants and desires and needs paramount in her life."

"That sounds remarkably—"

"Dull? It is." Jonathon nodded. "To my surprise, I found the appeal of such women was greater in theory than in reality. I cannot abide the thought of spending the rest of my life with a woman who has nothing more in her head than how to be a perfect wife." Jonathon shrugged. "It appears I too want a woman who is something of a challenge."

"Life will certainly never be dull with Elizabeth," Nick murmured.

"The question remains as to how you get to that life. Thus far, the plan consists of"—Jonathon ticked the points off on his fingers—"making it impossible for her to ignore you by closing her accounts."

"Becoming friends with her sons."

"As well as the rest of the family. Telling her how you feel about her."

Nick nodded. "How I've always felt."

"Admitting you made an enormous mistake ten years ago—"

"I have admitted my mistake already."

"But did you admit the sheer enormity of it? That this was the biggest mistake you have ever made in your entire life?"

"Perhaps not," Nick murmured.

"Grovel, Nicholas, grovel with enthusiasm and sincerity," Jonathon said firmly. "And finally, you must show her the price she pays for independence."

Nick raised a brow. "Is that all?"

"Probably not, but it is a plan of sorts." Jonathon grinned. "Neither organized nor succinct, but a plan nonetheless." His eyes widened with realization. "I've got it."

"What?"

"What Lizzie loses by being independent."

"Go on."

"Love," Jonathon said with a smug smile. "A grand passion."

"I thought it was a grand madness?"

Jonathon scoffed. "There's little difference between love and madness. Show her you love her, Nicholas, and more, show her she loves you."

"That actually makes a certain amount of sense." Nick stared at his friend. "You're really rather wise when it comes to women."

"No." Jonathon laughed. "Actually, I'm a complete idiot when it comes to women. I have no idea what I'm talking about." He sobered. "But I do know my sister. And I suspect until she accepts her feelings past and present for both you and Charles, and until she accepts that she too made a mistake ten years ago, there can be no future between you."

"That's an all too sobering thought," Nick said quietly. "Elizabeth is a remarkably stubborn woman."

"Still, I'd put your determination up against her stubbornness any day of the week."

Nick blew a long sigh. "Thank you. That's something, at any rate."

"Don't thank me." Jonathon grinned. "I could be wrong."

Chapter 14

Elizabeth swept into the foyer of Nicholas's house the moment Edwards opened the door. Miss Otis trailed a mere step or two behind.

"Where is he?" Elizabeth snapped, noting and disregarding Edwards's odd apparel.

"He, my lady?" Edwards's tone was calm and cool and rational.

"Sir Nicholas. Where—" Elizabeth started and stared at the butler.

Miss Otis's eyes widened, and her mouth opened to form a perfect O.

Edwards stared back blandly, as if there were nothing out of the ordinary whatsoever. As if he hadn't forsaken the usual reserved attire required of a butler for clothing of a more bizarre nature.

He wore no coat but instead sported a gold brocade waistcoat that reached to his knee in a style that had not been seen for more than a century. The sleeves of his white shirt were overly full, with a touch of lace at the wrists. He wore tall, loose-fitting boots, deeply cuffed, and if Elizabeth hadn't known better, she could have sworn that was a discarded eye patch hanging loosely about the butler's neck. At his waist—

"What is that?" Elizabeth pointed a shaky finger. "Surely that's not a sword?"

"Indeed it is, my lady," Edwards said without so much as a blink to indicate that wearing a sword was the least bit unusual for a servant in modern-day London.

"He looks like a blooming pirate, my lady," Miss Otis said, awe or perhaps shock coloring her voice.

"An aging pirate," Elizabeth said sharply.

Edwards's brow twitched.

Elizabeth narrowed her gaze. "What precisely is going on, Edwards, and where are my children?"

"His name, at the moment, is *Mr.* Edwards. First mate to the Pirate King." Nicholas's voice sounded from the shadows at the top of the stairs. "And I . . ."

Elizabeth looked up, her mouth dropped open.

Nicholas slid halfway down the curved banister on one hip, then leapt over the side of the railing and dropped a good four feet to land with a flourish lightly in front of her. "Am the Pirate King." He whipped a wide-brimmed, feather-plumed hat from his head and swept an exaggerated bow. "And I am at your service."

"Your Majesty," Miss Otis breathed and dropped a curtsy.

"He's not a Pirate King," Elizabeth snapped.

"He looks like a Pirate King," Miss Otis murmured.

"Thank you," Edwards said.

"Well, he's not." Elizabeth rolled her gaze toward the ceiling. "He's a madman."

"But you must admit, I do look like a Pirate King." Nicholas smirked. "And a handsome devil at that."

He did indeed look most impressive in a fanciful sort of way. His coat was as ancient as Edwards's, cut long down to his knees, of a slightly faded blue, embellished with gold trim and rows of gold buttons. The shirt beneath was opened halfway to his waist. His trousers were tucked into boots similar to Edwards's and he, too, had a sword at his waist. He looked every bit like a pirate who had just stepped from a storybook, and admittedly, the style suited him. He was indeed a handsome devil, and Elizabeth had always been rather partial to the idea of handsome, devilish pirates. She steeled herself against the most annoying impulse to throw herself into his arms and ignored the realization of how much she had missed him.

"I will concede the devil part of that statement." She waved the note she had clutched in her hand. "Now explain this."

He plucked it from her hand and scanned the brief lines. "It appears to be an invitation."

"You know full well it's an invitation. It's from you." She snatched it out of his hands and glanced at it. "Dated three days ago and addressed to Viscount Langley and the Honorable Adam Langley. For the purpose of tea and exploration. *'Tea and exploration'?"*

Nicholas shrugged. "Admittedly they preferred a rather sweet fruit drink my cook concocted to the tea."

Elizabeth narrowed her gaze. "And the exploration?"

"Look around you, Elizabeth." Nicholas gestured in a grand manner, ridiculous hat still in hand. "Have you ever seen a house more suited to exploration by young boys?"

Elizabeth glared. "Miss Otis informs me the boys have spent the last three afternoons here while I have been out."

"I am truly sorry, my lady," Miss Otis said quickly. "Sir Nicholas came to the house in the company of your brother. His lordship—your brother—swore their visits were appropriate as Sir Nicholas is their financial guardian and—"

"Yes, yes, I know, Miss Otis, you have explained it to me once already. I shall deal with my brother later." Elizabeth waved away her comment and turned to Nicholas. "As for you, you have a great deal of explaining to do about another matter that has come to my attention, but first I demand you hand over my children. At once."

"Children?" Nicholas drew his brows together. "Have you seen any children, Mr. Edwards?"

"No, Your Majesty," Edwards said in a level voice. "Only the Queen's men."

Nicholas gasped in mock horror. "The Queen's men!" He glanced from side to side quickly, as if the aforementioned Queen's men would burst into the foyer at any minute. "Aye, they are hot on our heels."

"Nicholas!" The man was definitely insane and, if she hadn't been so angry, possibly a touch amusing.

"What say you, Mr. Edwards?" Nicholas spun his hat through the air to Edwards, who caught it without effort. "Do we make a run for it? Or," his gaze slid from Elizabeth to Miss Otis and back, "do we take hostages?"

"Hostages I should think, sir," Edwards said coolly.

"My thoughts exactly. I'll take this one, you take the other." Nicholas grabbed Elizabeth's hand, spun her into his arms, and locked her tight against his side. "Aye, this one's a beauty."

"If you take so much as one step toward me, Mr. Edwards, I shall be forced to retaliate." Miss Otis raised her chin and glared at the pirate butler, who had not moved an inch. "I have brothers and I am well used to dealing with them. It will be difficult to use that sword of yours if you're doubled over clutching your—"

"Miss Otis, that's quite enough. I'm certain Edwards has no intention of taking you hostage or anything else." She glared at Nicholas. "Tell her."

" 'Tis true, lass." Nicholas directed his words at Miss Otis, but his gaze was fixed firmly on Elizabeth. "I fear ye will not fetch the price of her ladyship."

Miss Otis sputtered. "Well, I daresay."

"Aye." Nicholas tightened his grip and stared into Elizabeth's eyes. "This one will do. She's a comely wench, she is."

"I am not!" Elizabeth snapped, struggling to keep the reason for her presence in the first place foremost in her mind. And struggling as well to disregard how very exciting it was to be in his arms again and to ignore the impulse to banish Edwards and Miss Otis from the house and play, just for a moment or two, Pirate King and comely wench. "A wench, that is. Now unhand me."

"Ah, my lady, you are now the hostage of the Pirate King." He flashed her a wicked grin. "Enjoy it."

"I most certainly will not enjoy it! Release me at once. Your blasted sword is poking into me."

Before she knew it he had bent her backwards in his arms

and she was forced to cling to him or fall. She stared up at him and he leaned closer. "It's not my sword."

She sucked in a shocked breath. "Nicholas! Release me this very moment or I shall—"

"You shall what?" His voice was low and meant for her ears alone.

She lowered her voice to match his. "I shall grab that sword and twist it out of its scabbard until tears fill your eyes and you scream for mercy."

He winced. "Yow. That doesn't sound at all . . ." He paused, then shrugged. "Of course, it could be fun."

"Nicholas!"

"Don't worry, Mother, we'll save you," Christopher's voice sounded from above.

"We're coming, Mummy," Adam called.

Nicholas pulled her upright but kept a firm arm around her. She stared at the top of the stairs. Before she could utter a word of protest, two small, red-clad bodies slid into sight, riding the banister backwards at an alarming speed.

Her heart lodged in her throat. "Get off that banister this very moment!"

She started toward the stairs, but Nicholas jerked her back and spoke low into her ear. "I assure you, you've nothing to worry about. They're quite expert at it. Besides, they're not going nearly as fast as it looks."

"But they're children!"

"At the moment they are the Queen's men and they have come to rescue you. Do not ruin it for them. Now, prepare to be rescued," he tightened his grip, "and smile."

It was an exceedingly long banister and appeared exceptionally high even if, in a rational part of her mind, she knew it was neither. Besides, the boys weren't traveling nearly as fast as she had originally thought. Christopher came first, sliding with a surprising amount of grace, to thump against the newel post at the bottom of the stairs. Only then did she notice the pillow tied to the post. Apparently the banister had become a well-used route. Christopher leapt off the railing a split second before his brother careened down the banister after him, whooping all the way. Adam smacked against the newel post and, despite the padding, Elizabeth winced at the sound.

She breathed a sigh of relief, forced a brilliant smile to her face, and spoke low to Nicholas out of the corner of her mouth. "When this is over, you shall need someone to slide to your rescue."

Nicholas choked back a laugh.

Adam scrambled off the banister and adjusted his uniform. He wore a very old, red officer's coat, a good hundred years or so in age and style, that reached nearly to his ankles. The sleeves had been rolled up, and a wide, gold silk sash was tied around his waist in an effort to adapt the huge coat to the six-year-old. Christopher's apparel matched his younger brother's, and while he was not as overwhelmed by his coat as was Adam, both boys looked very much like caricatures of British officers from the last century. They were at once absurd and very, very dear. Elizabeth wasn't sure if she wanted to laugh or cry.

"In the name of Her Majesty, I command you to release her ladyship immediately," Christopher demanded with all the authority of the crown behind him.

"Unhand her at once you black-hearted devil," Adam said stoutly, then flashed a quick, wide-eyed look at his mother as he realized *black-hearted devil* might not be acceptable language. Elizabeth raised a brow but held her tongue, and her youngest son grinned with relief.

"Never!" Nicholas shifted her to his side and drew his sword. Immediately, the boys pulled out swords of their own and brandished them wildly in the air.

Elizabeth gasped but kept her voice low. "Swords? You gave them swords? How could you give them swords?"

"My dear Elizabeth, I would never give them real swords." Nicholas cast her a disgusted look. "Their swords are little more than rolled paper twisted and painted."

"Still—"

"Edwards did an excellent job, although they wouldn't fool anyone within two feet and are relatively harmless."

"They could poke their eyes out," she murmured.

"Release her, I say." Christopher's eyes narrowed. "Or I shall be forced to take action."

"And I shall be forced to help him." Adam waved his sword in the threatening manner only a small boy could make endearing. Elizabeth bit back a grin.

"Never," Nicholas shouted once again. "She's mine." He pulled her closer and spoke low into her ear. "If I were a real pirate I would kiss you long and hard right now, but as I am certain such an action would shock the Queen's men I shall forgo that." He released her, shoved her behind his back, and addressed the boys. "I warn you, I am an expert with the blade."

"Perhaps." Christopher brandished his sword. "But none are as well trained as—"

"The Queen's men!" Adam finished.

With a yell, Christopher and Adam launched themselves at Nicholas. The ensuing sword fight had all the drama of a badly but enthusiastically acted play, the mild thud of rolled paper hitting rolled paper a safe substitute for the ring of steel blade against steel blade. In spite of being outmanned, Nicholas held his own while still allowing the children to have the upper hand, such as it were.

In spite of the anger that had brought her here, the sight of the boys and this man, arguably simply a bigger boy, clashing paper swords and shouting and having a great deal of fun warmed her heart. She couldn't remember Charles playing with his sons like this. Of course, Christopher had been only five when his father had died. Still, she couldn't imagine Charles ever donning an absurd costume and pretending to be a Pirate King. They were his children, but he never would have considered staging a sword fight in the front foyer for their pleasure. It's not that he'd been a bad father; it simply wasn't done. He, like most men of his position, viewed children, sons most particularly, as something one was required to produce in life.

The fact that Nicholas was willing to go to such effort and, indeed, actually seemed to enjoy playing with the boys spoke volumes about the kind of man he was.

While the spirits of the combatants were willing, the

swords were of substantially weaker character. Within minutes, Christopher's was bent, Adam's was dangling limply from its handle, and Nicholas's was unraveling. Obviously, Edwards's swords were not crafted for serious battle.

Nicholas collapsed backward on the floor and at once was surrounded by the boys, aiming what remained of their weapons in a manner that would have been most menacing if indeed their weapons had retained more than a shred of their former glory.

"Do you surrender?" Christopher demanded.

"Surrender at once, you son of a sea dog." Adam glanced at his mother and grinned.

"Son of a sea dog," Miss Otis murmured, a hint of a sigh in her voice, no doubt in anticipation of dealing with the triumphant Queen's men for the rest of the day.

"Aye, aye, I surrender." Nicholas heaved an overly dramatic sigh. "But you have not seen the last of me, mateys."

"But he has seen enough of you for one day," Elizabeth said firmly to her children. "I suspect Sir Nicholas—"

"His Majesty, if you please." Nicholas got to his feet and planted his hands on his hips. "The Pirate King."

The boys grinned.

He did look exceedingly like a small boy's idea of a Pirate King—or perhaps their mother's fantasy. Elizabeth pushed the thought aside. Still, he was remarkably attractive in his absurd costume.

"His Majesty no doubt has a great deal of," she sighed in surrender, "*pirate* business to attend to. Miss Otis will see you home. I have a few matters still to discuss with Sir Nicholas."

"But Mummy." Adam's brows drew together. "We haven't found the treasure yet."

"He did steal it from the Queen, Mother." Christopher cast a suspicious look around the foyer. "It's here somewhere, and it's our sworn, sacred duty to get it back for her. It would make an excellent gift for Christmas."

"Although she might rather have a train than treasure." Adam looked pointedly at Nicholas. "She probably already has a great deal of treasure."

"Another day, lads. The treasure will be here waiting for your next visit. Now, do as your mother says." Nicholas's voice was firm but not unpleasant. The perfect tone for dealing with young boys. Elizabeth wondered how on earth this man of business had learned to deal with children.

"Go along with Miss Otis," Elizabeth said. "I'm certain she has any number of things to tell you about real pirates and how they were despicable and bloodthirsty and not to be emulated."

"Indeed." Miss Otis nodded. "They were a vile lot, they were. Pillaging and plundering and slitting throats without so much as a by-your-leave."

"Really?" Adam's eyes widened. "But Uncle Jonathon said there were Effingtons who were pirates."

"Privateers," Christopher said in that superior way older brothers have when dealing with younger siblings. "They were good pirates. For the crown and all that."

"Next time we shall be privateers," Nicholas said solemnly.

"With new swords?" Adam held his up sorrowfully. "Mine broke."

Nicholas glanced at Edwards.

"I shall see what can be done, sir," Edwards said in his monotone voice. He was at once totally correct and the most unusual servant she'd ever met. She couldn't imagine Hammond ever making swords for her sons.

"Excellent, Mr. Edwards." Adam beamed.

"Thank you for an enjoyable afternoon, Sir Nicholas," Christopher said in his most formal manner.

"The pleasure was mine, your lordship." Nicholas's tone matched the boy's.

"Mine too," Adam said quickly. He leaned toward his mother and lowered his voice in a confidential manner. "He's great fun, Mummy. Yesterday we got to dress like Indians with paint on our faces and feathers in our hair. It was grand."

"I'm sure it was." Elizabeth smiled wryly. "And did he teach you to slide down the banisters too?"

"Don't be silly, Mother." Christopher snorted. "That's not something one can learn in just an afternoon. Uncle Jonathon says it's a skill, like riding a horse. He taught us how last summer when we were at Grandfather's house in the country."

A vision of the great stairway at Effington Hall popped into her head and her stomach twisted. "I really must have a long chat with my brother."

"Come along, children." Miss Otis herded the Queen's men toward the door already opened by Edwards.

Adam's hushed voice trailed behind him. "It's probably a very good thing that we didn't tell her how Uncle Jonathon showed us the proper way to—"

Edwards closed the door firmly behind them.

"A very long chat." She shook her head, then turned her attention to Nicholas. "Look at what you've done to Miss Otis. You've ruined a perfectly good governess."

"Nonsense."

"She was terrified." Elizabeth ignored the inconvenient fact that Miss Otis might have been a tiny bit unhinged at the beginning of their encounter with the pirates but had certainly been nowhere near terrified. "She might well tender her resignation after this. She was hired to care for children, not fend off pirates."

"Often one and the same, I should think. But you're being absurd and you know it. I believe Miss Otis quite enjoyed it all, and beyond that, I didn't touch her, nor did any of my men go near the," he smirked in a wicked manner, "lusty wench."

"Stop it! Stop it right this very minute!" She resisted the urge to stomp her foot.

"Stop what?" His eyes widened innocently.

"Speaking like a pirate."

"I'm not speaking like a pirate." He strolled into the parlor, leaving her no choice but to follow. He shed his coat and draped it over the up-stretched hand of a marble garden nymph. "I'm speaking like a Pirate King."

"An annoying Pirate King," she snapped.

"But a Pirate King nonetheless." Nicholas sauntered to the ever-present decanter of liquor and poured a glass. "I would offer you a brandy, but I would hate to do anything to ease your annoyance with me."

"My justifiable annoyance."

"Probably." He took a sip of his brandy. "I like your children."

The comment caught her unawares. "You sound surprised."

He chuckled. "I am. Oh, I expected them to be well mannered and well behaved, which they are, by the way."

"Thank you," she murmured.

"But I never suspected I would actually like them. Enjoy their presence, their company. I've had little experience with children. This combination of children and Christmastime is extraordinarily potent. I find myself almost as excited as they are as the day approaches. And Adam was right, you know."

"Oh?"

Nicholas grinned. "We have had a grand time."

"Obviously." She smiled in spite of herself. "I do appreciate how kind you've been to them. Aside from my brother, who is unique in his own way, not many men would be so inclined."

"I am not like many men," he said loftily, then shrugged. "I know it is not fashionable to pay such attention to children or join them in play, but I recall my father playing various silly games with me in my childhood. I have no illusions about him, he had a great number of failings. But perhaps because he was not a practical man, and was, in truth, something of a perpetual boy himself, he treated me always as though I was an equal, someone of importance, of value to him. He and I had," he smiled, "grand times together. Those memories linger with me still."

"I see," Elizabeth said softly. Even a decade ago, Nicholas had not shared something this intimate with her. "Then I owe you my thanks for giving them a day they will not soon forget."

"They are good boys and very bright." He swirled the brandy in his glass and met her gaze directly. "They should have been mine."

Her heart caught and a dozen responses came to mind. About the choices he had made and the path he had chosen and the life he had lost. She pushed them aside and adopted a cool tone. "Well, they're not."

"They will be when you marry me. I quite like the idea of starting a marriage with two sons already in hand." He studied her thoughtfully. "Still, I should like a rather large family, though. Another son or two, I think, and several daughters as well. Six, or perhaps eight, children in all."

She stared in disbelief. "You're mad."

"How many does the queen have?"

"Eight, but as I am not a queen—"

"You will be once you marry the Pirate King."

"The Pirate King may find himself set adrift in the midst of an ocean before he has time to produce any offspring, let alone six or eight. As much as I do appreciate your attention to my sons—"

"I think it's important for your family to like the man who intends to join their ranks. I especially think it's important for your sons to like the man who plans to be their new father."

She ignored him. "The whereabouts of my children was but one of the reasons for my visit here today." She crossed her arms over her chest. "You have cut off my accounts at virtually every merchant I do business with. Do you care to explain why?"

"Not particularly." He shrugged. "However, just as a courtesy, mind you, I will say that I felt it was my duty as the legal administrator of your finances to save you from your own nature."

She raised a brow. "My frivolous nature?"

"Not at all. You and I both know the spree of indiscriminate spending you have engaged in in recent days is nothing more than a ploy to prove to me you are not the kind of woman I wish to marry. The woman I think you are, indeed, the woman I know you are now and have always been."

"Ten years ago you called me frivolous."

"I believe we've already established that I was something of a fool ten years ago."

"Still, one never tires of hearing it." She smiled brightly. "Now, about my accounts, I should like everything reestablished at once."

He shook his head. "I think not."

"Cutting off one's accounts at Christmastime is very much something Scrooge would do, you know."

"Probably."

"You have a great deal in common."

"Only in that he was an astute businessman." He swirled the brandy in his glass. "And we are both haunted by the ghosts of Christmas past."

She let the comment pass. She absolutely refused to allow him to distract her from her purpose, nor would she allow her anger to show. He enjoyed it far too much.

"As Christmas is nearly here, I have a great many unavoidable expenditures ahead."

"You should have thought of that."

"I am far and away too frivolous to think of such things." She sauntered over to him, plucked the brandy glass from his fingers, took a sip, and gazed into his eyes. "Nonetheless, my obligations remain."

A slight smile played across his lips. "Do they?"

"It has become something of a tradition among the women in my family to hold a tea as Christmas draws near. Tomorrow, I am to host the event. My mother, *the duchess,* will be there, as will my sister, all my aunts, and a fair number of cousins. All together I am expecting nearly thirty ladies to attend."

"It should be most enjoyable," he said mildly.

"It always is. However, my cook, while well able to handle the normal demands of my household . . ." She paused and gazed up at him. "Did you like the tarts?"

"They were excellent."

"The fruited cakes?"

"Quite tasty."

"The toffee?"

"Adequate."

She raised a brow.

"Only in the sense that I am more fond of baked goods than of candies." Laughter danced in his eyes. "I have always preferred tarts to toffee."

"As do we all," she murmured. "At any rate, she is not up to the task of producing the various treats a special occasion like this requires. Therefore I have chosen, as did my aunt Rebecca last year and my aunt Jocelyn the year before and my sister the year before that, to order a selection of delicacies for tomorrow's tea from Fortnum and Mason. Unfortunately, that's one of the many accounts of mine you have seen fit to close."

"You shall simply have to make do."

"Yes," she sighed, drained the last of his brandy, then put the glass back in his hands. "I suppose I shall, although I daresay the entire party will be ruined."

"You should have considered that as well." He narrowed his gaze. "What are you doing?"

"I'm not entirely certain." She trailed her fingers lightly along the open edge of his pirate shirt. "Flirting, perhaps?"

"I don't think this is merely flirting," he muttered.

"Probably not." She slid her hand slowly up the exposed area of his chest.

He sucked in a sharp breath.

"This is not at all what I intended," she murmured, reveling in the way the warmth of his flesh felt beneath her fingers. "I am furious with you, you know."

He swallowed hard. "Yes, well, I rather thought you would be."

She slipped her hand around his neck. "You should know as well that I'm fairly certain my mother, *the duchess,* won't be at all pleased by a family tradition being ruined. She likes this gathering of her sisters and female relations, and she will not look kindly upon your actions. It could well sour her view of you altogether."

He tossed his glass aside and wrapped his arms around her. "Yet I am equally certain your father," he bent and nuzzled the side of her neck, "*the duke,* as well as your brother," he kissed a particularly sensitive spot just below her ear, "*the marquess* will be pleased that I have not allowed you to squander your money in what can only be described as a frivolous manner."

Elizabeth leaned forward to brush her lips across his. "It appears we are at a stalemate."

"Indeed we are."

"I have missed you, Nicholas." She nibbled at his lower lip.

His arms tightened around her. "I have missed you as well."

"I have missed you rather a lot." Her fingers toyed with the hair at the nape of his neck.

"As have I."

"I am willing to reconsider, oh," she pressed her lips to his in a slow, easy kiss that belied the need swelling within her, "say, one of my conditions."

"Oh?" His lips trailed along the line of her jaw.

Her eyes drifted closed and she sighed with the pleasure of his touch. "You needn't vanish from my life after Christmas."

"How magnanimous of you." His lips whispered against her neck.

"Well?"

"I have no intention of vanishing from your life ever, as I intend to be your husband."

She groaned to herself, summoned all her willpower, and pushed out of his arms. "Why do you persist in this?"

"Why do you refuse to so much as consider it?"

"Because I prefer—"

"Yes, yes, you quite like your independence, running your own life, making your own decisions and so on and so forth. I've heard it before, and indeed, although you may think otherwise, I do appreciate your concerns. But I would hope that marriage, or marriage between the two of us, would not necessarily mean that you change your character. I am proposing that our marriage be a partnership of sorts, remember? I have no desire to lock you in a dungeon, keep you for my own pleasure." He paused. "Although that could be a great deal of fun."

"For one of us."

"Why do you refuse to understand?" His brows drew together in frustration. "Your independent nature, your self-reliance, your intelligence are exactly the attributes that I find so irresistible. I have no desire to change any of that."

"Then why change the very lovely arrangement we could have for as long as we both wish? Why muck it up with marriage?"

"I want to muck it up with marriage."

She raised a brow.

"That's not what I meant and you know it." He shook his head. "I've never given much consideration to marriage, but now I find I want it and all it entails. Family, children, and whatever else comes along. And I want it with you. Only you. I want you as my wife and my lover and, God help us both, my partner." He grabbed her hand and pulled her back into his arms. "Now and when we are both old and doddering."

She stared up at him. It would be so easy to give in and agree to marriage and anything else he wanted. At this very moment, it seemed that life and a future with Nicholas would be nothing short of perfect. But she had had perfect, and it had proved to be nothing more than an illusion.

She pulled out of his embrace and moved away. "Some things were not meant to be, Nicholas."

"And some things were." He stepped toward her. "Damn it all, Elizabeth, I was a fool a decade ago, need I pay for it for the rest of my days?"

"Pay for it?"

"I made a mistake ten years ago and now I want to rectify it."

"I am not a mistake to be rectified."

"I didn't mean it that way."

"How did you mean it?"

"I don't know!" He huffed. "I'm not entirely sure what I do or do not know when I am around you. I am not used to having good, solid offers refused. It's extremely disconcerting." He narrowed his gaze. "Most women would jump at the opportunity to marry me, you know. I am wealthy, knighted, and will inherit a respectable title." He stretched his arms in a wide, helpless gesture. "What in the name of all that's holy is wrong with me?"

"Not a thing," she murmured. *Especially not when dressed as a pirate.* She thrust the thought, and the accompanying rush of hot desire, out of her mind.

"Then we need to discuss this rationally."

"Can we?" Was there anything more ridiculous than discussing the subject of marriage with a knight dressed like a pirate? "It's not a business proposition, it's marriage, and it's fraught with emotion."

"Nonetheless, it can be considered in a rational manner."

She bit back a smile. "Benefits versus disadvantages? That sort of thing?"

"Exactly." He clasped his hands behind his back and paced an erratic course around the overstuffed room. "You told me you do not trust me and you do not trust the institution of marriage. I can certainly understand the first part." He glanced at her curiously. "Or have I recovered your trust yet?"

"No." Even as she said the word she knew it wasn't entirely true. How could one not trust a man willing to dress like a pirate and pad his newel post with a pillow for the benefit of one's children? After all, there were far easier ways for a wealthy man to entertain children than by playing with them himself.

"I can accept that for the moment. Very well, I shall have to earn your trust." He studied her curiously. "Now, why don't you trust marriage itself?"

She considered the question. How could she tell Nicholas, of all people, about the imperfections of her marriage? That she had apparently not been enough to make Charles happy. That they had not shared what her brother had called a grand passion. That her husband might well have found that with another woman.

Still, once, long ago, Nicholas had been the only person in her life outside of her family to understand she was more than she'd appeared. She'd trusted him with the truth of her own nature then. The first step toward trusting him today might well be trusting him with the past. Perhaps it was the warmth she'd already found in his arms or his unexpected kindness to her sons or the way he made her laugh in spite of herself, but at this very moment, she wasn't especially adverse to taking that first step.

"Charles had a mistress," she said simply.

Surprise flashed across his face. "I find that difficult to believe."

"No more so than I," she said wryly. "I frankly had no idea."

"Are you sure?"

She nodded. "Oh, there's no question."

"Did you tell Charles of your suspicions?" he said slowly.

"They were not mere suspicions, Nicholas." She drew a deep breath. The only other person she'd ever told of Charles's infidelity was Jules, and that had been in the immediate wake of Charles's death. Revealing this secret to Nicholas now was far more difficult. "Charles was rather sentimental, and he'd saved this woman's letters. Silly of him, really, and I've often wondered if he didn't want me to find them."

"And you did find them," Nicholas prompted.

"A few days before his death, actually."

"What did Charles say?"

"Nothing." She shrugged. "I never had the opportunity to confront him. I was a bit of a coward about it." She paused to gather her thoughts. "The problem with discovering your husband is unfaithful is the myriad of emotions such a discovery unleashes. I was furious, of course."

He nodded. "Understandably."

"And hurt. There was an overwhelming sense of betrayal."

"Yes, of course, there would be."

"Followed by a certain amount of guilt."

"Guilt?" His brow furrowed. "But you said you hadn't had a chance to tell him."

"Not his." She laughed wryly, rather pleased to note she could now see the irony, even the humor, in it. "Mine."

"Nonsense," he said firmly. "You had no reason to feel guilty. You did nothing wrong."

"Didn't I? I'm not entirely sure of that." She ran her finger idly along the edge of a large, round brass tray balanced on a carved horn base. "I had never questioned the, well, *perfection* of our life together. I had always thought we were both content with our lives. Obviously, when it came to Charles, at least, I was wrong."

"Charles was a fool," Nicholas said quietly.

"Was he? I don't really know." She shook her head. "I

don't doubt that he always loved me, but perhaps the kind of love we shared was not," she thought for a moment, "enough, I think. My brother talks about a grand passion."

"A grand madness," Nicholas murmured.

"One and the same, no doubt." She looked at him. "I do wonder if that grand passion, or madness, is what Charles found with this other woman. What he had with her was apparently quite intense and, well," she sighed, "lasting. At least according to her letters."

"Do you know who she was?"

"She signed her letters with nothing more than a term of endearment. I have no idea who she was. It's nothing more than morbid curiosity on my part, mind you, but I would rather like to know her name. It scarcely matters now, of course. Still, I do wonder if knowing who she was might be the one thing that would write 'the end' on the last page of the final chapter of the book of our marriage. It's an odd idea, I know, but she was such an important part of his life." It was surprisingly easy after all to talk to Nicholas about this. As easy as it had once been to talk to him about anything. She drew a deep breath. "The letters span nearly four years."

"Four years?" He stared in disbelief. "But that's—"

"More than half the length of my marriage." She shrugged. "That was perhaps more shocking than anything else."

He studied her for a moment. "You seem to have accepted it rather well."

"Now, I have. It has been three years, after all." Elizabeth uttered a short, disparaging laugh. "You needn't look at me like that. I'm not a saint."

"I never suspected sainthood," he said with a slight smile. "Hence my surprise that you are not still angry with him."

"Life continues, and one must continue with it." She heaved a resigned sigh. "I was too shocked to do anything at first, and Charles was dead a scant two days later. I never had the opportunity to confront him. I very much regret that, so much between us remains unsaid and unsettled, but it may have been for the best."

"Why?"

"This woman might well have been the grand love of his life, his grand passion. I'm not sure if, at the time, I could have understood that, let alone accepted it. I know I was loved by him as well, if not in the same way, and I probably couldn't have accepted that either. The passage of time has allowed a certain amount of perspective. I think now I might well have been his dearest friend rather than his greatest love. Pity we did not realize the love we shared, the comfortable sort of undemanding love we had known since childhood, was not, in the end, enough."

His gaze met hers. "For either of you?"

She raised her chin slightly and realized that what she was about to say was an admission she could not take back. "Perhaps."

"Perhaps it is not too late." He drew a deep breath. "For a grand passion."

Her heart thudded in her chest. "Or a grand madness."

"The best kind of madness." He stepped toward her. "I would be faithful to you, Elizabeth."

"Would you?"

"In this at least you can trust me." He paused. "In point of fact, I have been faithful to you. Always." The sincerity of his manner clashed with the absurdity of his apparel and his words.

"What?" She snorted in disbelief. "Oh, come now, Nicholas. Surely you cannot expect me to believe you have not been with another woman for ten years? You've admitted to other women in your life."

"But not in my heart," he said staunchly. "I have been faithful to you in my heart, in my soul."

She crossed her arms over her chest. "It's easy to be faithful in one's heart and soul when one's trousers are down around one's ankles."

"Nonetheless, I have never loved another woman the way I love you," he said staunchly.

She stared. "You love me?"

"I always have."

Her heart leapt and it was all she could do to keep from throwing herself into his arms. Caution shoved the impulse firmly aside.

"Are you certain you are not confusing love with lust? The desire for another ship or a fruit tart?"

"Absolutely not." Indignation sounded in his voice. "I love you now and I loved you then and I am fairly certain I never stopped loving you. It's different, of course, as we are both different now than we were then, but it's love nonetheless."

Love had not entered into their relationship thus far, and she'd spent so long telling herself she hadn't loved him that his admission and her own reaction bore further scrutiny before she acted in any way at all.

"Really?" She narrowed her gaze. "Yet you allowed me—no, you made certain I would marry Charles."

"I thought it was for the best. I thought, as did everyone else, I might add, you and Charles were meant to be together. I thought he would make you happy."

"I was happy. I lived a pleasant, uncomplicated, comfortable life in which all of the decisions regarding that life were made for me. A perfect life in which happiness and, indeed, perfection itself was an illusion."

"When you describe it that way," he said uneasily.

She moved closer and stared up into his dark eyes. "And what would I have had with you?"

Indecision flashed in his eyes, and he blew a long breath. "I don't know."

"And now?"

"Everything."

She shook her head. "I have become too independent and used to handling my life on my terms. You are too stubborn and too used to getting your own way. We would drive one another mad."

He smiled slowly. "Ah, but what a grand madness it will be."

Her smile matched his. "Reopen my accounts and I will consider marriage."

He shook his head. "I don't think that would be especially wise."

"Then we have nothing more to discuss today." She reached up and kissed him. "Rather a pity I think, I have truly missed you." He reached for her, but she danced away. "However, aside from your declaration of love, which I shall consider, by the way, I am intrigued by this whole question of trust. Can I indeed trust you?"

"Absolutely," he said staunchly.

"My mother and the rest of my family will be at my house tomorrow at half past four." She started toward the door. "As you have not seen fit to restore my accounts, I leave what they find entirely in your hands and *trust* that I will not be disappointed."

"What?" He stared in confusion.

"Consider it a test. Of trust and faith." She lifted a shoulder in a casual shrug. "Possibly even of love."

"And if I pass?"

"The question, my dear Pirate King, isn't so much what the prize is if you pass but what you lose if you fail."

"I do not intend to lose."

"Your confidence is impressive."

He shrugged. "As well it should be."

Something in his voice caught at her, and she paused to study him carefully. Even as she asked the question she was afraid of the answer. "Why?"

"It's simple, my dear Elizabeth. It took a mere three years for you to forgive Charles for his transgressions. Even as enormous as they were it's apparent you are no longer angry with him."

"Yes?" she said cautiously, knowing almost before he said the words the truth of what he was about to say.

"Yet ten years have passed, and after all that time, you have just as obviously never forgiven me, nor has your anger with me eased significantly. It is most telling; whether you are as yet willing to admit it or not scarcely matters. Some things were very much meant to be, my dear Elizabeth." A smug, knowing smile spread across his face, and he did look very much like a Pirate King. An annoying and practically irresistible Pirate King.

"And you and I are one of them."

Chapter 15

"In truth, I am torn." Elizabeth sipped her tea, her manner as casual as her tone. As if she were discussing nothing of any significance whatsoever.

"I'd be rather surprised if you weren't," Jules murmured.

The sisters stood side by side, surveying the ladies gathered in Elizabeth's parlor, all at the moment seated clustered in chairs or standing together in groups of threes or fours or more. All engaged in the sort of animated conversation, punctuated liberally with delighted laughter and the occasional gasp of disbelief or surprise, that occurs when women who truly like one another are kept apart too long. Sharing the latest news and, more importantly, hearing the latest gossip, both within the family and without, was an opportunity not to be missed. Everyone was here, of course: her mother and her mother's sisters, Aunts Emma, Jocelyn, and Rebecca. Her father's sister, Aunt Gillian, a great-aunt or two, and any number of cousins and second cousins. Between the aunts and the various and assorted other relations, it was an impressive showing of Effington females.

And while not a single lady present had failed to quirk a brow at the simple plates of fruited cakes and sugared biscuits Cook had frantically prepared since Elizabeth had discovered the state of her accounts yesterday afternoon, no one had actually commented aloud on the meager offering either, although she was fairly certain there were more than a few quiet observations and possibly some concern expressed as to her abilities as a hostess as well. The Effington ladies' Christmas tea was traditionally a lavish affair with a friendly rivalry between relations as to who could produce the most delightful—and impressive—afternoon.

This year's tea was decidedly understated. At least, thus far.

"Do you really think he will come to your aid? Rescue you from social disaster?" Jules studied her sister. "After all, it is already past five."

"Yes," Elizabeth said without hesitation and noted with a small measure of surprise she truly meant her words. "I presented it as something of a test. A challenge of sorts. Nicholas is a man who can never turn away from a challenge." *And he claims to love me. To have loved me always.*

"Still, he is merely a man. He might well think something like a ladies' tea," Jules nodded at the assembly, "to be relatively insignificant and not worth his effort."

"Regardless, he wants the family to like him. Half of the family, indeed some might argue the half most difficult to please, is in this very room."

"As far as I can recall, the family has liked him since he first came to live with Lord Thornecroft. Most of us anyway, and I have certainly changed my opinion."

"Do lower your voice, Jules. I'd prefer not to have the details of my life as the primary topic of discussion among every female in the family."

"You may well be too late." Jules scoffed but lowered her voice nonetheless. "Every woman here is wondering why you have seen fit to offer nothing for tea but biscuits and cakes, and most are speculating on the reasons behind it. Some are certainly questioning the state of your finances, but Mother and her sisters suspect there is something far more interesting than mere money involved."

"They would, wouldn't they?" Elizabeth glanced at her mother. The duchess caught her gaze and smiled pleasantly, but there was an assessing look in her eye. As if she was trying to piece together an intriguing puzzle. Her mother always had liked puzzles.

Jules's gaze followed her sister's. "I daresay she wouldn't be overly pleased to know you have shared Collingsworth's bed, although, given Mother's unusual way of looking at the world and her penchant for romantic tales, I rather suspect she would not be terribly condemning."

"I should prefer not to find out, thank you."

"Still, Mother's curiosity, even her opinion, pales in comparison to the question of what you will do about Sir Nicholas. You cannot play this game with him forever." Jules paused thoughtfully. "Can you?"

"Of course not. Nor do I wish to." Precisely what she did wish had been on Elizabeth's mind constantly since yesterday's encounter with Nicholas.

His declaration of love, of course, was paramount in her thoughts. She wasn't entirely sure if it changed everything or nothing at all. Either way, it produced the most delightful feeling of something rather like joy within her. But it was his observation about her attitude toward Charles and himself that nagged at her.

Why was it that she had forgiven Charles his infidelity after a scant three years when she still harbored a fair amount of anger with Nicholas for merely discarding her a decade ago? To Nicholas she'd dismissed it as insignificant, but the truth of his words had struck her deeply. After all, it was not as if he had made any promises to her. Not as if they had been betrothed.

In point of fact, aside from a few kisses and any number of candid conversations, their relationship could well have been called nothing more than friendship. The anger and the resentment she'd harbored against him all these years was not at all proportional to his crime. Indeed, as sins went in this world, Charles's had been much more heinous. Yet, in the years since the discovery of his mistress and his death she had not only forgiven him but perhaps even understood his indiscretion. She had come to believe, rightly or wrongly, that her husband might well have found something with this unknown woman that he had not found with her. And she'd cared for him too much, possibly, she now thought, in the manner of a dearest friend more than a lover, to even now begrudge him that.

Yet, while she had worked diligently for a decade to put all thought of Nicholas out of her mind, she had never really succeeded or forgiven him.

Perhaps it was time to face the reasons why.

"If you ask me, not that you have but you should," a firm note sounded in Jules's voice, "I think you would be the worst kind of fool if you do not snatch him up right now and drag him to the altar."

"I don't wish to marry," Elizabeth said without thinking.

"Marriage is beside the point. Do you still want him?"

Elizabeth sipped her tea. "I believe I've already made myself clear on that subject."

"For the rest of your days?"

Did she? Could she consider the rest of her life without him? And hadn't she already spent far too long without him? She heaved a resigned sigh. "Yes."

Jules cast her a smug smile. "In this day and age that is referred to as marriage."

"Still and all—"

"Do you trust him?"

"With my finances, even with my children, but"—Elizabeth drew a deep breath and met her sister's gaze directly—"he broke my heart, Jules."

"I know." Jules shrugged. "I've known since the very first time we spoke of him."

"You could have mentioned it to me," Elizabeth said wryly.

"You have denied it far too long. You would not have believed me. So." Jules paused to sip her tea, her tone deceptively casual. "Do you love him now?"

"The question isn't if I love him but when I loved him." Elizabeth shook her head. "Did I truly love him ten years ago? And if I did, when did I stop? Or did I ever stop? Did I marry Charles all the while loving Nicholas? Do you know what that says about me and my entire life?"

"Nothing of significance as far as I can see." Jules stared at her sister. "You might well have married one man when your heart truly belonged to another, yet did Charles ever suspect?"

"Most certainly not." Indignation rang in Elizabeth's voice. "*I* did not suspect."

"Did you do all in your power to be a good wife?"

"Absolutely. I was an excellent wife."

"To my mind, you were a far better wife than Charles was a husband. Lizzie." Jules leaned closer to her sister. "You would be well advised to put the past firmly in the past. And the best way to do that," she grinned, "is to snatch Nicholas up right now and drag him to the altar."

Elizabeth stared at her sister for a moment, then laughed. "That might well be the perfect solution."

"The perfect solution to what?" Mother's voice sounded beside them.

Elizabeth braced herself. She and Jules had been too engrossed in their own conversation to note their mother's approach.

"Nothing really, Mother," Jules said smoothly. "It's just that Lizzie had far more extensive refreshments planned, but for some reason they have not yet arrived from Fortnum and Mason."

"Yes, that's it." Elizabeth breathed a sigh of relief.

"Really? They are usually so efficient." Mother's voice was thoughtful. "However, that does explain the intense nature of your discussion."

"I thought it would," Jules murmured.

"We were just saying how I should send someone to inquire at once," Elizabeth said brightly.

"Excellent idea, my dear daughters." Mother smiled pleasantly. "Although I suspect Fortnum and Mason might not deliver any order if an account has been closed."

"Oh look, Aunt Jocelyn is waving to me. It's been forever since we've chatted. I really should speak with her." Jules started toward her aunt.

Elizabeth grabbed her arm and yanked her sister back to her side, then raised her chin and met the Duchess of Roxborough's gaze. "Whatever do you mean, Mother?"

Mother raised a brow.

Elizabeth blew a resigned breath. "How did you know?"

"Your brother let something slip to your father, who then insisted on the full story, and he, of course, told me."

Elizabeth traded glances with her sister. "What exactly did Jonathon say?"

"He told us of the clause in Charles's will giving control of your finances to Sir Nicholas. I must say I am quite disappointed in your late husband." The duchess shook her head. "Ridiculous to think you could not manage your own affairs."

"Thank you, Mother." Elizabeth should have known this would be her mother's reaction. Still, it was lovely to hear.

"I wish you had seen fit to confide in me about all this."

"Quite honestly, it was rather humiliating. I preferred to keep it to myself." Beyond that, Elizabeth wasn't entirely certain the confession of the revelation of Charles's last wishes wouldn't have led to any number of other confessions about her involvement with Nicholas. Confessions that she would prefer not to make to her mother. "Did Jonathon say anything else?"

"Only that you and Sir Nicholas have been at odds over the management of your funds since his return to England, culminating in irresponsible spending on your part and the closing of your accounts on his." Her mother's eyes narrowed thoughtfully. "Is there more?"

Elizabeth shook her head. "Nothing of any significance."

"He wants to marry her," Jules said with a grin.

"Between you and Jonathon it's a wonder I have any privacy at all," Elizabeth muttered.

"Does he? How wonderful." A delighted smile spread across her mother's face. "I have always liked Nicholas Collingsworth, you know. Certainly he was overly serious as a youth, rather too intense, I always thought. Now, however, I find him most delightful."

Elizabeth drew a deep breath. "I don't know that I want to marry again."

"She takes after her mother," Aunt Rebecca said in a low voice that nonetheless carried across the room.

Elizabeth's gaze slid past the duchess, and she groaned to

herself. She'd been so intent on the conversation with her mother that she had failed to notice the silence that had fallen in the parlor. And failed to notice as well that the attention of each and every lady present was on her.

Her mother's brows drew together. "I can well see why you might feel that way, dearest. I know I myself was reluctant to wed. I had plans for grand adventures. Indeed, I led your father on a merry chase." She smiled at the memory. "It was great fun as I recall." Her expression sobered, and she took her daughter's hands. "Dearest, you must go on with your life. Charles is gone, and you cannot mourn him forever."

Jules scoffed. "She's not mourning Charles, Mother. She simply doesn't want to give up the independence his death has afforded her."

"That's certainly understandable," Aunt Gillian murmured.

"Not at all, it's utter nonsense," Aunt Jocelyn said firmly. "Sir Nicholas has an impressive fortune, will inherit a fine title, and is exceptionally easy to look at, as well. She should marry him at once."

"Even so, independence is extraordinarily difficult to come by," a cousin said from the far side of the room.

Another relation scoffed. "She would be a fool to let him escape."

"Marriage is the preferred state for any female," someone else added.

At once the room exploded into animated debate over the relative pros and cons of Elizabeth wedding Sir Nicholas. Not an aunt or cousin failed to have a definite opinion, and not one hesitated to express it. Indeed, the volume of voices in the room rose to an impressive level.

Jules grinned at her sister.

"I don't find this the least bit amusing," Elizabeth said grimly. "Each and every female here is convinced she knows best how to run my life. Can't you stop them, Mother?"

"Not yet, darling, everyone is having such a lovely time of it." Mother chuckled and scanned the gathering. "Not a single woman here does not believe that she, and she alone, knows what the right course of action is. And there is nothing women, particularly Effington women, like better than expressing their opinions. Why I daresay you have provided them with the best possible Christmas tea. Nothing is as entertaining as deciding what someone else should do with her life."

Elizabeth sighed. "Yes, I suppose, but—"

"And I suspect the entertainment has only just begun." Mother nudged her and nodded toward the door.

Nicholas stood framed in the doorway studying the ladies with a definite expression of amusement. His gaze caught hers, and his grin widened.

"I love you now and I loved you then and I am fairly certain I never stopped loving you."

Her heart caught, and for the first time, she didn't ignore the feelings his presence aroused in her.

Mother leaned toward her, her voice low and for Elizabeth's ears alone. "Marriage is not always a grand adventure, my darling." Her mother's gaze searched hers, as if somehow she knew that Elizabeth's marriage to Charles had not been as perfect as it had appeared. "But with a man you love, it can be the greatest adventure of all. And well worth any compromise." She turned her attention back to the door and raised her voice. "Sir Nicholas, how delightful to see you again."

Nicholas strode toward them. The room quieted at once, all eyes on the tall, handsome knight crossing the floor toward her. Elizabeth could certainly see why so many of her relations thought she'd be a fool to allow him to get away.

"Your Grace." Nicholas took her mother's hand and raised it to her lips. "You are looking as lovely as ever."

"Very good, Sir Nicholas. You and my son have a great deal in common. I suspect the two of you practiced your charming manners together in your youth," Mother said wryly.

Nicholas laughed. "Only to make you proud of us, Your Grace."

"I am proud, Nicholas." Mother's gaze met his. "Of both of you."

"That means a great deal to me, ma'am," Nicholas said softly.

They smiled at one another for a long moment, as if exchanging secrets Elizabeth wasn't privy to; or perhaps reaching an accord.

Her mother raised a brow. "I suspect this is not merely a social visit?"

"Not entirely." Nicholas cast Elizabeth a quick, if decidedly smug, smile. Oddly, it didn't bother her at all. "I must, however, apologize for my tardiness. It was unavoidable." He turned toward the door and nodded. At once, a parade of waiters entered the parlor, each bearing a tray of Fortnum and Mason's best.

"Oh my," the duchess murmured.

"Well done, Sir Nicholas," Jules said with a grin. "Well done indeed."

There were delicate slices of duck encased in pastry, lobster salad, morsels of partridge and truffles in aspic. Trays were piled high with dainty cakes and fanciful biscuits and decadent chocolates. And if that wasn't enough, there was Bavarian cream and tarts and terribly expensive out-of-season berries.

"I heard of Lady Langley's," he cleared his throat, "*dilemma* and thought the least I could do was provide whatever assistance I could."

Elizabeth quirked a brow. "It was indeed the very least, given that you—"

"I think it's delightful and most thoughtful." Mother beamed at Nicholas, who had the good grace not to look too pleased with himself. "And impressive as well. I would have wagered a great deal that a gentleman would not have had the vaguest idea what to provide for a gathering of ladies."

"I cannot take full credit for that, I had excellent assistance as well as unlimited funds. Both of which can accomplish a remarkable amount in a relatively short period of time." His voice was as polished as his manner. "I would hate for your Christmas tea to be a disappointment."

Jules choked back a laugh.

Her mother cast her a quelling glance, then smiled at Nicholas. "And it is most appreciated." She nodded at her younger daughter. "I suspect you and I should sample some of what Sir Nicholas has provided before it has all been devoured." The duchess cast her gaze over the room and sighed. "They are a ravenous group, especially at Christmastime. Indulgence is in the air and we, and admittedly I include myself in that number, are most susceptible to it. After Twelfth Night we shall all have to cinch our corsets a bit tighter. Still," she grinned in a wicked manner, "excess at this festive time of year is well worth the price."

Nicholas chuckled but wisely held his tongue.

The duchess nodded, and she and Jules moved to join the others.

Nicholas stepped to Elizabeth's side and surveyed his handiwork. "Well? Did I pass your test?"

*Oooh*s and *ah*s washed through the room at the discovery of every new offering. All in all it was both excessive and impressive and served the multiple purposes of providing Elizabeth's guests with sustenance as well as another topic of conversation. Or rather a refinement of the previous topic. And judging from the snatches of conversation she caught, it appeared that those family members who had initially argued for independence rather than marriage now conceded wedded bliss with Nicholas might well be worth a fair amount of sacrifice.

The man certainly had every reason to look smug.

Elizabeth surrendered. "Without question."

"And?"

"And what?" Still, he was a bit annoying.

"I should think a word of thanks would be in order." A sanctimonious note sounded in his voice. "A semblance of gratitude. Something of that nature."

"I am most grateful," she said coolly. "Or rather I would be if the blame for my *dilemma* couldn't be laid squarely at your feet in the first place. If you had not taken it upon yourself to close my accounts simply to assert your authority." She smiled up at him sweetly.

His return smile was just as pleasant. "Which was in direct response to the absurd point you were trying to make about your nature by a binge of rash, reckless spending."

She clenched her teeth. "Which was only necessary given

your intractable stand regarding the control of my finances, indeed, the control of my very life."

"In many ways they sound already married," the voice of one of her aunts drifted to her. Once again, Elizabeth had failed to note the silence in the room.

Heat flushed up her face.

Nicholas leaned closer. "I'd say it appears inevitable."

She met his gaze, his dark eyes shaded by amusement and something deeper, something important, something . . . forever.

The ladies in the room, the very room itself vanished. She existed only in the look in his eyes, the thud of her heart. And in that very moment she surrendered to what indeed was inevitable and so very right. For the first time in ten long years she faced the truth of what, somewhere deep inside, she had probably known all along. She'd loved him then, she loved him now, and she had never stopped loving him. He was and had always been her fate. Her grand passion.

Elizabeth drew a deep breath and smiled in a manner only slightly unsteady. "Perhaps some things were indeed meant to be."

Surprise flashed across his face, and he stared for a long moment. Then he smiled slowly and looked as if he wanted to pull her into his arms right here and now. Instead he took her hand and drew it to his lips. It would have been somewhat disappointing save for the promise in his eyes.

His voice was low and meant for her alone. "Will you join me for supper tonight, Lady Langley? Around half past eight, I should think."

She swallowed hard and gazed into his eyes, knowing full well that, regardless of what had passed between them up til now, supper with him tonight would truly be the beginning of what was meant to be.

A grand passion.

A grand madness.

"I should like nothing better, Sir Nicholas," she said softly.

"Well, I daresay I can't hear a blasted word," one of her cousins muttered somewhere in the distance. "What are they saying?"

"I have no idea," someone else murmured. "But from their expressions, I'd wager it's good."

He grinned down at her and she laughed up at him, not really caring at the moment what anyone else thought at all. "Until tonight then," he said quietly, released her hand, and turned toward her mother. "I should be off, Your Grace."

"You will not be joining us then?" A twinkle lurked in her mother's eye. "For tea, that is."

Nicholas shook his head. "I think not. Frankly, this is rather a formidable gathering, and I should feel much like a wolf in a herd of lambs."

"Nicholas, you are a delight," Mother laughed. "The fact of the matter is, in this gathering, it is the wolf who should have fear of the lambs."

He grinned that disarming grin of his. "Precisely my meaning, ma'am." He turned toward the assembly, the ladies hanging on his every word, and swept an impressive bow. "Ladies, felicitations of the season. I wish you all the merriest of Christmases."

"We will see you at the Effington Christmas Ball, will we not?" Mother said.

"I would not miss it for the world. Good day, Your Grace." He nodded at Elizabeth. "Lady Langley."

"Sir Nicholas," Elizabeth said with a cool nod of her own that belied the fluttering within her brought on, no doubt, by the acceptance of her own feelings and the anticipation of what was to come. Tonight and every night thereafter.

He strode out of the parlor, her gaze, and that of every lady present, following him until he disappeared from sight. As if on cue, his exit prompted an immediate upsurge in eager female voices all intent on describing and praising the charms, the thoughtfulness, and the appearance of Sir Nicholas.

"I wonder who assisted him," Jules murmured from somewhere behind Elizabeth.

"No doubt the people at Fortnum and Mason," Mother said. "Although it scarcely matters. The important thing to note is that he came to Elizabeth's aid. It speaks well of the man."

"It does, doesn't it?" Elizabeth said softly, still gazing unseeing at the door.

"You do realize you and Charles never argued," Mother said thoughtfully.

Jules snorted. "While you and Nicholas argue constantly."

"I think it's something to consider." The duchess paused for a moment. "And I think it's quite significant."

"You're absolutely right, and I should do something about that." Elizabeth turned to her mother and sister with a brilliant smile that seemed to emanate from somewhere deep inside her. From her heart, or perhaps her soul.

"Indeed, I would be a fool if I failed to snatch him up right now and drag him to the altar."

Chapter 16

Nick leaned back in the chair behind his desk and stared unseeing at the library door.

What in the hell was he supposed to do about this?

He drummed his fingers absently on the desktop. Elizabeth professed to want honesty between them, yet honesty was a vague and elusive thing, much given to individual interpretation. How much honesty did she really want? Was this something she needed to know? Besides, it was all over and done with, and firmly in the past. Wouldn't any revelation of the truth at this point in time simply hurt her, perhaps deeply?

Still, could he—in all good conscience and the interest of honesty—keep this from her? If they were to have a life together, and that had been his intention all along, shouldn't it indeed be based on honesty? Shouldn't they begin their future without secrets between them? Especially secrets of this magnitude.

He glanced at the Viennese clock on the mantel. Usually the automata in the base of the timepiece depicting a cobbler's workshop, the cobbler and his apprentice moving in consort with the clock movement, brought a smile but this evening he was only concerned with time. It was just past seven. He had more than an hour until Elizabeth's arrival. Plenty of time to dress for dinner. No time at all to come up with an answer.

Damnation. There didn't seem to be an answer. Not a good

one, at any rate. Nick blew a long, frustrated breath. He couldn't remember the last time he had been this unsure about anything. It was this pesky business of being in love, no doubt. It fogged a man's mind and destroyed any possibility of rational thought.

He didn't know how on earth he could tell her, but he knew full well that if he held his tongue and she found out, she would never understand that his only interest had been in protecting her. And she might never forgive him.

He stared at the cobbler's workshop, the apprentice's hammer striking off the seconds on the sole of a shoe. One . . . two . . . three . . .

He should definitely tell her. There was simply no need to tell her today. His mood brightened. Or even tomorrow, for that matter. He smiled at the apprentice. Why not wait until they had shared five years of wedded bliss together? Or better yet—ten. Even twenty. That would put it all nicely in perspective. Why, there was a very good chance that with the passage of a great deal of time she would find his revelation no more than mildly interesting.

A sharp rap sounded at the library door, followed almost at once by Edwards.

"Beg pardon, sir, but Lady Langley is here."

"Already?" Nick got to his feet. Her timing was decidedly fortuitous. A few minutes earlier and it would have been most awkward indeed. Even so . . .

He grinned. Elizabeth's early arrival might well mean that she was so eager to see him she could barely wait for her guests to depart. Certainly he wanted nothing more than to be with her. To take her into his arms. To accept her gratitude, graciously of course, for the success of her tea in whatever manner she wished to express it. Hopefully, naked and sprawled across his bed wearing nothing but a corset. Red, if he was very, very lucky, although he couldn't imagine Elizabeth owning a red corset. Wearing one but not owning one. Perhaps a gift was in order? For Christmas. Privately given, of course. And stockings. Definitely stockings. The finest available and nothing the least bit practical.

"Nicholas." Elizabeth swept into the room with a curt nod, her chin held high, her shoulders back, her breasts straining at the fabric of her dress. Oh yes, he could definitely imagine Elizabeth in a red corset.

"You're early."

"I could scarcely wait." The words were right, but there was something definitely amiss in her tone.

He narrowed his gaze. "Did your guests have an enjoyable time?"

"Yes," she said coolly.

He studied her carefully, the corset in his mind even now fading to a serviceable, practical, well-washed white. She was obviously annoyed about something. Or rather annoyed at him about something. He racked his brain, but he really hadn't done anything. Not yet, that is.

"Elizabeth," he said slowly, "is there—"

"Do you have something to tell me?" Her voice was overly casual, her manner idle. Her gaze was firmly on him, but she absently picked up a small Ming ginger jar.

"What are you doing with that?"

She glanced at the jar in her hands as if she was unaware that she held it. "I had rather thought I had cured myself of this habit." Her brows pulled together. "Until you returned, that is."

"What habit?" He was almost afraid to ask.

"I have become a vase thrower, Nicholas." She shrugged as if she held some worthless piece of penny pottery and not a priceless relic.

"Yes, I've noticed." He eyed the ginger jar. "Only vases?"

"Primarily vases. Sometimes a pot, crockery, the occasional dish, every now and then a glass."

"Ah well, then, specifically, that is a ginger jar."

She smiled. "Ginger jars."

"I don't remember you as a vase thrower."

"I didn't used to be a vase thrower." Her brow furrowed. "I don't remember when I started throwing vases. When life became rather frustrating, I suspect."

"Frustrating?"

"Oh, I don't know. That may well be the wrong word." She shifted the jar from hand to hand in the manner of a small boy with a ball. He did wish she wouldn't do that. "There is an astounding amount of satisfaction in throwing something with weight to it." She glanced up at him. "This has a nice throwing weight, by the way."

"I'm sure the Ming dynasty created it with that in mind," he murmured.

"And it is appreciated." At least she didn't seem quite as annoyed as she had a moment ago.

"That is an exceptionally valuable piece." He circled the desk. "Quite rare and very, very old."

"You have plenty of money."

"It's irreplaceable."

"Ah well. Rather a pity then." She studied the blue underglazed jar. "I believe I started after Christopher was born. I don't remember exactly what prompted me to throw my first vase, but I do remember the intense sense of satisfaction and, well, relief, I would say. The heft of the object in my hand. The release of letting it fly. And the enormously satisfying crash as it shattered against the wall. Precisely why I prefer vases, you see."

"I'm afraid I don't." He directed his words to her but kept a careful watch on the pottery.

"Glasses, especially crystal, are light and rather inadequate to the task." She shook her head. "Not like a good vase."

"Ginger jar," he corrected and chose his words carefully. "What, pray tell, is prompting you now?"

"Ah yes, the matter at hand." She narrowed her gaze. "Do you have something you want to tell me?"

Not if he wished to save his jar from certain destruction. "I don't think so."

"No?" She raised a brow. "Nothing at all?"

"No?" It was more a question than an answer.

"About Miss Godwin?"

"Teddy?" His heart sank. How much did she know, or did she merely suspect? "Why would you think—"

"Come now, Nicholas." She glared at him. "I saw her leave.

Not more than ten minutes ago. I refuse to be placed in this position again, knowingly or unknowingly. I will not stand for it."

He stared at her for a long moment. Relief washed through him, and he grinned. "You're jealous."

"I most certainly—" She huffed. "Yes, apparently I am jealous."

His grin widened. "How delightful."

"It's not the least bit delightful," she snapped. "It's maddening. I have never been jealous a day in my life."

"Charles never made you jealous?"

"No." She heaved a frustrated sigh. "Never. I would have been possibly, if I had known of his *activities,* but as I didn't. . . ." Her eyes narrowed. "What is your relationship with Miss Godwin?"

"As I told you the last time you were jealous, Teddy is a very old and very dear friend. Indeed, she helped me with the order from Fortnum and Mason. She has a gift for that sort of thing." He crossed his arms over his chest and leaned back against the desk. A jealous Elizabeth was rather intriguing and most amusing. "I daresay I couldn't have done it without her."

She studied him with obvious suspicion. "And she stayed here all the while you were at my house and afterwards?"

"Not at all. If you must know, we met this morning. She guided me in selecting items for the tea and was most instrumental in convincing Fortnum and Mason to put the order together at once." He met her gaze. "Her charming persuasiveness coupled with a great deal of my money is why your tea was such a success." He raised a brow. "It was a success, wasn't it?"

"Rousing," she muttered. "Why then was she here this evening?"

"My, you are jealous." He chuckled. "It's most appealing."

"It's not the least bit—"

"Teddy stopped by on her way to the theater to see if all had gone well." It was the truth as far as it went and, for now, he saw no need to tell her anything else. "Nothing more than that."

Elizabeth considered him for a long, silent moment, then

sighed. "I feel like something of a fool." She set the ginger jar down. "Again."

"Jealousy, brought on by jumping to conclusions, will do that."

She shook her head. "Even so, it's a part of myself I am unfamiliar with, and I do not like it."

"I, however, find your jealousy and your foolishness rather charming."

"I should send Miss Godwin a note of thanks," she murmured. "And my apologies as well."

"No need to apologize," he said quickly. He could not conceive of anything more dangerous than a true friendship springing up between Elizabeth and Teddy. No, it was in the best interest of all involved to keep these two women as far apart as possible. "She has no idea of your erroneous conclusions. Besides, it would simply embarrass her."

"I suppose. But a note of thanks—"

"Would be most appropriate. Now then." It was past time to get the subject off Teddy and onto something far more important. "About this jealously problem of yours—"

"I do not have a problem with jealousy." A reluctant smile lifted the corner of her lips. "My problem is you."

He resisted the urge to move toward her. "Oh?"

"Yes, well you see." She clasped her hands together and glanced around the room, her gaze falling anywhere except on him. "That is to say . . ."

"Yes?"

"I have given this matter a great deal of thought. Due consideration, that is."

He nodded. "Go on."

"And I have decided, well"—she drew a deep breath and met his gaze—"I will marry you, Nicholas."

"Will you?" he said slowly.

They were the words he wanted to hear. The words he'd waited for. Why then wasn't he overjoyed?

"Yes, I will." She nodded firmly.

"Why?" At once he realized there was something here that he'd missed. Something that nagged at the back of his mind.

"Why?" Her eyes widened. "What do you mean, why? You've given me any number of reasons why I should marry you. For one thing, you control my finances."

"Ah yes, of course." He forced a light note to his voice that belied the sinking sensation in his stomach. "You want me for your money. Not very flattering."

"That's not it, Nicholas," she said quickly. "And you well know it."

"No, I didn't think it was. What I do think"—even as he said the words he couldn't believe he was saying them—"is that, at the moment at least, marriage between the two of us might well be a mistake."

"What?" Shock rang in her voice.

"I'm not entirely sure marriage right now would be the wisest course."

"Why on earth not? It's what you've wanted all along."

"Yes it is and I still want it."

"Then—"

"You jumped far too quickly to the conclusion that there was something between Teddy and myself."

"That's what this is all about? Most men would be flattered." Her voice rose. "Besides, why wouldn't I be jealous, Nicholas? She is a lovely, desirable woman, and you—"

"Yes?"

"You are," she drew a deep breath, "everything a woman could ever want."

"Thank you. Nonetheless, I don't think you should enter into marriage with a man you don't trust."

"Nonsense, Nicholas. I might not have trusted you initially. You did break my heart after all, and that's not something a woman forgets easily, but you have more than proved to me the kind of man you are."

"Did I break your heart?" he said quietly.

"It's taken me a decade to admit it, but yes, you did. Regardless, I am certain you are now a man I can trust with, with," she lifted her chin, "with the rest of my life."

"Can you? You say you've never known jealousy, yet you assumed the worst when you saw another woman leave my door."

"Obviously because I cannot bear the thought of you with someone else. Did I mention you should be flattered?"

He shook his head slowly. "I'll not pay for another man's sins."

"What?" She shook her head in confusion. "Whose sins?"

"A few moments ago, when you thought there was something more than friendship between Teddy and myself, you said you would not be put in that position again."

"I see." She nodded. "And rightfully so. You can scarcely blame me for that."

"I don't." He chose his words with care. "When I told you that I had been faithful to you in my heart all these years, as trite as it may have sounded, it was the truth. I have never loved another woman."

"You . . ." Her voice caught. "I never imagined—"

"When we met again a few weeks ago," his gaze met hers, "I asked you if you were at peace. You didn't answer."

She scoffed. "Because it was a silly question."

"Because you aren't at peace. Not with Charles."

"Charles is dead." She crossed her arms over her chest. "Dead and buried and gone."

"And you never had the chance to confront him. To resolve things between the two of you. He shared his life secretly with another woman for more than half of your marriage. You can't tell me that you don't have any number of questions about that relationship."

"Oh, I suppose I do. It would be only natural to have a certain amount of curiosity—"

"As much as you claim to have forgiven him, you said it yourself: He is an unfinished chapter in your life."

She shook her head. "Even so—"

"He betrayed you."

"I know that," she snapped. "And you broke—"

"Damn it all, Elizabeth. I did what I thought was best for *your* life and *your* future and *your* happiness, and I am bloody well tired of apologizing for it. It was the biggest mistake of my life and the noblest thing I've ever done. I did what I did in the manner I did to assure you would marry the man I thought, the man everyone thought, the man *you* thought, was right, indeed, *meant for you*. To assure your happiness."

"Well, you were wrong!"

"Only in hindsight. The years may have proved my actions in error, but given the same circumstances I would do precisely the same thing again. *For you.* And the mistakes made ten years ago were not mine alone!"

"Charles wasn't—"

"I'm not talking about Charles, I'm talking about you."

She gasped. "Me? Surely you aren't saying that I—"

"Oh, but I am. You could have argued with me. You could have refused to accept my edict. You could have fought with me, for me, *for us*. Damn it all, Elizabeth, you could have followed me!"

"Don't be ridiculous! There was no conceivable way that I . . . I didn't know . . . I wasn't sure . . ." She paused, and he could see the memory of their parting flit across her eyes. She squared her shoulders. "I was very young."

"We were both very young, but I loved you enough to give you up."

"And I was as big a fool as you to have allowed you to do so! Is that what you want to hear?"

"I don't know." A weary note sounded in his voice.

"What do you want me to do, Nicholas? To close this chapter? Shall I go to his grave and yell at the top of my lungs? Shall I find a spiritualist to contact his ghost?" She searched for the right words. "If I have forgiven him it's because I had no choice. If I have justified his actions it's because I didn't know what else to do to make it all make sense."

She turned away and paced the room. "Until his death I thought our life together was perfect. I had never noticed that it was not a *grand passion*, but I was content. I thought he was content. Until your return, I didn't realize that content was not enough. I didn't realize that I had, in all likelihood, married the man who should never have been more than a dear friend and allowed the friend who was very possibly *my* grand passion to walk out of my life."

"I would never betray you," he said simply.

"I know, and yet I am . . ." She fell silent for a long moment.

Nicholas wished he'd held his tongue. Taken her acceptance of his proposal and ignored the rest. But while he was willing to spend the remainder of his days atoning for his mistakes, he would not pay for Charles's. He wanted Elizabeth more than he wanted life itself, but not at this cost. And he feared through the years to come it might well destroy them both.

"I am afraid." She met his gaze. "I am afraid of admitting that I have loved you always. Of admitting my life thus far has been," she uttered an odd, short laugh, "a grand mistake."

His stomach twisted. He was an idiot. She was willing to marry him. And she loved him. Nothing else really mattered. "Elizabeth."

She ignored him. "I think now I survived Charles's infidelity, even his death because, while I did love him dearly, he was never half of my soul." She drew a deep breath. "You are."

"Elizabeth." He started toward her.

"Please don't." She held out a hand to ward him off. "When I stormed over here I never considered any of what we've just discussed. But you're right: I trusted Charles implicitly and he betrayed that trust. However, even in those few days when I knew about his mistress, before his death, I was never jealous."

"It would have been understandable."

"But I wasn't. Yet every time you so much as look at another woman I think the worst when you have given me no reason to do so. And either I care for you more than I have ever thought possible or you're absolutely right. I am holding you responsible for Charles's failures." She turned and started toward the door, then swiveled back. "In truth, I think I might well blame you for everything."

"What?" His brows drew together.

Sparks flashed from her green eyes. "If you hadn't been so bloody self-sacrificing. If you had listened to your heart instead of everyone else—"

"Including you," he said pointedly.

"Oh, believe me, I count myself in that number," she snapped. "And I am probably as big a fool as you. But if you hadn't taken it upon yourself to make a decision that would affect both our lives without so much as a by-your-leave—"

"I was being noble!"

She snorted in disdain.

"And this is not all on my head." He narrowed his eyes. "If you hadn't been so concerned with convincing the world that you were nothing more than pretty and frivolous and empty-headed, perhaps Charles would have realized that you were not the right match for him in the first place. That you and he were not *meant to be*. Maybe, if you'd had the courage to be who you truly were with anyone other than myself, you would have had the courage to admit your feelings and stop me from walking out of your life!"

"You scarcely walked. You fled!"

"Fleeing certainly has a great deal of appeal at the moment!"

"On that, Sir Nicholas, we agree!" She turned on her heel and stalked toward the door, then turned back. "Christmas Eve and the Effington ball are the day after tomorrow. You needn't bother to escort me, I shall be at Effington House most of the day with the children."

"As you wish," he said curtly.

"I shall expect your decision as to the management of my finances then as well."

"Certainly."

She glanced at the ginger jar. "There would be a great deal of satisfaction in throwing that now."

"If you're asking my permission, you don't have it."

"I neither want it, nor do I need it." She grabbed the jar, hefted it in her hand, then met his gaze defiantly. "Is it really valuable?"

"Priceless."

"Good." She nodded, then flung the jar with all her strength.

Somewhere, in a more rational part of his mind not colored with anger, he noted that her throw was straight and true, obviously the result of a great deal of practice, and aimed right for his head. Without thinking he put his hand up and caught it. The smack of porcelain against flesh echoed in the room. Remarkably, given the sting in his hand, the jar held without so much as a crack. His admiration for the long dead artisans who'd lovingly created it notched upward.

"You caught it." She stared in disbelief. "You caught my vase."

"I caught *my* fifteenth-century, blue underglazed, porcelain, Ming dynasty ginger jar." He set the jar carefully on a nearby table. "And that was exceedingly childish of you."

"And no doubt frivolous as well."

He shrugged in agreement.

She studied him for a moment. "I told you I would not throw myself at you again. I did not think that tonight . . . That scarcely matters now as well, I suppose."

With that she nodded, turned, and stalked from the room, slamming the door behind her.

Nick stared at the door unseeing and slowly unclenched his fists. Odd, he hadn't noticed he had clenched them.

He drew a deep, calming breath. This evening certainly hadn't gone as he'd planned. No. He glanced at the clock. It was not yet eight. The evening he had anticipated shouldn't even have begun yet, let alone be over.

What on earth had happened? The woman drove him mad, but it was his fault, of course. He should have simply kept his mouth shut. But while he was more than willing to shoulder the blame for his own mistakes, he'd be damned if he'd be saddled with her late husband's as well.

He made his way around the assorted obstacles in the room to the decanter of brandy and glasses perched precariously on a tray balanced on an African tribal drum, poured a glass, and tossed it back.

He wanted her, he always had and suspected he always would. He wanted her heart, her hand, and, God help him, her trust. Was any of that possible now?

Still, it wasn't all bad. She'd admitted he'd broken her heart. He winced. That knowledge wasn't especially good, but it did mean she had cared for him then. She'd admitted loving him then and loving him now. "Half of her soul," she'd called him. Of course, there was indeed a fine line separating love and hate, and it was apparent she was now tottering between the two.

Obviously his talk with Teddy had put all this in his head in the first place. If only . . . well, there was no point in regrets. All that had passed between Elizabeth and him tonight could never be taken back.

This evening was a disaster, and he had no idea how to set things right and no idea if it was even possible. Perhaps they both needed more time before rushing into marriage, although one would have thought a decade was time enough. Was it simply his pride at stake or his own sense of honor? He had no idea what the answer to that was either.

There was one way to close the door once and for all on her life with Charles. One way to write the end to that chapter and give her the answers and the peace she deserved.

He ran his hand through his hair. He could not live the rest of his life without her. That was not in question.

The question now was whether or not he could live the rest of his life with her.

Chapter 17

"You look dreadful." Jules eyed her sister over her teacup.

Elizabeth paced the breakfast room. "I feel dreadful."

"I don't believe I have ever seen you look quite this bad."

"I've never felt quite this bad." She halted in midstep and looked at her sister. "How bad?"

"Rather like you've been dragged through the streets of London behind a carriage." Jules's gaze skimmed her sister from head to toe. "The very *worst* parts of London."

"That bad," Elizabeth murmured, glanced down at her dress, and winced.

She did look somewhat bedraggled and haphazard. Not at all her usual self. Certainly, she hadn't waited for her maid this morning and had thrown on the first thing she could don unassisted. *This morning* being a relative term, given the fact that she had had absolutely no sleep and darkness had simply slipped to dawn at some unnoticed point. She'd spent much of the night prowling restlessly through the house or staring through her windows at Nicholas's house. Noting the light burning in his library well past dawn. Wondering if he was as distraught as she. At least a half dozen times she'd found herself at the front door fully prepared to go to Nicholas and do whatever was necessary to mend this rift between them. Up to and including throwing herself at him once again.

She was stopped only by the realization that she had absolutely no idea what to say and, worse, what to do.

"I am such a fool." Elizabeth wrapped her arms around herself and resumed her pacing. "He's right, you know. About everything."

"Not at all."

Elizabeth glanced at her sister. "You don't think he's right? About Charles and me and *everything*."

"Oh no, I definitely think he's right. In point of fact I think his assessment was rather brilliant. I wish I had seen it myself. I simply think he's as great a fool as you."

Elizabeth raised a brow. "Do you?"

"Well," Jules smiled. "Perhaps not as great."

"Thank you." Elizabeth glared. "It's so good to know I have the unwavering loyalty of my sister."

"Loyalty is not the issue. However, honesty is. I think you are both fools. Total and complete idiots. Lunatics of the highest order." Jules set her cup down in a firm manner. "He should have snatched you up and dragged you to the altar the moment you agreed to marry him."

"Is that your solution for everything?"

"Yes, and it's a damnably good one too," Jules said sharply. "Right now we should be celebrating your betrothal and perhaps even planning a Christmas wedding. I have no idea what the procedure is these days, but Father or Lord Thornecroft or Nicholas himself could have certainly talked to some official somewhere, or even bribed someone if necessary. I'm certain arrangements could have been made to have you wed on Christmas Day itself."

Elizabeth stared. "Why, Jules, I never suspected, but you are a romantic. A rather diabolical romantic, but a romantic nonetheless. And overly optimistic as well."

"We romantics are all optimistic," Jules said in a lofty manner. "Besides, it's the season of hope and goodwill and that sort of thing. When we were girls I used to say anything was possible at Christmas." She met her sister's gaze. "I still believe it."

"Christmas is inevitable. It will dawn in two days regardless of what else may happen in the world." Elizabeth shook her head. "I fear a future with Nicholas is not."

"Oh, do stop it, Lizzie. I've had quite enough." Jules folded her arms on the table and leaned forward. "Stop feeling sorry for yourself."

"I'm not feeling sorry for myself."

Jules raised a brow.

"Very well then." Elizabeth sighed and collapsed into a chair. "I'm feeing a bit sorry for myself. I haven't felt this helpless in, well, ever. Since Charles's death I have become accustomed to solving whatever problems have arisen. Indeed, I can't conceive of a problem I cannot solve. Except this. I simply don't know what to do."

"What do you want to do?"

"I want to break every piece of his Chinese pottery," she said, forcing a pleasant note to her voice. "Preferably over his head."

"That sounds like a plan," Jules murmured.

Elizabeth snorted. "Satisfying perhaps, but futile." She traced the rim of her teacup absently with her forefinger and considered the situation. "I can't understand how one can want someone so badly yet at the same time have an overwhelming compulsion to strangle him."

Jules smirked. "I believe that's called love."

"It certainly does not have a lot to recommend it." Elizabeth stopped and cast a wry glance at her sister. "And it's remarkably different than anything I felt for Charles."

"Wrong kind of love," Jules said, eying a plate of tarts on the table.

"Which brings us back to the very beginning. I," Elizabeth paused dramatically, "am a fool."

"We've established that. Now, what do you intend to do about it?"

"Excellent question." Elizabeth stared at the painted floral design on her cup as if it held the answer. "I have considered going to him, apologizing—"

"Oh, I wouldn't apologize if I were you."

"Why not?"

Jules raised a brow. "Were you wrong?"

"No. But I wasn't very pleasant."

"Nor was he, from what you've said. Besides, he should be accustomed to your unpleasantness. You weren't very nice when he returned to London."

"Dear Lord, I'm a shrew." Elizabeth rested her elbows on the table and buried her face in her hands. "How could he possibly want me at all?"

"One does question his sanity. Regardless, he does love you in spite of the flaws in your character. I think it's rather wonderful of him. Now." Jules thought for a moment. "You have admitted you were as much to blame as he for what happened in the past?"

"More or less," she mumbled.

"And you've told Nicholas that you love him?"

"I believe I mentioned it in passing."

"You should probably do more than simply mention it in passing, but that is a minor problem and easily fixed. And you've accepted his observations as to your unresolved state in regards to Charles?"

"As upsetting as they are—"

"As insightful as they are."

"Yes, yes, I suppose I have." Elizabeth lifted her head. "There is nothing that can be done about that."

"Probably not. But there is a great deal that can be done about Nicholas." Jules studied her sister thoughtfully. "However, if I were you, I should wait until the ball to do anything at all. It will give you both a bit of time to reflect. Besides, your relationship ended at the Christmas ball, and it's only fitting that it should begin there once again."

"Fitting?" Elizabeth raised a brow. "I'm not certain how fitting it is, but it does bring things full circle."

"Talk to him at the ball."

"I shall not grovel."

"I'm not sure a certain amount of groveling isn't called for on both your parts. Nonetheless, you should probably wait to see if he grovels first."

Elizabeth smiled reluctantly. "Nicholas does not strike me as a man who takes well to groveling."

"One has to make sacrifices for love," Jules said in a superior tone. "On second thought, you might be well advised to grovel a tiny bit yourself. You were, after all, oh, what is the word I'm thinking of?"

"Wrong?"

"Exactly." Jules nodded. "About a great many things, but most of all for not sharing the blame for your parting and your life."

Elizabeth frowned. "What do you mean, my life?"

"Come now, Lizzie, if you hadn't been so determined to hide the brains God had seen fit to bestow on you, so intent on appearing flighty and empty-headed, simpering and—"

"I did not simper! I never simpered."

"Well, perhaps my memory fails me in that area." Jules shrugged. "Even so, the fault lies as much with you—"

"Yes, yes." Elizabeth waved off the comment. "I know that and I have acknowledged it. What still remains though is what to do about this business of trusting Nicholas. I thought I did trust him, but apparently, thanks to Charles, I don't." She tapped her fingers on the table. "To be honest, Jules, I'm not sure that my jealousy in regards to Nicholas has anything whatsoever to do with Charles. Perhaps I was never jealous where Charles was concerned, not that he ever gave me a reason to be, mind you, because the love that I had for him wasn't even remotely like what I feel for Nicholas."

She got to her feet and resumed pacing, searching for the right words with every step. "Loving Charles was an easy, peaceful sort of thing. There was no particular effort to it. Loving Nicholas is tempestuous and frightening and," she rested her hands on her stomach, "exciting in a queasy sort of way."

Jules nodded wisely. "A grand passion."

"I do hope so. It's all rather a lot of trouble to go through for anything less." She met her sister's gaze. "I can't promise him I shall never be jealous."

"Tell him. I think a certain amount of jealousy is to be expected and condoned when one has a grand passion."

A discreet knock sounded at the door and Elizabeth's butler

stepped into the breakfast room. "Beg pardon, my lady, but you have a caller."

"Sir Nicholas?" Elizabeth brushed her hair away from her face and glanced at her sister. "I can't possibly see him now. Whatever will he think?"

"He'll think you've spent as dreadful a night as hopefully he has," Jules said. "And he'll probably think you look charming."

"Still, I—"

Hammond cleared his throat. "Forgive my interruption, my lady, but it's not Sir Nicholas. It's a woman."

"A woman?" Elizabeth sighed. "I have no desire to see anyone at the moment. Please tell her I am indisposed."

"She said to tell you it's a matter of some delicacy and quite important."

Jules huffed impatiently. "Out with it, Hammond, who is it?"

"A Miss Godwin," Hammond said with a distinct note of disapproval in his voice.

Elizabeth and Jules traded glances.

"Well, this should prove interesting." Curiosity gleamed in Jules's eyes.

"Show her into the parlor. We shall join her in a minute." Elizabeth nodded at the butler. "And do ask Cook to prepare a tray. Some of those tarts, I think, and tea."

"Very well, my lady." At once Hammond took his leave.

"I wonder what she wants?" Elizabeth murmured.

"There is only one way to find out." Jules grinned. "And I for one can hardly wait."

Theodora Godwin stood by the window gazing absently out onto the street. Tall and striking and dressed in the latest fashion, the actress had an air of grace about her that was most compelling. It was no wonder she was acclaimed on stage. What woman in her right mind would not be jealous of such a vision?

"Miss Godwin?" Elizabeth stepped into the room, Jules right at her heels.

The actress turned toward her with a nervous smile. "Teddy, remember?"

"Yes, of course, Teddy." Elizabeth returned the smile. "And you've met my sister?"

"At Lord Thornecroft's." Teddy nodded at Jules. "It's lovely to see you again." She looked at Elizabeth. "I had rather hoped we could speak privately."

"Oh, you shan't even know I'm here," Jules said brightly.

"My sister was just leaving." Elizabeth cast Jules a firm glance. "She has a great many errands to attend to, what with Christmas being two days away and all."

"I could certainly stay."

"But we would hate to keep you." Elizabeth took her sister's elbow and escorted her to the parlor door.

Jules leaned close and spoke softly into Elizabeth's ear. "You will promise to tell me everything later, though."

Elizabeth smiled. "Probably."

Jules frowned with annoyance, then glanced back at Teddy. "Apparently I have a great number of errands to run. Good day, Miss Godwin."

Teddy laughed lightly. "Good day."

Jules cast her sister a last hopeful glance, heaved a resigned sigh, and sailed out of the room. Elizabeth closed the doors firmly behind her.

"She may never forgive you for that," Teddy said with a smile. "Your sister is extraordinarily curious."

"She always has been." Elizabeth stepped to the sofa, sat down, and gestured for the actress to take a seat. "But I must confess, at the moment, I share her curiosity."

Teddy settled on the edge of a nearby chair. "You're surprised then? That I'm here?"

"Very much so."

"To be entirely honest, I hadn't really planned on calling on you, but I had forgotten my parasol at Nicky's yesterday. I have just been to his house."

"Oh?" Elizabeth said in as casual a manner as she could muster. "And how is Sir Nicholas today?"

Teddy studied her thoughtfully. "You're not very good at this, are you?"

"Good at what?"

Teddy smiled. "Acting."

"I wasn't . . ." Elizabeth sighed. "I used to be very good at it, pretending to be someone I wasn't, that is."

"It's a skill you've lost."

Elizabeth chuckled in spite of herself. "I haven't needed it." She sobered and leaned toward Teddy. "How is Nicholas?"

"Terrible. Simply awful." The actress shook her head. "I have seen any number of men at their very worst through the years, but I'm not sure I've ever seen a man in such a state."

"Really?" Elizabeth brightened.

Teddy nodded. "He has been up most of the night drowning his sorrows, and today he is in the foulest of moods, most unpleasant I assure you, which simply mirrors his appearance. He looks," she thought for a moment, "like he's been drug through the streets behind a horse."

"A carriage," Elizabeth murmured.

"Exactly." Teddy pulled her brows together. "I must say you look rather . . . well . . . *weary* yourself."

"You're being kind." Elizabeth grimaced. "I suspect my appearance is comparable to Nicholas's, and I know I feel exactly the same way I look."

"He's miserable."

"Good." Elizabeth heaved a heartfelt sigh. "I should hate to be miserable alone."

Teddy hesitated for a moment, then set her shoulders squarely. "He talked to me rather freely about the two of you. I don't think he would have under other circumstances, but this morning he is, well—"

"Intoxicated?"

"Oh no, I think that's worn off but for the lingering effects." Teddy shuddered. "As I said, he's quite miserable. At any rate, I felt compelled to come here and speak with you myself."

"There's really no need. I know I've been foolish, but I

can't seem to help myself." She met the other woman's gaze. "I love him, you see."

"As well you should. I would love him myself if I didn't think of him as something of a brother." Teddy grinned wryly. "I've often thought that was rather a pity. I think Nicky is a wonderful man."

Elizabeth stared. Perhaps her jealousy was not entirely far-fetched.

"You really needn't worry." Teddy leaned forward, her manner as sincere as her words. "He loves you. He has loved you for as long as he can remember, and I daresay he always will."

"Has he?" Elizabeth said softly. The mere fact that Nicholas was willing to admit his feelings aloud to someone other than her was deeply significant and filled her with a lovely sort of warmth.

"Indeed he has."

"Still, one has to wonder, I don't know." Without thinking, Elizabeth's gaze drifted to the window that looked out at Nicholas's house. "Is love enough? There is so much that has passed between us. So many recriminations and regrets." She shook her head. "I do not want to lose him again, but I am at a loss as to how to prevent that. He has this theory, you see, about trust, and it's"—she met the other woman's concerned gaze—"not entirely absurd. But I have no solution."

"I see." Doubt flickered across Teddy's lovely face.

Elizabeth studied Teddy carefully. The actress was decidedly unsure about something. "Forgive me for being blunt, but is there something you wish to tell me?" Her stomach lurched and she braced herself. "About Nicholas?"

"Oh, no, not at all."

Elizabeth breathed a sigh of relief.

Teddy hesitated, as if she was debating the merits of her next words. At last she nodded slightly, more to herself than to Elizabeth. "Although there is something on my mind. It has nothing whatsoever to do with all of this, but I would truly appreciate some advice."

"I'd be happy to help." Elizabeth smiled in a confidential manner. "I've always rather liked giving advice."

"Excellent." Teddy drew a deep breath. "A friend of mine is writing a new play and he has a role he thinks will suit me." She met Elizabeth's gaze. "I told the story to Nicky yesterday evening."

"A play?" Elizabeth winced. "Oh, dear. I know nothing about the theater, and, Teddy, I'm not really—"

"Do humor me, Elizabeth. I could use the opinion of another woman."

"My thoughts may not be all that helpful today," Elizabeth said wryly. Still, Teddy's play might well take her mind off her own problems. And the least she could do was listen, given Teddy's kindness in coming here to mend matters between Elizabeth and Nicholas. "Very well then, do go on."

Teddy drew a deep breath. "I would play the role of a foolish woman who falls in love with the wrong man. A man who is already married."

Elizabeth scoffed. "It doesn't sound very original thus far. I daresay I've heard this plot before."

"Perhaps." Teddy smiled. "The character I would portray has always thought of herself as honorable and had never before considered any sort of involvement with a married gentleman. Yet when they meet, there is something between them that is irresistible. Almost as if they were meant for each other. As if their souls were bound together."

"A grand passion then?"

"A grand passion?" Teddy nodded thoughtfully. "Yes, I like that. I suppose it was. He was indeed the grand passion, the great love of her life. Even so, they were not free to be together."

"Because he was married?" Elizabeth was intrigued in spite of herself.

"Exactly. So, the character I would play decides to put him out of her mind and flees the country. To America, I think, where she meets a gentleman she had met once before but now they become very good friends. They have a great deal in common, you see. Both are far away from home, and he too is trying to put out of his mind the memory of the woman he loved but was not free to be with."

"In America," Elizabeth said slowly. Where had she heard this story before?

"Neither of them reveals the names of their loves, and eventually she returns home determined never to see the gentleman she loves again."

"But she did." It was a statement more than a question.

"Yes, she did. She didn't want to, but it was inevitable, part of the plot."

"Yes, it would be, wouldn't it?" Elizabeth murmured, realization growing within her.

"They are together for years. A secret, private relationship she keeps even from her closest friends."

"It must be quite difficult."

Teddy shrugged. "It is all in the name of love. It is not the life that she had wanted, but it is all they have. He never offers to leave his wife and she never asks. My character believes the gentleman truly loves his wife, it was simply a different sort of love."

Elizabeth's heart thudded in her chest. "Not a grand passion?"

"No." Teddy shook her head. "But real and important to him nonetheless. He had known her and her family much of his life. At any rate, the gentleman dies and my character is left alone with nothing but the memories of a love she could never reveal."

"It's a very sad play." Something oddly like panic washed through her, and Elizabeth rose to her feet. "I don't know that I wish to hear the rest. I'm not at all sure that I like it."

"But it's not over." Teddy stood, her gaze intense. "My character runs into her old friend from America again. And this is where the play takes a twist. It turns out the woman he loves, the woman he could never be with, is the wife of the very gentleman she loved."

"That is a twist." Elizabeth held her breath. "And?"

"It seems the wife knew about the other woman but not soon enough to confront her husband before his death. And the friend realizes that if the wife knew her husband had truly found the love of his life, she would at last be free to be with her true love. She would be at peace."

Elizabeth struggled against the lump in her throat. "And is she?"

"I don't know. The end hasn't been written."

Teddy's gaze locked with Elizabeth's, and they stared for an endless moment.

At last Teddy drew a deep breath. "I must go. I am already late for a costume fitting."

"Will you do the play then?"

"I don't know that either. As you said, it's very sad."

Elizabeth drew a deep breath. "I am so sorry. For your character that is, and the husband."

"You needn't be, it's just a play." She studied Elizabeth for a long moment. "If I might give you a piece of advice, Elizabeth. Nicky is a good man. Don't lose him again."

"I don't intend to." Elizabeth forced a smile. "Thank you."

"I wish the two of you all the best." Teddy started toward the door, then turned back. "She didn't blame the husband, you know, or the wife for that matter—my character, that is. She was simply grateful for the happiness they had shared."

The back of Elizabeth's throat burned and she could barely get out the words. "What happens to her?"

"She goes on with her life. Alone."

"I daresay there will not be a dry eye in the house." Elizabeth struggled to keep her own emotions in check. "I am not an expert on the theater, but don't audiences usually prefer an ending where the heroine lives happily? I know I always have."

"Oh, but my dear Elizabeth, I should have mentioned it before. My character is not the heroine of the piece. She is merely a secondary player. The lead roles in the production, indeed, the love story itself," Teddy smiled, "is between the friend and the wife."

Teddy nodded and took her leave.

Elizabeth sank down on the sofa and let the tears she had held back fall freely.

She'd been right all along about Charles. It was in many ways gratifying to know for certain that she had understood her husband's nature far better than he had understood hers. Poor, dear Charles. He had found the love of his life when it had been too late to do anything about it. Perhaps if Elizabeth had found the strength and independence of character during her marriage that she had found since, he might have had the courage to confess all to her. They might well have gone their separate ways. Even possibly divorced. But she'd appeared a dependent, vulnerable sort of creature, and he'd been too honorable to abandon her.

Was there indeed peace to be found now in the truth?

Possibly, but no great aura of calm and serenity fell upon her. No overwhelming sense of tranquility swept through her. Simply a terrible sadness and deep regret.

There was, however, a measure of comfort in knowing that Charles had indeed found a grand passion and a joy and a happiness he had not had with her. Elizabeth had cared for him too much to begrudge him that.

She'd always thought she had indeed put the past behind her, until Nicholas had walked back into her life and forced her to face any number of things she'd never had. It struck her that she was as much haunted by the ghosts of the past as Scrooge. Still, settling with the past gave her no clue as to what to do about the future.

Perhaps she needed to put not merely her trust but also her faith in Nicholas and in love and possibly even in fate. And needed as well to put her faith in the magic that shimmered in the air at this special time of year. And heed the words of her sister and believe.

Anything was possible at Christmas.

Chapter 18

Effington House was as festive as ever it was at this most festive time of year. Swags of holly and ivy and laurel adorned every railing, topped every door and each and every window. Not a ledge or a nook or a cranny remained untouched. The guests at the Christmas ball were adorned as well and matched their surroundings in their merriest attire and most celebratory mood.

Even in her current state of apprehension, Elizabeth could not fail to appreciate the scent of evergreen and gingerbread that wafted through the halls of the house like a jolly, festive specter. The ghost of Christmas Present, no doubt.

Christopher and Adam and their cousins, together with a sizable number of parents, aunts, and uncles, had spent the better part of the day, as they had every twenty-fourth of December since Elizabeth's childhood, decorating Effington House for Christmas. It was always a delightful time for children and those who fancied themselves adults at any time of year save this. Servants and family bustled about with preparations for the ball and Christmas itself, the work so filled with fun and good cheer that it was scarcely considered work at all but rather a rollicking good time.

The day had started with the dispatch of a sizable contingent, led by Jonathon, a tradition he'd laid claim to years ago, to the Covent Garden market to select a trio of the largest fir trees available. Two would be decorated with all manner of glass fruits and silk ribbons to flank the ballroom doors. The third, decorated as well with a variety of ornaments made by Effington children through the years, including those ornaments that were originally edible but were now more sentimental than palatable, would be placed in one of the parlors to shelter the family's gifts to one another. Inevitably, his mother would comment that the trees were really not as big as she had wished and vow that in the upcoming year, they would grow their own at Effington Park and transport them to London for Christmas. Whether that vow was abandoned for practical reasons or simply slipped her mind with the passage of the season no one knew, nor did anyone ask. That too was a family tradition.

Excitement and anticipation sparkled in the air and sounded in the voices of the children and shone in the eyes of those youngest in age and, as well, those merely young in spirit.

Elizabeth was not immune to the magic of the day. Indeed the joyous laughter of her children and the assorted other Effington relations served to occupy her mind with something other than thoughts of Nicholas. At least for a moment or two.

In the day since the revelation of Teddy's play, Elizabeth had come to any number of conclusions. In many ways, Nicholas was right: She had not found peace, or more accurately made peace, regarding Charles. She had indeed fabricated an excuse for his behavior in her belief, or perhaps simply her hope, that he had found a grand passion. Knowing now that she'd been right lifted a weight she had not realized she carried.

But Nicholas was wrong about trust. Her jealousy was not a matter of trust but of fear. The fear that once again he would vanish from her life under the mistaken assumption that his actions were in her best interests. She wondered now if her initial resistance to having anything whatsoever to do with him upon his return to London had been some sort of instinct to protect herself, or rather, protect her heart.

What Nicholas hadn't realized, what had only struck Elizabeth herself sometime shortly after dawn this morning after a second long, sleepless night, was that the weight she had lived with since Charles's death was not due merely to her questions about his actions but to her own sense of guilt. To the nagging suspicion, deep down inside, that somehow she was to blame for Charles's turning to another woman. That in some manner, she had failed. She hadn't, of course, and could now truly understand that Charles had been as fated for Teddy as Elizabeth was for Nicholas. Still, destiny was not necessarily easy.

Loving Charles had been safe. Loving Nicholas risked her very soul. She was nearly thirty years of age and had spent much of her life on the sure and safer road, where walking was scarcely any effort at all. It was past time to take the course fraught with peril, where a misstep could send her flying off the edge of a cliff to crash on the rocks below. Ah, but wasn't the view and even the fall itself glorious and well worth the price?

Elizabeth had survived losing Charles to another woman and then to death. She knew, as she'd known nothing else in her life, that she could not survive losing Nicholas.

And she did not intend to do so.

Tonight Elizabeth and Nicholas would come full circle. Jules was right as well. It was more than fitting that all should be settled between them on this of all nights. To begin again where everything between them had once ended.

And, in truth, wasn't Christmas Eve the beginning of hope, the epitome of joy, and the embodiment of love?

Elizabeth hadn't the vaguest idea what she would say to Nicholas or indeed what she would do, but she would absolutely not end this night without a clear understanding between them. He was her grand passion, the love of her life, and regardless of what she had to do, up to and including the admission, again, that she'd been wrong, even perhaps shaded with a hint of groveling, as well as throwing herself at him, so be it. By Christmas Day Nicholas Collingsworth, Sir Nicholas, the future Earl of Thornecroft, would be hers forever. And she would be his.

Precisely as it was meant to be.

Now, all she had to do was find him, which proved to be rather more difficult than she had expected. Certainly, it seemed the crush of guests this year was greater than ever, but that could simply be in her own mind and due entirely to the fact that she was intent upon finding one guest in particular. In addition, each and every person in attendance seemed determined to keep her from her goal with calls of "Felicitations of the season!" and jovial greetings of "Merry Christmas" and more often than not rapt discussions that began with, "Did you hear about . . ." It was virtually impossible to avoid any of these conversations, and, even as impatient as she was, Elizabeth gave each and every encounter her full attention.

Still, she kept a sharp eye out for Nicholas, although she had yet to see him. A heavy weight settled in the bottom of her stomach. Surely he hadn't decided not to come at all? No, he had to be here. His uncle was here. Admittedly, that was scarcely significant as the two men no longer shared the same house and therefore would probably not arrive in the same carriage. But Nicholas had promised her mother that he'd be here, and while he might break a promise to Elizabeth, he would never do so to the duchess.

Jonathon would know if Nicholas had made an appearance. Of course, Elizabeth scanned the ballroom, Jonathon was nowhere to be seen either. At once the answer of where he might be struck her. She rolled her gaze toward the ceiling, made her way through the crowd, out of the ballroom, and headed toward the library. It was past time Jonathon found a wife, if only to keep the library free during events like this. Once everything was resolved between Nicholas and herself, she would make it her purpose in life to find the perfect match for her brother. Whether he liked it or not.

She reached the library door and yanked it open to come face-to-face with a very flustered Jonathon.

"Did you, by any chance, see anyone . . . someone . . ." He craned his neck to see around her.

"Someone?" She stepped past him into the library. "You mean a woman? Very pretty? Rather upset?"

"Yes," Jonathon said with an eagerness that was most intriguing.

"No." In truth, she'd seen no less than a dozen female

guests who could conceivably have come from the library, but she'd been too intent on her own purpose to pay heed to any one of them beyond a murmured exchange of greeting and a practiced smile.

"I see." Jonathon's expression fell, and Elizabeth studied him curiously.

There was something about the look in his eyes that indicated this might well be more than simply another Christmas Eve encounter. This would bear further examination at a later point. At the moment, she had her own *tryst* to arrange.

"Have you seen Nicholas?"

"Nicholas?" Jonathon said absently, still staring down the passageway.

"Yes," she snapped. She had no time at the moment to waste on one of Jonathon's amorous intrigues. "Nicholas Collingsworth? Sir Nicholas? Your dear old friend?"

"Yes, of course." Jonathon cast one last, longing look, then slipped something hidden in his hand into his waistcoat pocket. At any other time, that gesture would have piqued Elizabeth's curiosity, but not at the moment. He heaved a sigh and turned toward his sister.

"Well? Have you seen him?"

"Briefly. In this very room actually, not more than half an hour ago." Her brother narrowed his gaze. "I gather you and he had words."

"You could say that." She shook her head. "We haven't spoken since, and I had hoped, no, I intend to speak with him tonight."

Jonathon considered her for a thoughtful moment. "He's leaving, you know."

"What?" Panic raised her voice. "What do you mean leaving? Leaving London?"

He nodded. "He was inquiring about train schedules."

"Train schedules? To where? When?"

"I don't recall."

"Think, Jonathon! Where is he going and when?"

"Damn it all, Lizzie, I am thinking." Jonathon drew his brows together. "I had other things on my mind, you know."

"It wasn't Southampton, was it?" Her heart stilled. "He has ships docked at Southampton. He's not going back to America, is he?"

"I don't remember." Jonathon shrugged helplessly. "It's a possibility, I suppose. Southampton has the right sound to it."

For a moment, fear rooted her to the floor, then resolve rushed through her. "Absolutely not. I won't allow it."

"*You* won't allow it?" Jonathon raised a brow. "How do *you* intend to stop it?"

"I have no idea, but I will. And if I can't." She set her jaw in determination. "I shall go with him or I shall follow him. I shall take the boys and we shall all go after him."

A grin broke over her brother's face. "Will you indeed?"

"Yes, I will." She started toward the door. "And do try to do something about that I-knew-it-all-along smirk of yours. It's not the least bit becoming."

"The satisfaction isn't in its appearance." Jonathon's grin widened, if possible. "But its significance."

"I don't doubt that."

"Wait, Lizzie." He grabbed her arm. "You stay here, I'll find him for you. I failed you ten years ago. I should have stopped Nicholas then. For you." He smiled and met her gaze. "Allow me the privilege of doing so now."

"Jonathon." She swallowed hard. "There are moments when you, well, you can really be quite a wonderful brother."

"I am a saint," he said in a most unsaintly manner. He leaned forward and brushed a kiss across her cheek. "I shall locate Nicholas and drag him back to you."

She frowned. "If you have to drag him—"

He sighed. "I daresay it's ten years too late for pride, Lizzie."

"Oh, it's not a question of pride. At least not mine. I simply don't want him hurt." She grinned. "Not overly, that is."

"I shall do my best." He waved a salute and started out the door. "By the way," he called over his shoulder. "That package on the desk is for you. From Nicholas."

She glanced at the desk and her smile faded. Slowly, she crossed the room, her gaze fixed on the small, fabric-wrapped package. In size and shape it looked like a book.

Her breath caught.

She stared at it for an endless moment. Or a lifetime. Or simply a decade.

Lizzie turned to the paper on the desk, thought for a moment, then penned a few lines. She sat back and studied them. Personal, but not too personal. Affectionate, but not overly so. One could read her words in any number of ways depending on the reader's own feelings. Yes, it would do.

She reached for the gift, noting and ignoring the tremble in her hand. The catch in her throat.

She'd been lucky to find one still available. The bookseller said they could well be sold out entirely before Christmas. She opened the small volume, drew a deep breath, then carefully wrote the decided-upon lines on the flyleaf and waited for the ink to dry.

Elizabeth pulled off the ribbon, knowing even before she drew off the fabric what would be revealed.

It was the perfect Christmas gift for a man she might or might not love. A man who might or might not love her. The perfect gift for an old family friend about to embark on endless travels or someone who might well be very much more than a friend.

It was not exactly as she remembered. The gilt was nearly worn from the cover. The corners were rubbed and bumped. In appearance, it looked a book that had been well read, even loved. A book that had not merely been opened once a year for a Christmas story but paged through often throughout the years with affection and remembrance and love.

Elizabeth opened the book gently and stared at the sentiment she had written so long ago.

May this token keep memories of home and the spirit of Christmas always in your heart.

Yours fondly,
Elizabeth

And beneath her words, other lines had been added.

You are always in my heart.

Forever,
Nicholas

The writing on the page blurred. The back of her throat ached, and tears fogged her eyes.

"I did not intend for you to open that yet," Nicholas's quiet voice sounded from the doorway.

"Why?" She sniffed hard and looked up at him. "Did you prefer that I wait until after you had gone?"

"No," he said slowly.

"Well, I won't permit it." At once the fear that had lodged in her heart the moment she'd seen the book was dashed aside by determination fueled by anger. "Not this time. Not again."

"You won't?" He stepped into the room cautiously and closed the door behind him.

"Absolutely not." She waved the book at him. "I am a far cry from the girl who wrote this."

"Are you?" He moved closer.

"Indeed, I am. I have no doubts as to my abilities or my competency or, for that matter, what I want!"

"And what do you want?" A slight hint of a smile quirked the corners of his mouth.

She stared in disbelief. "You think this is amusing?"

He nodded in a somber manner that didn't fool her for a moment. "Possibly."

"How could you?" She glared. "I am trying to tell you that I shall not allow you to vanish from my life once more. And if you insist on leaving England, on fleeing, *again,* I shall go with you. Or failing that, I shall follow you. All the way to America, if need be."

"Really?" He raised a brow and stepped nearer, close enough to touch. Or to grab tight. Or to throttle. "To America?"

"Yes." She stared up at him and held her breath. "Is that where you're going then? To America?"

He studied her curiously. "Why do you think I'm going anywhere, let alone to America?"

She searched his dark eyes and couldn't read a thing save that annoying glimmer of amusement. Surely, if he were really leaving her . . . "Jonathon told me."

"He did?"

She nodded. "He told me you were inquiring about train schedules."

"Trains don't run to America."

"I know that." She grit her teeth. "But they do run to Southampton and some of your ships depart to America from there and—" Elizabeth drew her brows together. "You're not going to Southampton?"

"I rather expect I shall make regular trips to Southampton in the future, but I have no immediate plans to do so."

"Then where are you going?"

"Birmingham."

"Birmingham?" She stared in confusion. "There are no ships in Birmingham."

"Which works out nicely, as there are no ship docks."

"Then you're not leaving England? You're not going to America?"

"Not any time soon, no."

"Jonathon led me to believe . . ." She narrowed her eyes and tried to ignore appealing images of her brother running for his very life.

Nicholas chuckled. "Jonathon is a very good friend, and I shall have to thank him."

"If he lives that long," she muttered. "I can't believe he said, or rather he led me to think . . . it scarcely matters at the moment, I suppose."

"He told me you were here and you wished to speak to me." Nicholas's dark gaze met hers. "Fortuitous, as I wished to speak with you as well."

"Indeed, I do. I—" She drew a deep breath. "You were right."

"I was wrong," he blurted at precisely the same moment.

Her eyes widened and she brushed aside her own comment. "You were?"

"Indeed, I was." He nodded. "I have given this a great deal of thought. The past cannot be changed. Charles is dead, and there is no conceivable way to answer the questions you have about his actions and his emotions."

"There isn't?" she said slowly.

"No." His manner was firm.

She studied him closely. "I suspect his mistress could probably tell me a great deal. Possibly lay any curiosity I might have to rest."

"Perhaps, but as you said, she did not sign her name to her letters. Therefore you have no way to find her. Besides," he paused to choose his words, "I think there is every possibility, regardless of what you might think now, or indeed what I thought, that what you may discover could hurt you deeply. I scarcely think the peace you might derive is worth whatever pain you might suffer."

She stared at him for a long, astonished moment. He knew full well that Teddy had been the woman in Charles's life, yet he wasn't going to tell her. In spite of his theory that said knowledge would ease her mind and possibly even smooth the difficulties between the two of them, he was going to keep this from her because he feared it might hurt her.

Ten years ago he had made a decision at the price of his own happiness because he'd thought it was best for her. Now, he was doing exactly the same thing for precisely the same reason and with a similar cost attached. In the back of her mind, Elizabeth noted that she should be furious that he had once again made a decision that would dramatically affect her life, yet oddly she wasn't the least bit angry. Instead a lovely sense of joy washed through her and a bit of awe as well that he could love her so much as to be willing to do whatever was necessary to keep her from being hurt.

"I see." She nodded thoughtfully. "Still, you said you would not pay for another man's sins."

"Oh, I have no intention of doing so, yet I do realize, given our own past, that I may have to continue to earn your trust over time. I shall endeavor to do so."

"Will you?" Her solemn smile belied the sheer happiness that bubbled up inside her.

"Indeed I will. However," his voice was firm, "I will not abandon old friends, nor will I promise never to cast an appreciative eye at another woman."

"As long as your eye is all you cast." She reached out and trailed her fingers lightly along the lapel of his coat.

He caught her hand. "I can agree to that."

"You should be aware, though," she drew a deep breath, "I suspect I will be jealous of every appreciative look you cast and all such looks cast in your direction. I shall try not to be a shrew about it, but I am fairly confident that it has nothing whatsoever to do with Charles and everything to do with how I feel about you."

"And how do you feel about me?" He pulled her hand to his lips and kissed her palm.

She shivered with delight and anticipation. "I thought I made my feelings perfectly clear the other night."

"Tell me again." He fairly growled the words and pulled her tight into his arms.

She raised her chin and looked squarely into his eyes, as intense and smoldering now as they had been when she'd first gazed into them. First wondered what it would be like to be in his arms. In his life. For the rest of her days. "You are now, and have always been, my love. My grand passion."

"And you . . ." He leaned closer and brushed his lips against hers. ". . . are my madness."

"Grand?"

"Exceedingly grand," he murmured, and his lips met hers in a kiss that held the grandest of promises for this Christmas and all the Christmases to come.

Without warning he drew back and stared down at her. "I have reconsidered."

She drew her brows together. "Reconsidered what?"

"In regards to our partnership, marriage, that is, after a great deal of thought—"

She grinned. "Due consideration?"

"Exactly." He nodded. "I am willing to offer you forty percent, but I can go no higher."

"Oh, but I think you can." She wrapped her arms around his neck. "I shall take no less than forty-nine."

"Forty-nine? Which leaves me only fifty-one percent? Exceedingly bad business practice, Elizabeth." He shook his head, then shrugged. "Agreed." He grinned. "And to seal this agreement—"

His lips claimed hers once more, and Elizabeth noted this was much better than a mere handshake or a written contract. Love for this man surged through her, and she knew it was in equal measure on both sides. And wondered as well if it was truly necessary to return to the ball, or could they—

Abruptly she drew back and stared at him. "Why are you going to Birmingham?"

He laughed. "Mr. Dickens is to do his first ever public reading of *A Christmas Carol* in Birmingham in a few days. I have arranged admissions, and I thought you, and Christopher and Adam, of course, would enjoy it."

"Nicholas." She swallowed hard. "That's wonderful of you."

"I am a saint," he said modestly.

"St. Nicholas?" She raised a brow. "Father Christmas?"

"There's a distinct resemblance," he said in a lofty manner, then sobered. "Elizabeth, you first gave me Mr. Dickens's story of second chances on Christmas Eve. It seems only fitting that I give you his words as he truly meant them to be read."

"Oh, my." Her voice caught. "I don't think I've ever received such a gift."

"No, my dear Elizabeth." He stared at her for a long moment. "The true gift is love, and it is I who has never received such a gift."

Her heart lodged in her throat, and she stared into his dark eyes, smoldering once more with passion and promises. And knew without question she would always share the sense of wonder she saw reflected there, and the love.

The ghosts of Christmas Past that had always lingered between them could now be set firmly in the past, where they belonged. The ghost of Christmas Present could be feted with love and joy. As for the ghost of Christmas Yet to Come, he was not to be feared but welcomed.

Life with Nicholas would be neither perfect nor easy, but she had had both. Grand passion had a price, and it was well worth any cost. With Nicholas by her side, this Christmas and every Christmas—indeed, every day from this one forth—would be filled with love and tears and laughter and everything that was her life, her heart. Her family, her sons, and Nicholas. Her grand passion. Her grand madness.

As it was always and forever meant to be.

Epilogue

He had no further intercourse with Spirits, but lived upon the Total Abstinence Principle, ever afterwards; and it was always said of him, that he knew how to keep Christmas well, if any man alive possessed the knowledge. May that be truly said of us, and all of us! And so, as Tiny Tim observed, God Bless Us, Every One.

—*A Christmas Carol,* Charles Dickens, 1843

Christmas Yet to Come
Christmas Day, 1858

"He had no further intercourse with Spirits . . ." Frederick's voice rang in the theatrical manner he insisted *A Christmas Carol* demanded.

Nick grinned and wrapped his arm around his wife.

Just as he had done every Christmas Day since Nick and Elizabeth had wed, Uncle Frederick sat reading aloud to the children. Whether it was his overly dramatic interpretation or simply the power of Mr. Dickens's words, the children listened with rapt attention—even Christopher, who had claimed he was far and away too old to be read to this year and it was time to put such childish amusements aside. Adam, who emulated his brother in everything, agreed he was probably too old as well, but since Uncle Frederick did so love reading the story, Adam could certainly listen out of affection and respect for his elders. And because it was, after all, Christmas Day.

James, barely four years of age, had dozed on and off throughout Frederick's reading and was even now curled against Christopher's side. It never failed to amaze Nick how well the boys had taken to their new brother. Indeed, they were already planning the day when he could join them in their exploits and adventures. Adventures no doubt originally inspired by their Uncle Jonathon, who, now that he had children himself, was getting a bit of his own back.

The twins, of course, were still far too young for the Christmas reading and were upstairs under the watchful eye of Miss Otis, who had proved herself more than capable of the care of his daughters as well as his sons.

". . . he knew how to keep Christmas well, if any man alive possessed . . ."

Frederick's voice swelled, and Lady Thornecroft bit back a grin. No one had been more surprised than Nick, or possibly Frederick himself, when Frederick had at long last married, and to a woman suspiciously close to his own age at that. Nick suspected there was an interesting story behind it all, but when asked, Frederick would only shake his head, grin in a wry manner, and mutter, "should have married her years ago."

". . . as Tiny Tim observed, God Bless Us, Every One."

Frederick closed the small book with a flourish. "Well? How was I? As good as Mr. Dickens himself, I should think."

The older boys traded glances and grins. Frederick asked the same question every year and received the same answers.

"Absolutely, Uncle," Adam said staunchly.

"Better than even last year I would say," Christopher added.

"Exactly as I thought," Frederick said in a lofty manner and winked at his wife.

Nick chuckled and gazed over his family with the sense of contentment and deep gratitude only a man who has truly found everything he has ever wished for can know. Even now it was difficult to believe. Certainly, their lives weren't perfect and the world itself was an ever more difficult place, but, for the moment, they were happy and healthy and together. And whenever he met Elizabeth's gaze, he saw his own love and passion reflected there. Mad and grand and forever.

He glanced at his wife. Elizabeth watched her family gathered together, and a slight smile played on her lips. Her voice was soft, barely more than a whisper, probably not meant for any mortal ears at all. "God bless us every one."

"My dear Elizabeth." Nick tightened his arm around her and smiled into her green eyes. "He already has."